THE GOLDEN THREAD

MONICA CARLY

Matador
9 Priory Business Park,
Wistow Road
Kibworth Beauchamp
Leicester LE8 0RX, UK
Tel: (+44) 116 279 2299
Fax: (+44) 116 279 2277
Email: books@troubador.co.uk
Web: www.troubador.co.uk/matador

ISBN 978 1780880 167

British Library Cataloguing in Publication Data.
A catalogue record for this book is available from the British Library.

Typeset by Troubador Publishing Ltd, Leicester, UK

Matador is an imprint of Troubador Publishing Ltd

Printed and bound in the UK by TJ International, Padstow, Cornwall

MIX
Paper from
responsible sources
FSC
www.fsc.org FSC® C013056

This book is dedicated to my family in gratitude for their unfailing love and support.

A sister is a gift to the heart, a friend to the spirit,
a golden thread to the meaning of life.'

Isadora James

CHAPTER 1

She stood in front of them all knowing it was the moment when she must speak, but unable, for once, to find the words. The sea of young faces swam before her eyes, wave after wave of children, filling the hall, sitting on the floor before her in ascending order of age. The little ones in the front gazed up in some perplexity, not appreciating the significance of this moment. The older ones further back fidgeted impatiently, their minds elsewhere, longing for the talking to be over.

'Why's she leaving?' Craig whispered behind his hand.

'Cos she's old,' hissed back Ben.

'How old d'you reckon?'

'Oh, 'bout a hundred, probably.'

To the watching children Claudia Hansom, in her dark grey suit and white blouse, grey hair cropped short in a mannish cut, must indeed have looked at least as old as their grandmothers. Perhaps even older! They were used to seeing her firm expression, her upright stance, dark-rimmed spectacles perched on her nose. They were also well aware of their headteacher's reputation for sternness. This might be her last day at the school but they weren't going to take any chances. Suppose she decided to keep them in today of all days! They wouldn't put it past her. A low profile was best.

As deputy, Brenda Walsingham knew, better than anyone, how much Kingdown Primary School owed to Claudia's total dedication over the past thirty years, and especially as head teacher during the last seventeen. Brenda concluded her farewell speech by saying that Claudia would be sorely missed when the new school year began by staff and pupils alike.

'Hear, hear!' was the audible comment from members of staff ranged at various points around the hall, keeping sharp eyes on their charges, ready to nip any sign of misbehaviour in the bud.

'Like a hole in the head,' was the less detectable comment from Peter Rawlinson, teacher in charge of geography, whose dedication to duty had been called in question more than once by Claudia.

'I can't help noticing that there is only a very small visual display of your project with Year 5 on Antarctica,' Claudia had remarked, having summoned him to her office. 'I would have thought there were countless opportunities for drawings and pictures relating to the climate, the wild life, the stories of exploration. I expected to see far more evidence of your progress by now.'

'My class did very well last term! You said so yourself! Their final assessment was well above average!'

'That may be so, and I agree that was pleasing. But we must build on it quickly – it's important not to let things slip this term.'

'She's on to everything,' he had grumbled when back in the staffroom for his precious mid morning break, angrily gulping down a cup of coffee and making short work of a couple of KitKats.

'She doesn't miss a trick!' Joan Baldwin had had her knuckles rapped when, as teacher in charge of Year 3, she had tried to introduce some basic yoga techniques into her classroom as a way of calming some of the unruly pupils. Claudia regarded it as a waste of valuable class time and told Joan that she did not wish to see it happen again.

Today Claudia, renowned for her ability to address an audience competently, even at short notice, was clearly ill at ease. She clutched the large bouquet of flowers that had just been presented to her and tried to control the tight band across her chest. The children, sensing their head teacher was, for once, uncertain of herself, became restless.

Meena Patel, in the third row, wriggled uneasily. She remembered the day her father had brought her to school because her mother was in hospital. He wasn't used to the routine and had left her lunch box behind. Meena, sobbing quietly, had walked down the corridor with her hands jammed into her eyes, trying to stem the flow of tears. Claudia had spotted her and enquired gently what the trouble was. In no time the secretary had been instructed to try and contact Mr Patel and soon the missing lunch box was produced. The little girl, her happiness restored, had clutched it tightly for the rest of the morning.

Claudia cleared her throat. 'I'd like to say a very big thank you to you all – to you, Miss Walsingham, and to all the members of staff for the fascinating book on ancient Greece. It will afford me hours of pleasure, I know, and I look forward to studying it.'

She was nearing the end of her few words. A hush had fallen on the assembly.

'And thank you, children, for the beautiful card you have designed for me. You have given me much to treasure – but best of all are the memories.'

She mustn't let any emotion show. It had been difficult to hold her feelings in check earlier, in the staffroom, when she had been given that beautiful book. Carefully wrapped in blue paper, the gift had been presented by Brenda with the words, 'This is a small token of our esteem and our gratitude for all you have done to keep this school consistently up to a high standard. Please accept it with our love.'

Claudia had let out an involuntary gasp when *The Glories of Greece* emerged from its wrappings. She quickly turned the pages noting the comprehensive text and the variety of its many photographs and illustrations.

'You could hardly have given me a more appropriate gift. This will give me hours of pleasure! Thank you so much.'

She smiled, clearly touched by their thoughtfulness. Normally she kept social interaction with her staff to a minimum. She never discussed personal issues or talked to anyone about her private life. Her colleagues were aware that she lived alone with Socrates, her cat. Once, when Socrates was ill, she had broken her own rule and confided to the pleasant reception class teacher, Sophie Longman, how worried she was about him and that she would take him to the vet that afternoon. The next day Sophie had put her head round Claudia's study door to enquire whether Socrates' health had improved, to be rewarded with a fairly brusque, 'He's much better, thank you.' Claudia then immediately changed the subject.

On this, her last day at the school, a new and surprisingly relaxed mood prevailed. Carried along on a tide of celebratory events Claudia found an unfamiliar warmth and jollity in the way her staff spoke to her. They even teased her a little.

'So, Miss Hansom, tell us how you will fill all that wonderful leisure time you will have at your disposal. You can always mark some of my books for me, should you find yourself in need of a diversion!'

The others laughed jovially. Mary Salter, in charge of English, waited for a response, secretly wondering if she had overstepped the mark. But before Claudia could reply Jean Farley, an art teacher, jumped on the bandwagon.

'I'd love to have the chance of visiting art galleries whenever I chose. Imagine being able to wallow in all those Old Masters without worrying about the time, or without having to supervise a dozen pupils who can't see the point of any of it! I do envy you!'

Had she lost out on the camaraderie that obviously existed in the staffroom? The position of head teacher inevitably put you in a lonely place, but this was a necessary part of making it clear who was at the helm. While all the other members of staff exchanged cheery words and banter in the staffroom, she had her own office where people came if they needed to speak to her.

Claudia responded to their questions. 'As it happens I do have a project lined up.'

'Why doesn't that surprise us?' Mary smiled encouragingly.

'And your kind gift will start me on my way. What I've been planning is to do some writing – I thought I'd write a book on the art and architecture of classical Greece.'

Her enthusiasm took over, and she found herself wanting to tell them – to tell someone – the ideas that had been taking shape in her mind. She loved that period in Greek history when she felt that the quality and originality of the work reached their highest point.

'What I want to do,' she said, leaning forward eagerly, 'is to present the art and architecture of that period to young people so that it comes alive. There's so much they could be interested in – pottery, sculptures, coin design, painting – and yet the sad fact is that most of them will grow up quite unable to appreciate any of it.'

'Well, if anyone can put it in a way that appeals to the young, you can.'

Brenda voiced their thoughts, and they all nodded. Claudia was known for her gift of presenting difficult concepts to children in a way they could grasp. This is what had marked her out as a good teacher from the start, and this was what had made teaching such a gratifying occupation. Every time she saw the light dawn in a child's eyes and knew that at last they had understood, she felt rewarded. She specialised in maths, a daunting subject for many children and she was often up against a wall of apprehension, as they doubted their own ability to come to terms with a new topic. But the children knew that when Miss Hansom took the class, the atmosphere might be strict but they would learn something, and, however long it took, she would remain patient.

'I'm planning to do a great deal of research into the subject, so you see how welcome this lovely book is.'

Claudia picked it up once more, and was just opening it when Sally Winston, the supply teacher who had only been in the school for two weeks, spoke out. 'I expect you're looking forward to being able to spend lots of time with your family!'

A gasp of horror was audible from the rest of the staff. Unwittingly the poor woman had just committed the cardinal error. As far as anyone knew Claudia had no family – she never spoke of anyone, and no relative had ever attended any school functions. Brenda Walsingham knew that on her confidential papers, under next of kin, she had mentioned a sister with a rather odd surname –

the name Fox came to mind, but she knew it wasn't that, although she couldn't remember what it was – but it was an unwritten rule that 'How are you?' was just about the only acceptable personal enquiry. Unfortunately, the new supply teacher, who had come in at the end of term when the other members of the staff were at their busiest, was not aware of this.

An awkward silence stretched interminably. Claudia studied the contents page in her book. Finally some forced chatter relieved the awkwardness.

This, her last day at the school, was nearly over. As she stood in front of everyone at the final assembly she tried desperately to frame her closing sentence, knowing they were waiting for her to finish. Now was the time to say that she would miss them, but she hesitated, fearful that her inner feelings might become uncontrollable. She took a deep breath.

'Goodbyes are never easy. Teaching has been my life, but now it's time for me to leave and start a new one. I wish you all the very best. Remember, children, work hard, listen carefully to your teachers and always be a credit to the school.'

'Yeah, yeah, yeah. Whatever,' muttered Lola Butchers, skewed round sideways in the back row, sighing loudly.

'Shut it!' hissed her neighbour. Bernadette Robinson had enjoyed the dubious honour of being Lola's best friend throughout the term. This had resulted in a number of incidents earning the displeasure of their teachers, until the inevitable happened and they found themselves in their head teacher's office. After a severe reprimand Claudia had dismissed them with the words: 'Your teachers have complained several times about your disruptive behaviour. You must both turn over a new leaf. I do not care for your present attitude.'

'And I don't care for yours, neither.' Lola expressed her defiance the moment the door was shut.

'They've got it in for us,' said Bernadette. 'Why they keep having a go at us? It's not fair.'

'It's cos we're black, innit?'

Now, as Claudia turned to move away, Lola whispered, 'Man, that woman's got a sour face. At least we don't have to look at it no more. Hey, Bernie – d'you fink she's ever had a man?'

'What, her?' Bernadette put on a look of mock incredulity. 'Do me a favour!'

They both dissolved into uncontrollable giggles, hugely enjoying the joke.

Claudia walked away from centre stage, keeping her head down in an attempt to prevent anyone noticing the tears in her eyes. Members of staff made their way back to the staffroom.

'Thank God that's over!' Peter threw himself down on a chair, scrabbling in his pocket for a biscuit.

'I felt sorry for her.' Mary voiced sentiments silently shared by others in the room. 'And it's my view that this school will be the poorer without her. When all's said and done, she's had this place running like clockwork.'

'Her standards were high and she made jolly sure ours were too. I think that was no bad thing,' said Joan, siding with Mary.

'Well I can't wait to let mine slip a bit next term!' Peter started collecting his things, anxious for the summer holidays to start.

'I have every reason to be grateful to her.' Members of staff paused in their preparations to go home to listen to Jenny Lewis, who rarely voiced an opinion. She had just completed her first year as a teacher and still lacked confidence both in the classroom and with her colleagues. 'I felt so incompetent at times, when I first came,' she continued. 'In fact, I'll confess I'd more or less decided teaching wasn't for me. I went to see Miss Hansom who made me feel a lot better about things … she gave me bits of advice and was quite encouraging. She actually said I could come and talk to her whenever I wanted. I know I'm still not much good now, but I'd have left long ago if it wasn't for her.'

The moment had arrived. She had cleared her desk of any personal possessions, leaving it ready for her successor. Now it was time for Claudia to start her journey out of the school where everything had become so familiar over the years that it felt like home. Outside, she turned to look back at the characterless buildings with their peeling paint. Had the school represented a place of security – or a prison? She was now being released into a world of new freedoms, with no ties or responsibilities – and she was afraid. Here at the school she was a person with a key role and a position of authority. Once she had left it behind she became a nobody. Just an ex-head teacher, living alone, with her cat.

There was no going back. She must walk through those gates. Brenda had come with her, to see her off.

'Goodbye! Enjoy your retirement!' Come back and see us sometimes!'

'Thank you. Thank you for the send-off you've given me. I shall write my appreciation shortly.'

She turned to go. Summoning up her resolve, she walked through the gates for the last time and stepped into her future.

CHAPTER 2

The next day dawned grey and dismal. Claudia, looking out of her bedroom window, saw homes shrouded in mist, their true identities hidden behind a haze that blurred their outlines. Rivers of rainwater ran purposefully down window panes, only to trail off aimlessly, joining the puddles on the impervious pavement below.

Socrates, the black cat who had been Claudia's companion for the past ten years, waited for her in the kitchen, anticipating his customary morning milk. Just as expected, at the usual time, Claudia appeared. The night before, when she went to bed, she had picked up her alarm clock, and after some initial resistance, had moved the alarm hand forward an hour. It felt decadent and self-indulgent, but her colleagues had enthused on her behalf about the joy of not having to make early starts any more, and it did seem the sensible thing to do. Her body clock, however, refused to be adjusted as easily and she was wide awake at the usual time. There seemed little point in continuing to lie in bed.

Socrates greeted her with his familiar sound – a strange little noise that was a cross between a purr and a mew. Whether he was aware of the traumatic change in her life, who could tell? He was as enigmatic as his Greek namesake. Claudia often felt his black, furry head contained more wisdom than the heads of many humans. He would look at her as if he understood what she was thinking and she drew comfort from his presence. She would return home at about six o'clock each evening, having stayed on for some time after the pupils had left, in order to deal with any problems and prepare for the next day. At the sound of her key in the front door, Socrates would jump off his chair and run into the hall to greet her. He always welcomed her, rubbing up against her calf and making little purring sounds. Bending down to stroke him she would talk to him as one adult to another. But he would only allow this indulgence for a short time, soon returning to his chair and his own private thoughts.

Later in the evening, a short time before bedtime, Socrates would stir, stretch, groom himself with elaborate licking motions and then slowly approach her, jumping up onto her lap. This was the time she liked best of all. As her hands caressed his silky fur, her pent up emotions were allowed expression. Yesterday evening, after her final day at Kingdown School, she told him she had lost her *raison d'être*, and did not know how to find the incentive to start again. Would there be enough to occupy her and satisfy the active mind that refused to wind down? The future stared emptily at her. Well, this was no good. She must pull herself together and get on with things. She got up to make her evening drink of hot milk. She put the saucepan on the cooker and lit the gas under it.

Her thoughts strayed back to the events of the day. It was a beautiful bouquet they had given her, and in a vase on the table in the lounge, the flowers seemed to take over the whole room. The accompanying card stood on the mantle piece. Suddenly she couldn't stand its sentimental phrases, the 'abundant good wishes for a happy retirement', with its platitudes about 'standing at the threshold of a wonderful new life'. She grabbed the card from its prominent position and took it into the spare bedroom where a small chest of drawers housed papers and other relics from the past.

In the bottom drawer were a few envelopes containing photographs. She picked one up and opened it. Inside was an old black and white picture of a lovely young girl with shoulder-length curly hair and a coquettish smile. A stabbing pain caused her to drop the picture as if it had burned her fingers. At the same moment she remembered the milk! Rushing back to the kitchen, she was just in time to see the frothing liquid rise up to the top of the pan and spill over the edge. The flames spluttered and died and the room was quickly filled with a pungent smell. Claudia mopped the mess up as best she could. Then she went back into the lounge, sat down in her chair and wept.

That night she could not sleep. A vision of Maria kept dancing before her closed eyes – the sister with whom she had had no contact for almost forty years. Maria – who had grown into a beautiful young girl, with curly light brown hair, dazzling smile and delightful figure – had been her constant companion and closest friend from the moment she had arrived on the scene, when Claudia was three years old. Now Maria was all she had left in the world. Their mother had died early, when the sisters were only fifteen and twelve. As a result a special bond had grown up between them and they had become accustomed to sharing a great deal of their lives with each other. What would Maria look like now, with grey hair and an ageing complexion? What had she done with her life? Was she happy? Claudia knew she had married. What family did she have? Claudia sighed. The day had been emotionally draining enough as it was, so why allow thoughts from the past to torment her? There was enough to cope with, getting used to becoming a nobody – or nobody who counted with anyone any more.

So did you only exist in the minds and estimation of other people? At school everyone had known who she was, the important role she played in the life of the school having been firmly defined. Of course they could have managed without her for a few days, if necessary, but she was the anchor, or perhaps more accurately, the captain at the helm. Outside the school walls she was a shadowy figure, with whom a few people were acquainted, but she made no difference to their lives. If she suddenly disappeared one day, no one would be any the wiser – and no one would care.

Claudia woke to the sound of teeming rain. The first decision to be made was what to wear. Her wardrobe was full of suits. They were her school uniform. She always bought them at Marks & Spencer's because her shape was inconsistent. Her shoulders were narrower than her frame suggested and over the years her hips had expanded.

The great advantage of shopping in her favourite store was that she could match up a size 14 jacket with a size 16 skirt. There was a row of such suits which she had used over the years, and very useful they had been too. But suddenly they were no longer appropriate wear for her new lifestyle. She would take most of them to the charity shop and just keep a couple in case any special occasions presented themselves. What special occasions? Bitterly she reflected that they were unlikely to arise, but perhaps it would be as well to be prepared. Even in school holidays she had worn the suits, as she frequently went into school and did not wish to suggest to anyone who might have seen her that she let her standards slip simply because the pupils were not present.

She would begin this new phase of her life by going to buy some suitable leisure clothes. Braving the elements, she took a bus to the High Street, where she made her way to the Marks & Spencer's store. Searching among the rails she tried to find what might be considered suitable attire for ladies of retirement age. Dismissing the idea of anything in the younger sections she arrived at the range headed 'Classics'.

Two other ladies of about the same age came up, chattering and laughing together. They started rifling through the clothes on the nearby rails.

'Don't think much of these!' said one in tones of disgust. 'They look like grannies' clothes!'

'You are a granny.'

'Doesn't mean I have to look like one!'

They bustled off, leaving Claudia hesitating among rows of skirts and blouses. For a moment she watched their retreating figures, then turning back to the rails of clothes they had spurned she began to make her selection.

* * *

Freedom! For an hour or two anyway – Paula knew she mustn't presume on Edith's kindness for very long – she had time to herself!

How lovely to be able to concentrate on shopping without the complication of small children. Mind you, already she was missing them and longing to see them again, but it did simplify matters if she didn't have to hump pushchairs about or answer endless questions to satisfy an inquisitive little mind. Paula hurried about her business hampered by the weather. Shoppers were scurrying along the wet pavement, weaving eccentric patterns as they attempted to avoid the worst of the puddles.

How sad that Jack had missed the birth of his new little daughter. She knew soldiers had to go where they were sent, and she had accepted that there would be times of separation when she married him, but she regretted that duty to join the force invading Iraq had resulted in his missing this very special moment in the life of their family.

He adored Isabel, now nearly five, never tiring of playing with her during his precious days of leave. Paula feared he might be disappointed at the lack of a son but he had sounded so thrilled when he had managed to make contact after the birth, just three weeks ago. What a perfect little baby girl had arrived! So pink and delicate and … well … beautiful!

And she was lucky to have a really supportive mother-in-law – those old jokes were totally inappropriate. Edith was like the mother she missed so badly, adoring the children and doing everything she could to help. Well, Paula had finished her errands and would soon be with them all again at home. Her car was parked just round the corner – if only all these people didn't keep blocking her path! Just at that moment a gust of wind tugged at her umbrella, whipping it inside out.

In front of her was an older lady clutching a Marks & Spencer's carrier bag. She was struggling against the wind and with her head down did not see a large man bearing down upon her from the opposite direction. Taking a sudden step towards the kerb to avoid a puddle he banged into the older woman's side, knocking her off course. Mumbling an apology he hurried on his way, but the woman had lost her balance. For a moment she teetered looking as if she would be able to right herself, but then lost control and went down on the wet pavement, her carrier bag flying out of her grasp. Paula nearly tripped over her.

Several people stopped, one retrieved the bag and someone else said, 'Are you all right?' Strange how that's the first thing people say to someone who obviously isn't, thought Paula. A trickle of blood had started to run down the woman's leg.

'Yes, yes, perfectly, thank you. Please don't worry.' Various hands helped her back onto her feet.

'If you're sure.' The other shoppers melted away. The woman looked rather shaken.

'Do you live far away?' asked Paula.

'No, just a bus ride. Thank you, I'm quite all right.'

'That leg wants mopping up. Look, my car's just down the next side road, I'll run you home.'

'Oh no, really, there's no need. Please, there's really nothing wrong – nothing of any importance.'

The woman tried to brush some muddy marks off her coat and started to walk on, but stumbled a little. Paula grabbed her arm.

'No, really … I insist. I saw it all happen. That man bumped straight into you and he hardly even stopped! I hope your shopping hasn't suffered. Come on, my car's just over there.'

'But it must be taking you out of your way. Don't you want to get home? Where do you live?'

'Oh, I'm just round the corner from Kingdown School – do you know it?'

'Yes, yes, actually I–'

'We're hoping our little girl will be going there in September! She's longing to start big school.'

'How old is she then?'

'Isabel's nearly five, and so full of questions! There's never a dull moment. And now I've got a new baby – just three weeks old.'

'A new baby! How lovely for you – what's the new baby's name?'

'Maria.'

'Oh!'

Surprised at the exclamation Paula turned to look at the woman beside her. She was very white.

'Look, here's the car. I'm glad I'm giving you a lift … you really don't look too good.'

'It's very kind of you. I keep saying there's no need.'

'Nonsense. Hop in. I'm Paula, by the way – Paula Munro. What's your name?'

'Claudia …' Before Claudia could get any further Paula had shut her into the passenger seat and was going round to the driver's side.

'I'm afraid I'm making your car rather dirty.'

'Don't worry about that. The car gets all sorts of clutter in it.'

'Where are your children? I mean, you've been out shopping …'

'My wonderful mother-in-law offered to have them for a while this morning. She's besotted with the new baby. Well, so am I. Do you like babies?'

'I haven't actually–'

'It's their little hands I think are so amazing. So tiny, yet so perfect, and those miniature fingers that are still strong enough to wrap round yours and grip you. Mind you, they all grow up to be a handful, don't they? What do you do … are you retired?'

'Yes, I have just–'

'I expect you find you're busier than ever! I've heard retired people say they never seem to have a minute, and don't know how they ever fitted work in!'

They were drawing up outside Claudia's flat.

'I was wondering … I don't know whether you'd like to come to tea, and see the children? Would you like to come tomorrow? It would be nice to know you're okay.'

'Tomorrow? I'm not sure if–'

'No, I expect you're far too busy. But look, if you ever find a slot, and you think you'd like to pop in, you could always give me a ring. I'll write my telephone number down for you.'

'It's very kind of you. You've been extremely kind. Thank you for bringing me home. I really do appreciate it.'

'Not at all … do hope that leg's not too badly injured. I think you'll have to throw the tights away!'

'Goodbye, and thank you again.'

Claudia stood outside her flat, her bag of shopping in one hand and the scrap of paper with the telephone number on it in the other.

Paula waved cheerily. 'Do come!' she called out of the car window. Claudia nodded.

Funny woman, thought Paula as she drove away. She hardly said a word. I can't believe I asked her to tea! Oh well, I don't suppose she'll come. In fact, I don't suppose I'll ever see her again.

CHAPTER 3

The library was an oasis of calm. Browsing among the shelves of books never failed to lift Claudia's spirits, particularly the reference section. Ancient Greece was, for her, an endless source of fascination. Given the time, she could spend hours studying illustrations of the art of the period. She revelled in the quietness that surrounded her. There was something soothing about rows of bound volumes sitting there patiently in readiness for their moment of glory – like flower buds waiting for their time to blossom.

Once again the previous night had been restless. Thoughts held at bay during the years when she had immersed herself in her work now seemed impossible to stifle. Images had flooded through her brain triggered by innocent words from the young woman who had come to her rescue the previous day. She grimaced at the thought of how she had fallen smack down on that dirty pavement. Her raincoat would have to go to the cleaners and she had collected a number of cuts and bruises on her hands and legs. The incident had left her feeling embarrassed and stupid, but fortunately there was no great damage.

The hurt had come from some of the things Paula, in all innocence, had said. For a start there had been the name Maria to reawaken echoes from the past. And fancy the woman asking her to tea! Claudia knew that, if she went, she would be expected to drool over the new arrival while the mother stood there beaming with pride. This was a role she had often fulfilled at school when a parent had shown a new baby to the headteacher for her to admire. She had always done her best, knowing that before her there was potentially another pupil to attend her school in five years' time. But sometimes it had been hard work when the occupants of the prams had looked a little odd, as newborn babies can, almost subhuman, Claudia thought.

On the other hand, some of the new babies were startlingly beautiful and she could be mesmerised by the sight of an enchanting little girl. That was when the pain went deep. Last night she had finally fallen into a troubled sleep which brought no relief, her dreams full of images of a tiny baby whose little fingers gripped her mother's hand. Then someone came and cruelly prised those tiny fingers away.

Day time was much better. Then thoughts could be concentrated on objective topics of interest rather than the introspective, bitter emotions that had plagued her over the last two nights. In the lending section Claudia discovered a book on classical architecture that she hadn't seen before. She took it over to the counter for scanning. The librarian smiled at her.

'That looks interesting,' she remarked. 'I'd love to have time to devote to reading something like that. What with working and running round after my family ….'

'I've just retired,' Claudia replied, 'so now I can start on some major projects. Things I've been wanting to do but I've been too busy.'

'Lucky you! I've got another twenty years to wait! It can't come soon enough for me.' The librarian hesitated. 'By the way, had you thought of joining the Fine Arts Society? I could give you a leaflet. I hear they have some very interesting talks.'

'Thank you, I'll bear that in mind. But what I'm really interested in ….' She trailed off, as the librarian was distracted by some girls who had come in chattering loudly.

'Excuse me … I'll have to go and have a word. They don't seem to realise ….'

Picking up her book, Claudia made her way home. Socrates was waiting for her return, and so, on the doormat, was a letter. Claudia picked it up and examined the envelope. She wasn't expecting any

18

post and rarely received personal mail. There were no clues as to the identity of the sender.

A letter opener lay on the hall table ready for use as Claudia hated envelopes that had been roughly torn and left with jagged edges. This one was a business letter bearing the name of some sort of agency by the name of *Seekers.* The name meant nothing to her. Claudia read the letter with mounting bewilderment.

It seemed that a third party wished to contact a certain Miss Claudia Hansom, on behalf of a relative with whom there had been no communication for many years. The agency, wishing to ensure that the correspondence had been sent to the right person, asked Claudia to confirm some personal details, including her occupation and the first names of her parents.

What could this mean? Surely it could only have come from one source … who else but Maria? Or rather, from someone on behalf of Maria, for there were no other relatives. Claudia sat down and read the letter over several times, trying to understand what lay behind it. So had Maria died? Perhaps there was a will, and she had mentioned Claudia. Well, Claudia had no wish to inherit any kind of legacy from her sister, although, if there were a sum of money, she might as well have it and pass it on to a cats' home.

All the same there was an uncomfortable feeling in the pit of her stomach at the thought that her sister had died. To feel such a pang was hardly logical since, in reality, Maria had been dead to her for almost forty years. The rift that had resulted from the events of that time had never been healed. Claudia always refused to allow her mind to return to memories that were still capable of distressing her. Her first reaction was to crumple the letter up and throw it in the bin. But on second thoughts, might it be better to provide the details that had been requested, so that she could at least find out what it was all about?

Before she could change her mind she grabbed a sheet of paper, wrote a quick response to the letter, giving as briefly as possible the facts required, and sealed the envelope.

With a sigh she sat down, her mind whirling. So much for her cherished belief that all those incidents were dead and buried beyond reach! It was impossible now to prevent the memories from returning. Unable to fight any longer, Claudia lay back in her chair and let the past live again.

CHAPTER 4

'Everyone must sit still and pay 'tention!'

Ranged in a semi circle, the pupils sat obediently before her, staring unblinkingly at their teacher as they waited for the educational gems Claudia, aged five, prepared to disseminate. Her students, mostly a selection of teddy bears, stuffed toys and dolls, were models of perfect behaviour apart from the one disruptive element in the centre whose unruliness destroyed the peaceful learning environment Claudia was attempting to create, thereby sabotaging any chance of educational advancement for the class as a whole.

'Maria! Sit down! You've got to sit still!'

But Maria had other ideas. To her two-year-old mind there were far more engaging pursuits than listening to her elder sister running through the alphabet or reciting tables. What did she care whether A was for apple or B for bear? And numbers were a closed book to her.

Claudia, proud of her accomplishments so far, felt a burning desire to share them but was constantly thwarted by a somewhat less than receptive audience. Her reading was well above average for her tender years, but what she really enjoyed was her number work. She could count up to a hundred without hesitation, recite her two and three times tables accurately and was in the process of mastering her four times table. At school her teacher commended her quickness to learn, noting her early promise. A future in teaching was already Claudia's main goal in life. How frustrating, then, to find her younger sister so totally uninterested.

Sometimes Maria would stay quiet for a few minutes, sucking her thumb and grasping her favourite doll against her chest. But soon she would start to move away from her cushion, grabbing one or two of her classmates as she went, staggering on wobbly legs to play one of her favourite imaginative games. If Claudia tried to restrain her forcibly, the blood-curdling screams that ensued would have Anita running in to reprimand Claudia for her treatment of her small sister.

One day, foiled as usual by Maria's unwillingness to concentrate on the important matter in hand, Claudia went to find her mother who was busy with one of her culinary projects in the kitchen.

'She won't listen, Mummy! It's not fair. How can I practise being a teacher if Maria won't let me teach her?'

Anita tried to reason with Claudia, suggesting that her expectations of her small sister were perhaps a little too high.

'What is it about teaching that attracts you so much?' she asked. 'You're very young to have decided on a career already.'

Claudia struggled to put into words why she was so sure this was what she wanted to do with her life. As they talked, Anita suddenly became aware of the smell of burning and at the same moment there was an urgent banging on the front door. An alarmed neighbour had come to report that flames could be seen leaping out of the top of the Hansoms' chimney!

Anita rushed into the lounge to find Maria, who had managed to push the fireguard aside, chuckling as she gleefully threw her classmates, one by one, onto the fire.

'Eliminating the opposition seems a rather drastic method of achieving top-of-the-class status,' remarked their father, when he was told of the escapade that evening. 'I think Claudia will probably achieve it by fair means, without resorting to foul.'

That day marked the end of Claudia's teaching practice sessions. Instead, forced to confine her activities to lesson preparation until Maria grew a little older, she set about creating an arithmetic book to help her sister learn the rudiments of mathematics.

Claudia loved school, quickly revealing an aptitude for number work which convinced her teachers that they had a talented pupil in their midst. She had learned to read early without any difficulty and shone in most subjects, picking up information quickly and assimilating facts without effort. For her age she seemed to know an amazing amount about the world she lived in. She could find most countries on the globe and knew their capital cities by heart. Historical projects were a source of particular delight, the ancient world proving to have an endless fascination for her. The longer ago the time in question, the more it awakened her interest.

Maria was clearly cast in a rather different mould since it was the social aspect of school life that delighted her. Quickly making friends, she was popular with her classmates who were attracted by her sense of fun. Her reports of what she had done centred on who had sat next to her and what games had been played. Lessons scarcely featured in her accounts of her school day.

One day Claudia decided to put her sister's reading ability to the test.

'Bring me your storybook of Goldilocks and the three bears. Let's see if you can read it.'

Maria, opening the book at the first page, started on an imaginative account of the whole story, remarkable in its detail but bearing no relation to the actual words on the page.

'You're not reading it!' Claudia interrupted.

'I am! I am!'

'No you're not. You're just making it up.' This sent Maria running to find her mother, wailing loudly that Claudia was being horrid to her.

By the time Maria was in her second year at school the teachers were all too well aware that history was not repeating itself. Jane Singleton, Maria's teacher, remembering Claudia from three years previously, remarked on this to her colleague, Betty Chalmers, who currently had Claudia in her class. 'Maria's a charming little girl – never really naughty – just mildly mischievous, but she shows no real interest in learning. I can't help comparing her with Claudia at that age. She was hungry for knowledge and progressed by leaps and bounds!'

'She still does! She's a joy to teach,' replied Betty. 'That girl will go far. I'm pretty certain she's university material.'

Claudia's weak point was in the area of imagination. It did not come easily to her to invent stories, with the result that her creative writing tended to be about things she had done, thinly disguised. Nor did she much enjoy reading fanciful tales. Where was the point of a story that could never have happened? By way of compensation, her grasp of grammatical correctness and her neat handwriting made her work a pleasure for her teachers to read.

Maria's writing, by contrast, flowed spontaneously as the inspiration came flooding in. Her spelling and punctuation may have been unconventional but her stories had strong imaginative appeal, captivating the reader with a narrative full of drama and unexpected twists and turns. By contrast, her mathematical ability was abysmal. She had no interest in trying to work something out in a logical way. Where was the fun in that?

Anita encouraged Maria's imaginative play, entering into it with childlike delight. They would build their own village in the lounge by laying down pencils on the carpet to mark out the streets and then placing little houses at various points in which their invented characters lived. Then, each taking a doll, they would walk them along the streets until they met, whereupon a lively exchange would take place, probably starting with the weather and then moving on to more personal family matters.

Anita would be so caught up in their game that only a burning smell from the kitchen would remind her she had put a cake in the oven some time earlier. She may have had little formal education, but she could weave magical stories and invent games which she delighted in playing with her children. At bedtime she would read to them for hours, although once Claudia had mastered the art for herself, she preferred to read her own books.

Their father rarely arrived home in time to say goodnight to his girls. Dr Hugh Hansom, university lecturer in physics, was a remote figure who stayed at his place of work for as many hours as he could without incurring the wrath of his wife. Deeply immersed in his world of scientific experiments, he could forget everything else and only come back to reality after frantic telephone calls from Anita who had had to throw one ruined dinner into the dustbin and start afresh. He could think of little to say to his girls when they were very young.

Once Claudia's scholastic abilities became clear, Hugh began to take pleasure in asking her about her latest projects and achievements. The older she grew, the more she enjoyed conversing with him, describing articulately the progress she had made in certain areas, and what she enjoyed most about her work. If she had any problems, which wasn't often the case, he could usually shed light on what was puzzling her, to their mutual satisfaction.

Hugh then tried the same approach with his younger daughter.

'What have you learned at school today, Maria?'

'Oh, the teachers didn't bother with much today. They let us make up stories.'

'So what was your story?'

'Mine was about a deep, deep forest where a beautiful young girl with long fair hair went off to play – but she got hopelessly lost, and the more she tried to find her way out the more the tangled branches caught her and held her so that she struggled and struggled in vain! And then a handsome prince came riding by ...'

'How did he manage to ride in the forest if it was so thick with overhanging branches?'

Maria stopped mid flow, looking nonplussed.

'Now you've interrupted me, Daddy, and I can't think where I was.'

'You were in the middle of this deep, deep forest – or, at least, your beautiful young girl was.'

But Maria had lost interest, realising her audience was not as captivated as the girls at school had been.

Sunday lunch was the one time when the Hansoms sat down together as a family to enjoy the culinary delights Anita would set before them. After a typical menu such as succulent roast beef, light-as-a-feather Yorkshire Pudding and crisp roast potatoes, followed by apple pie, Hugh would lean back contentedly in his chair and beam at his family. He considered himself an extraordinarily lucky chap although it was an unfathomable mystery that an old stick-in-the-mud like him should be so blessed by the presence of a beautiful wife – but he was unfailingly grateful for it.

'Thank you, my dear, for an excellent meal, as always. Now, girls, what are you going to do this afternoon?'

'I'm going to help Mummy with the washing up,' said Maria, quickly, believing that was the best way out of what might be a rather tricky conversation. Anyhow, it was always fun being in the kitchen with Anita.

'And you, Claudia?'

'Well, if Mummy doesn't need me I thought I'd have a go at those maths problems I told you about.'

'Well done,' approved Hugh.

'How boring!' muttered Maria under her breath, almost spoiling the good impression she had just created. Anita frowned at her, urging her to carry some plates out to the kitchen.

Despite their differences in temperament, the girls became close companions. Claudia was protective of her younger sister, shouldering a responsibility for Maria's well-being which wasn't always well received as Claudia could be dictatorial at times.

'You must finish your homework before you start to play, Maria,' she would say, day after day, with little effect.

'Stop being so bossy, Claudia. Mummy, Claudia keeps being bossy. Tell her to leave me alone.'

'She's only trying to help you, darling. You really should get your homework done, like she says. Look, come and help me make some scones, and then get on with it after that. Would that be a good idea?'

'Oh yes!'

And Maria was off to the kitchen before Claudia could say anything else. But in the evening, before bed, Maria would come into Claudia's room and chatter away, telling her all about her day at school and who had started being friends with whom, and what had been so funny that they had all giggled until they got into trouble. She took comfort from knowing that if she needed help she could always turn to Claudia and it was difficult to say how much of Maria's maths homework was actually done by her. Claudia had become adept at faking Maria's handwriting.

'I do hope we don't ever get separated,' sighed Maria one evening, when Claudia had come to her rescue once more. Maria had lost her exercise book in which she had done her latest piece of homework and was about to get into dire trouble. Claudia had managed to find it lurking in the depths of her satchel, covered up by a number of magazines that Maria and her friends shared with each other. 'I'm sure I couldn't manage my life without you.'

'Don't worry. We'll stay together through thick and thin. Though I do think you're going to have to become a bit more responsible one of these days.'

Maria pulled a face.

But soon there would be changes. When Claudia was eleven she won a place at the local grammar school. Maria knew she had little hope of following her there – nor would she have wanted to do so – but she wondered how she would fare at school without Claudia's support.

She did have one gift that Claudia lacked – an ability to charm people. She was already discovering that this was her best method of extracting herself from potential trouble and achieving her own ends. Her ready smile meant she was always surrounded by a large number of girls who all wanted to be her friend. She was too young and innocent to understand that this talent could prove a two-edged sword.

CHAPTER 5

'Mummy! Mummy! Where are you?' Claudia, now aged fifteen, had arrived home from school, aglow with news of her latest achievements, but the house was silent. Anita, who usually made a point of being at home to greet her children, was nowhere to be seen.

Claudia finally found her mother in the bedroom, lying on the bed.

'Are you all right, Mummy? What is it?'

'I'm so sorry, darling … I just came over a bit faint … I thought I'd better lie down for a few minutes … I must have dropped off to sleep. I'm so sorry. How did you get on today?'

'Fine – I got full marks in that maths test – but you are all right, aren't you? I mean …. You're not ill, or anything?'

'No! Of course not! I'm fine – really I am. Be an angel and put the kettle on – I'd love a cup of tea. Then I'll come downstairs. Oh, by the way, don't say anything to your father … I don't want him to get worried. There's really nothing to worry about.'

Claudia couldn't help feeling disturbed. She tried to believe there was nothing wrong but her mother looked so pale. She would say something to Maria when she came back from having tea with one of her friends.

Maria found the idea of their mother not being well very frightening. 'Shouldn't we tell the doctor? Or should we disobey Mummy and tell Daddy?'

'Let's see how she is,' Claudia decided. 'If she really is all right then I think we needn't do anything about it.'

'Good idea,' Maria agreed. 'Perhaps it's nothing – after all grown-ups do faint occasionally, don't they?'

The girls were used to helping around the house. Anita had brought them up to take a share in some of the basic chores, so it didn't come as a particular surprise when they were asked to help with clearing the tea things away, or washing up. As far as they could tell Anita was back to normal, if perhaps a little tired.

But two days later there was a loud crash in the kitchen followed by the sound of breaking crockery. Both girls rushed in to find Anita on the floor, a tea towel nearby and fragments of a broken plate scattered everywhere.

Claudia rang Hugh's work number and the secretary managed to get hold of him. He told Claudia to ring the emergency number for an ambulance and said he would come immediately.

The diagnosis was cancer, and it was only a matter of time. Had she seen a doctor earlier, perhaps something could have been done but now the disease had spread too far. Three months later Anita lost her battle and died.

Hugh, heartbroken and guilt-ridden, buried himself deeper in his work. He hired a housekeeper who coped competently, but the girls now lacked the emotional warmth their mother had always lavished on them. With Hugh still a rather distant figure, they turned to each other for comfort and support and the bond between them grew stronger than ever.

When Claudia reached the sixth form at school she worked single-mindedly in order to achieve her goal of university entrance. Maria was aghast at how much effort was required, and swore she would leave school just as soon as she got the chance. There was only one aspect of Claudia's sixth form life that appealed to her sister, and that was the school Hop. It was the custom of the school to make arrangements with a neighbouring boys' grammar school for a dance one Saturday afternoon each term, in an attempt to broaden the horizons of girls who, being at a single-sex school, might not have opportunities to mix with boys.

'Oh, Claudia! You are lucky! I wish I could go! What are you going to wear?'

'Nothing. I'm not going.'

'Oh, you must! Why ever not? It'll be such fun – just think! All those boys!'

'I can't waste my time on that! I've got lots of work to do over the weekend.'

'Oh come on! You never do anything but work! Don't you think you ought to get in a little practice at going to dances? After all, there must be fun things like that up at college. It can't be all work, can it?'

Claudia had to concede that Maria had a point. Perhaps she ought to give it a try. After all, the other girls were all getting excited about it and she didn't want to be a total stick-in-the-mud when she got to university. Maria was happy to advise her on what she should wear.

'Get something blue, Claudia – it's your best colour. You look lovely in blue.'

Claudia had no illusions. She knew Maria was far prettier than she was. As the years passed the differences between the two girls had become more marked. It wasn't just the way their minds worked – it was also their physical appearance. Claudia had stopped growing at five feet, five inches, and begun to thicken, her waist not being as well defined as she could have wished. Her hair was dark and straight, her face, although not unattractive, was unremarkable, and she required fairly thick spectacles for daily use.

Maria, a good five feet, eight inches in height, had shapely long legs that were the envy of her peers. With her light brown curls hanging below her shoulders, her striking facial features and her slim figure, she soon attracted the boys. Always laughing and bright, her friendliness made her popular with her classmates, who also admired her prowess on the sports field. Her teachers were less impressed since she skimped on the hours spent on her studies, but even they couldn't help liking her.

On the day of the hop Claudia did what she could, with a little help from her younger sister, to look her best and joined up with a couple of her classmates to go to the event.

That evening Maria rushed to the door to greet her. 'Well, how was it? Did you have an amazing time? Were their some fabulous boys?'

'There were a great many spotty, lanky youths, none of whom had a sensible word to say.'

'Did you dance with lots of them?'

'Oh yes. It was carefully arranged so that there was an equal number of boys and girls, and we did a Paul Jones, so we kept ending up with fresh partners.'

Maria squealed with excitement. 'I wish they had these hops at my school! Oh, Claudia, how marvellous! Surely there was one super boy there, wasn't there? There must have been at least one!'

'Not one, I promise you. They were all pretty unattractive and seemed so young. Not a Prince Charming in sight.'

'I bet there's a tall, dark, handsome stranger out there for you somewhere! One day, Claudia, you're going to meet him, and he's going to sweep you off your feet! You just wait.'

Despite their differing outlooks and talents, the girls remained attached to each other, and shared their various concerns. Of course they irritated each other intensely at times, as sisters commonly do. Claudia's habit of correcting any inaccuracies when Maria was recounting an event spoiled the flow of her story, and after all, it was the dramatic effect that mattered – as far as Maria was concerned – rather than a strict adherence to fact. Claudia could not understand this approach, nor could she comprehend how her sister could be content to grow up without any plans for the future, simply drifting along enjoying the present as if there were no tomorrow.

Claudia's way forward was clearly marked out. She planned to go to university – the Oxbridge option was certainly on the cards – to read mathematics, prior to embarking on a teaching career. It was impossible to predict what Maria would do. She saw no point in making any decisions, and took life as it came, happy to leave the worrying to others.

Claudia's plans fell neatly into place – she was accepted by St

Hilda's College, Oxford. As the time drew nearer for her sister to leave home, Maria began to experience some disquiet. She knew she would miss Claudia sorely and wondered how she would manage without this prop that had always been there for her. For once she kept her thoughts to herself. But there was no need to voice them. Claudia had been thinking along similar lines.

One day, after agonising for some time, she said to Maria, 'I've made a decision. I'm not going to take up my place at university. It isn't fair to leave you here on your own.'

Maria reacted immediately, and forcefully.

'No, Claudia, no! I can't have you make that sacrifice for me. I want you to go ahead with things, the way you've always planned.'

'But won't it be awful for you? You'll be so alone, with only Dad for company!'

'I know it won't be easy, but I couldn't bear you to give up everything you've hoped for and dreamed of because of me! I can't let you make that sacrifice! I'd hate myself, for the rest of my life, if I made you lose the chance of going to college! Please, Claudia, you mustn't think like that a moment longer.'

Claudia reached over and took her hand.

'What would I do without you? You're the best sister in the world! Look, we'll keep in touch all the time, and perhaps you'll be able to come and stay for a weekend occasionally, or I might be able to come home from time to time. Thank you, Maria. I shall never, ever forget this.'

They smiled at each other, happy in the knowledge that the bond between them was so strong nothing could mar it, for so it seemed to them both. Despite the pang the separation caused her, Claudia was happy when the time came for her to go up to Oxford. Maria, with a marked lack of enthusiasm, continued at school.

Hugh continued to be excessively proud of his elder daughter, and baffled by his younger one. Fortunately for him his work was utterly absorbing. Giving himself up entirely to its demands he was able, for the most part, to deny the existence of the outside world.

CHAPTER 6

Professor Hugh Hansom looked round his physics laboratory and smiled contentedly. Among his familiar apparatus, with his latest experiment set up and his lecture notes in a neat pile, he felt at peace with the world. Ever since his wife had died this was the environment that offered security, its familiarity providing comfort and the stimulation of the work absorbing his energies. He would happily have brought a camp bed in and stayed at night if that had been a practical possibility.

The laws of physics appealed to him because of their predictability. He liked things that you could rely on and understand. People were in a different category altogether; they were a source of bewilderment to him, and none more so than his own two daughters – or perhaps, more accurately, his younger daughter. Claudia, at least, seemed to behave in a way he understood, with her consistent approach to her studies, and her long-term objective of joining the teaching profession. But Maria! He had no idea how she functioned, or what was to become of her. This was one area where he bitterly regretted his wife's death. Anita had had a close relationship with both girls, and Hugh knew that they had easily confided in her. He had kept out of it, feeling he had very little to offer. If there had been a son, that would have been different, but girls! He simply couldn't cope with their silliness and their excitement about trivial and unimportant issues.

It occurred to Hugh that he probably had a better relationship with his students than he did with his own daughters, but that was perfectly understandable. They were on the same wavelength. They looked to him for guidance through their courses, and he was able to supply it. Nothing was too much trouble. He would take as much time as was needed to help those who found the work difficult, but he much preferred to be with the bright students, who immediately grasped the concepts he was putting forward, and who could discuss issues with him from a basis of understanding.

There was a tap on the door. He wasn't expecting anyone, but he looked up and called, 'Come in!'

Amanda Gosling appeared, advancing rather tentatively, and seeming ill at ease. A bright, second-year student, she had never appeared to experience any particular problems, and had settled into student life easily. He couldn't think why she might want to see him.

'Sit down, sit down,' he said. 'What can I do for you?'

The girl hesitated. Then she said, in a voice so low he could hardly hear, 'I'm afraid I have to leave.'

He looked up, startled. Then he noticed that her face was blotchy, and she was clearly feeling miserable. Even as he saw these things, she took out a tissue and blew her nose.

'Why must you leave? Your work is very good. I don't understand. Why on earth would you want to give up everything you've achieved here?'

'I don't want to,' she replied, looking up for the first time. 'But I have to. You see, I'm sorry to say, I'm ... pregnant.' Then her head went down again, and there was a great deal more nose-blowing and mopping of the eyes.

Hugh was flabbergasted. He had no idea what to say. Whatever did you say to girl students who found themselves in that position?

'Oh dear, how awful!' he said, which proved to be quite the wrong thing as it set off another bout of tears.

'Yes it is,' the girl sobbed. 'And I don't know what to do, and my parents are going to be so angry, and I'm so disappointed ... and so worried.'

'Look,' said Hugh, 'are you certain? I mean ...'

'Yes, I am certain, now. I kept hoping ... but it's no good ...

'What will you do, then? Are you going to …? I'm sorry, it's none of my business.'

'I don't know what to do … but the only thing I know is that I can't get rid of it. I've thought about it – night after night – but I can't do it. I shall have to have it.'

'Well, what about the father then? Is he going to–?'

'No! I certainly don't want to marry him! I've been so stupid – I can't tell you, Professor Hansom. Just once, only once in my whole life, I got drunk at a party, and I allowed a student I hardly knew … well, I think I must have … I've no memory of being forced … and it's the only time I've ever … and now …'

'Dear, dear. How very unfortunate.' He realised that the girl's life was in ruins, but at least he had the tact not to say so. Coming from a middle-class background as she did, her parents would no doubt support her in the end, but she'd probably never get over the shame of it, and her life at university was over.

'Look,' he said, 'thanks for telling me. Have you spoken to anyone else? I'm sure there's someone here who would be able to help. There must be someone who could give you advice.'

She nodded. 'I haven't yet, but I'm going to. I've found out who I need to speak to, and I'm going to do that now. But I wanted to tell you first, because … because …' She broke down again, sobbing convulsively. Then she stood up, and turned to go.

'Good luck!' he called after her. Then he chided himself for his stupidity. What an idiotic thing to say. It was her bad luck that had brought her to this point. The poor girl! He felt truly sorry for her.

Later that evening, as he thought about the scene that had taken place in his laboratory, it occurred to him that, as he had a daughter who was in her first year at university, perhaps he ought to say something to her. Should he tell her about poor Miss Gosling? Was it his fatherly duty to warn her of the dangers? The more he thought about it, the more unnecessary it seemed. Claudia was eminently sensible. She rarely went to parties, and he couldn't believe, for one moment, that the experience of the poor girl who had come to him today would befall his daughter. No, the more he thought about it, the more confident he felt. Claudia would never succumb to any kind of temptation like that. Not his serious-minded, intelligent Claudia. Never.

CHAPTER 7

Claudia had only been up at Oxford a few weeks when she received an anguished note from Maria. It read:

Dear Claudia

Please, please come back for a day, or more if you can. I'm miserable and unhappy and I badly need to talk to you. I miss you so much, and I do need to see you. But, of course, I'm very happy that you are there, and settling in well, by all accounts. Please reply straight away – I'll feel so much better if I know you're coming.

All my love, Maria

How could she refuse? In any case, it gave her an excuse to go home, and if the truth were told, she was feeling rather homesick. If she just went on Sunday, it wouldn't really impinge on her work. She'd just cram in as much as she could on Saturday. And probably she could get a bit of study done on the train. It would be wonderful to see Maria and her father again. She wondered what the terrible drama was, and guessed it was probably a storm in a teacup. But to Maria, experiencing the problem, it would be all-consuming.

She dropped a note into the post straightaway, saying she would come for the day on Sunday. It was already Thursday, so Maria would not have long to wait. In any case, it was quite likely that by the time she got there, the whole thing, whatever it was, would have blown over.

Maria's face lit up at the sight of Claudia, and she ran to her and hugged her. 'It's wonderful to see you! How are you? How are things going? Are you working terribly hard? I'm so pleased you're here – I've missed you so, and I've been longing to talk to you!'

There was no need to answer any of the questions – Maria wasn't interested in the answers. Obviously her own problems were still uppermost in her mind. Claudia greeted her father, who seemed pleased to see her, and after exchanging a few pleasantries with him, she followed her sister upstairs. Maria's bedroom was strewn untidily with magazines, an array of lipsticks lay on various surfaces and other items of make-up cluttered up the top of her dressing table. Various clothes were in evidence, either on hangers or lying on the bed. Claudia observed that nothing had changed.

'Well,' said Claudia, getting straight to the point. 'What is it? Why are you so miserable?'

'Daddy's cross with me and Diana won't speak to me!' wailed Maria. Diana Maitland had been Maria's best friend for several years now, and each was deeply involved in the other's hopes and dreams. At fifteen years of age both girls viewed social success as their top priority. Academic attainment meant nothing – neither could wait to leave school the following year so that they could embark on their adult lives.

'One thing at a time – what have you done to make Dad cross?'

'It's so unfair! He seems to think I should be working as hard for my exams as you did, and I can't, Claudia. I just can't. It all seems such a waste of time – after all, I've no intention of going to university!'

'So how much work are you doing?'

'Well, not a lot, I agree, but even if I did put in hours, I wouldn't get anywhere. I'm not like you, Claudia. I know I'm a disappointment to him, but I haven't got your brains and that's all there is to it.'

Claudia realised that her father probably had unrealistic ideas about his younger daughter, but at the same time she knew Maria made as little effort as she could get away with.

'Look, Maria, if you'll promise to try a bit harder, at least at English where you do sometimes get good marks, I'll speak to Dad and explain your side of it. Now what's the problem with Diana?'

Maria's face took on a tortured look. 'She won't speak to me any more and I can't bear having fallen out with her. I've tried ringing, and I've written lots of notes, and delivered them to her door – but she won't have anything to do with me!' Maria began to sob uncontrollably.

When she had finally calmed down, Claudia asked, 'What happened? Did you do something to upset her?'

'No! I didn't! I'm sure I didn't. Well, I never meant to upset her. I can't help it if Lance prefers me to her. How is that my fault?'

'Slow down a bit. Just try and tell me from the beginning.'

'Well, I was going out with Alex, and Lance was going out with Diana, so we decided to go out as a foursome. Only Diana and Lance had hardly been going out for any length of time, because I'd been going out with Lance until recently. Then Alex, who'd been going out with Lorna, got fed up with her, and started to ask me out, and I thought he might be more fun, so Lance started going out with Diana, only when we all went out together Lance started paying me attention, and in the end he took me home, and Alex got fed up, and took Diana home, and now Diana thinks I took Lance off her, and she won't speak to me!' More sobbing followed this convoluted explanation.

'It's hardly surprising she's not too pleased with you!'

'You're not going to take sides with Diana, are you? That's not what I asked you to come home for! How could I help it if Lance preferred to be with me! I didn't ask him to come back – I'd have stayed with Alex, even if he wasn't as much fun as I'd thought. But I hate having Diana, of all people, not speaking to me! We've been best friends for ages, and now she just ignores me! I can't bear it! It's awful at school with her avoiding me all the time. It makes me feel horrible.'

'What did you say in your notes to her?'

'I said it wasn't my fault that Lance came home with me, and it isn't fair of her to blame me. I didn't do anything.'

'That's hardly going to help.'

'How do you mean?'

'How about saying you're sorry, and that you miss her as your friend, and ask her what you can do to win her friendship back.'

'Oh, Claudia, I didn't think of that! Of course you're right! Thank goodness I've got a clever sister – I don't know how I'd manage my life without you to help me. I knew you'd sort it all out.'

'I've hardly done that. But perhaps it's worth a try.'

'I'm going to ring her up now, and say exactly what you said – that is, if she'll speak to me.'

Maria went downstairs to use the telephone. Claudia couldn't hear her words but she heard the tone, and it sounded contrite in the extreme. Then she heard the sound of crying, and went out to the landing to listen. It was clear they were both sobbing their hearts out, and Claudia heard phrases such 'missed you dreadfully' and 'don't let's ever quarrel again', and she smiled to herself. The friendship clearly mattered a great deal to Maria, and losing her friend had been a tragedy of the highest order. Claudia was glad they had become reconciled. She would have a word with their father before she left – she was sure he'd understand there was little to be achieved from pushing Maria where school work was concerned.

Of course Hugh was extremely interested to hear what Claudia was doing at Oxford. She told him about the syllabus she was following and the tutorials she attended. She said she was putting in a great deal of time, but she was enjoying her studies, finding them stimulating and rewarding. He congratulated her on making an excellent start and asked several questions. When she'd answered them all, she slipped in a few comments about Maria, trying to get Hugh to understand that her sister was unlikely to attain any great academic standard so it was probably best to let her move at her own pace.

Later in the afternoon she said goodbye to her sister who was restored to her usual sunny state, kissed her father, and took the train back to Oxford. She had really enjoyed spending a little time with Maria again, and there was something rather comforting about knowing you were being missed. Maria's life might, in Claudia's view, revolve around trivia, but she had to admit that there were times when she was rather lonely at Oxford. The familiarity of Maria's chatter and her unconstrained expressions of affection had warmed Claudia's heart. She loved the course she was doing but there was no emotional satisfaction in her college life and, whatever Maria's shortcomings might be, Claudia knew that her sister meant the world to her. Pleased that she had made the visit and that, for the time being, Maria had regained her usual cheerfulness, Claudia felt ready to pick up the cudgels back at Oxford once more.

CHAPTER 8

When Claudia came home at the end of her second year at Oxford her self-confidence was high. She had sustained an excellent level of marks throughout the last three terms, and knew she was heading at least for a good second class honours degree, and quite possibly for a first. Yes, the final year would be tough, but she could do it. She didn't mind how much time and effort she put in, because the end result would make it all worthwhile. She would be able to embark on a teaching career – an objective she had held for as long as she could remember.

That same summer Maria achieved her lifetime ambition – she left school. She quickly fell into a pattern of getting up late, telephoning friends, and going out in the evenings. Eventually Hugh put his foot down. This was not good enough – she must get a job. He was not prepared to support her idleness.

Maria grumbled, but conceded that he had a point, and began, in a half-hearted manner, to look at newspaper advertisements. However, with her usual luck, the ideal job found her, without any effort on her part.

On her daily journey back from school she used to pass Stroud's Fashions, a small shop selling ladies' clothes. She had often lingered to look in the window, and occasionally went in, as the selection was rather more interesting than the clothes she saw in the traditional department stores.

Out in town one day, on her way to meet up with a group of friends at a coffee bar, she passed by the shop and saw some dresses in the window that appealed to her. She went inside and browsed among the different items, enjoying their colours and fingering the different textures. The proprietor, Jennifer Stroud, not being particularly occupied at the time, came out from behind her counter.

'Can I help you? Are you looking for something in particular?'

'Isn't this dress amazing! I love this colour – it's such a gorgeous pink. And the material feels so soft and smooth.'

'It is beautiful, isn't it – but perhaps a little old for you?'

'Oh, I wasn't thinking of buying it – I haven't any money! I just like looking at lovely clothes. Sorry – I suppose I shouldn't have come in really. I'm wasting your time.'

'That's quite all right. It's nice having someone appreciating my choice of fashions. I suppose you're not looking for a job, are you? As it happens, I've been thinking of taking on a young person.'

The arrangement could hardly have been better. Beautiful clothes were what sparked Maria's enthusiasm, and the idea of being in a fashion shop all day was certainly attractive. For her part Jennifer was able to take on the assistant she'd been wanting comparatively cheaply, and she could see there was potential for development in this eager young girl.

Now Maria was up promptly each morning – much to Hugh's relief – happy to be going off to an environment she loved. She soon proved she had an excellent eye for what suited people and many satisfied customers left with outfits they would not have dreamed of buying had Maria not pointed out how the colours and style enhanced their appearance. She also proved to have a flair for window dressing, her efforts attracting the eye of passing shoppers who could not resist coming in to browse.

Jennifer Stroud was delighted with her new assistant's enthusiasm and the resulting increase in sales. After three months she gave Maria a small rise in recognition of the good job she was doing, and Maria felt that this, coupled with opportunities for socialising in the evenings, provided her with all she wanted in life. The past year had brought a marked change in her. Gone was the childish behaviour of the previous year. Diana Maitland had faded completely out of her life. She was a self-possessed young woman, and the greater level of maturity made her more attractive than ever, with the result that there was never any shortage of boyfriends.

Claudia was pleased to see that Maria had fallen on her feet, but she was troubled by the social aspect of her sister's life. Almost every evening Maria would rush home from work, wash and change with lightning speed, and then disappear through the door in a state of high excitement with the young man who had been lucky enough to book her for that evening. Mostly the boyfriends came to the door to collect her and the two young people would set off on foot, as the main attractions, such as the cinema and the coffee bars, were within walking distance. Greg Butchers, however, was the proud possessor of a Lambretta scooter, and his attendance at the family home to pick Maria up possibly equalled in frequency that of all the others put together. Claudia would hear the sound of the engine accelerating as the vehicle disappeared in the distance with Maria on the back, arms tightly wound round Greg's waist, clearly finding the experience exhilarating.

Then Claudia would wait anxiously for her sister to return. Sometimes, if she had been to the cinema, Maria would be back before Claudia had gone to bed. Then she would regale Claudia with an account of the latest film, the story punctuated with frequent giggles at some private joke she thought it better not to share. On many occasions, however, she came back so late that Claudia would give up waiting for her. Claudia might have retired to bed but this did not mean she could sleep. She would lie there worrying, wondering just what Maria got up to on these late evenings. Should she, as the older sister, say something? She knew only too well that her father would not see any need to intervene. He took very little notice of what Maria was doing, now she was settled in her job. It was at a time like this, when she did not know what to do, that Claudia found herself missing her mother acutely. Anita would have known how to handle the situation.

One night, as Claudia lay awake, she heard the unmistakable splutter of the scooter's engine approaching the house. She breathed a sigh of relief, and waited for the sound of the key in the lock. It did not come, but as her bedroom was at the front of the house she could hear the unmistakable sound of Maria's giggle, and also the gruff tones of a male voice. Then there was silence. Claudia got out of bed, and gingerly drawing back the corner of the curtain, peeped out. The two young people were locked in a tight embrace. Even as she watched they shifted position, and unmistakably the words, 'Stop it, Greg! Greg!' followed by more giggles, could be heard.

At last there was the sound of the front door being opened, and Maria's feet running upstairs, as the scooter roared away down the road. Claudia looked at her alarm clock – it was gone 3 a.m. She got up and opened her bedroom door. Maria saw her and grinned.

'Oh, Claudia!' she said. 'I had such an amazing time, I can't tell you. Do you know what we did? We–'

'You're very late, Maria,' Claudia cut in. 'Do you know what the time is?'

'Oh, fiddle the time.' Maria looked entirely unconcerned. 'Anyhow, what are you doing up, if it's so late?'

'Waiting for you to come back, and worrying because you haven't.'

'Whatever do you want to do that for? I'm perfectly able to look after myself. I'm only having a good time. What's wrong with that?'

'Come in, a moment. We don't want to wake Dad.'

Maria followed Claudia into her room, protesting, 'Must I? You're not going to be stuffy and start lecturing me, are you?'

'Look, Maria, it's just that I feel responsible, with no mother here to guide you. You're out with a string of boys, you come back at all hours, and I don't know what you're doing.'

'I told you – I'm just having fun. We go to the pictures, or meet up with some of the others …'

'Yes, but I worry about what you do when you're out with these boys … well, what I mean is … how far do you go?'

'Not far at all – only into town. Except when it's Greg, of course, with his mean machine, as he calls it. Then we can–'

'That's not what I meant. I saw you both outside this evening. You were ...'

'Oh, Claudia! So that's what you're worrying about! Do you really think I'd risk getting pregnant? I can tell you, a baby's the last thing I want at the moment – and not for ages! Life's far too good the way it is.'

'Are you sure, Maria? Are you sure you know what you're doing? It all looked pretty intense outside just now.'

'So you were snooping! Just stop clucking over me like a mother hen. I promise you, *that's* not going to happen. I'm not a schoolgirl now. I know all about these things. You don't have to worry.'

And with that she got up, smiled sweetly at Claudia, and disappeared into her bedroom. Claudia felt relieved to a certain extent, while still wondering just how much Maria's assertions were to be trusted. Well, she had done what she could.

It was time to go back to Oxford, for the final push. Claudia knew it would be hard work, but she was prepared to make the effort. She was on the way towards achieving her goal. She and Maria continued to keep in touch, frequently exchanging letters. The sisters settled back into their separate ways of life, each drawing comfort from the knowledge that the other would always be there for them.

CHAPTER 9

'Claudia! Are you there? I'd like to have a word with you.'

It wasn't often Hugh sought her out – usually they lived parallel lives, communicating infrequently, but always civilly. Hugh was very proud of his undergraduate daughter, delighting in her successes throughout her course. Claudia was in her third year now and only the last hurdle remained to be overcome – her Finals were in three months' time.

Maria was amazed when Claudia came down for her first vacation and immediately drew up a schedule of study. She had assumed Claudia would be on holiday when she came home, not realising the amount of work to be covered, and when she saw it for herself she was all the more glad she had not stayed on at school any longer than she had to!

'Fancy having to spend all your free time working! Where's the fun in that? It looks like slave labour to me!'

Claudia patiently explained that new work came at a fast rate, and it was her responsibility to use the vacations to revise and prepare for the next term's work, but Maria soon lost interest.

'You don't seem to have much of a social life. It wouldn't suit me!'

Claudia agreed that indeed it wouldn't suit her sister. She had been kept informed, on the whole, in their weekly letters, of the procession of young men who came and went – each successive one being the amazing specimen of manhood who was going to whisk Maria away into the sunset – only to be abruptly superseded by another young hopeful. Claudia, for her part, had had no wish to embark on any sort of relationship. It would have been too distracting. She got on satisfactorily with her fellow students, and was happy to leave it at that.

It seemed her father had a proposition to offer her.

'A colleague of mine knows of a young Italian who will be doing business for his company in England and who wants to improve his English. He's looking for someone competent to give him some tutoring – the pay would be good, I understand, and I wondered if you would like to consider it – while you're at home?'

'Oh, I couldn't possibly! I've far too much to do. I've got my studies all planned out.'

'I really don't think it would take up too much of your time. I believe he speaks quite well – it's just that he wants to get a bit more confident, and master colloquial English. Well, think about it.'

Inclined to reject the idea initially, Claudia started to wonder whether, perhaps, there might be some merit in it. If it wasn't going to be too onerous, it would be a useful way of accumulating some funds – something she might need as she embarked on a teaching career, possibly moving away from home. Her father was always ready with his support, but she preferred to be as independent as possible. Perhaps it would be fairly easy to manage an hour here and there; after all, she did schedule in breaks, otherwise she wouldn't have been able to keep up the high level of concentration required. And it would be a kind of introduction to teaching. She agreed to meet this man, thinking she could discuss his needs, and then make a decision.

She was unprepared for the handsome Italian who presented himself – tall, dark, good-looking, athletic build, with an engaging smile, wonderfully penetrating blue eyes and a charming manner.

'Miss Hansom! It is kind of you to invite me to your home. Your father has told me that you study very hard now. It is admirable – your cleverness with mathematics. Do you think you could help me learn English?'

'You don't seem to need too much help. You're speaking quite well, as far as I can see.'

'Ah, you are a very kind lady, signorina, but I know that I do mistakes. My English is – how you say – textbook? I need to speak like the English people, so there is no problem for me when I make business.'

'What business will you be doing?'

'I work for the renowned Italian firm, Carbotti – you have heard of them, no? We use beautiful leather and make lovely handbags and other accessories to make the signoras and signorinas look most beautiful.'

Claudia laughed. She had never met anyone quite like Stefano, and decided a slight diversion wouldn't do her any harm. They reached an agreement about times and dates – he would have three hours a week, on separate days – and they would do oral work, for the most part, but she agreed to make notes for him during the lesson so that he would have some reference material afterwards.

It took considerable determination to stick to her studies. She was eager to do a little research into some basic Italian words and phrases, knowing nothing of the language. She found herself looking forward to their sessions.

On the first occasion she encouraged him to tell her about his background – his family, his work and what he wanted to achieve from his lessons. He talked easily about all his sisters and brothers, and their family home near Milan so that the hour ran quickly by. Every now and then she stopped him and corrected a word here or a phrase there – sometimes changing the order of words into a more natural English style. Every time she intervened she noted the point down so that when he got up to go he was already aware of a number of improvements he could make.

He held out his hand to her, and bowed a little, thanking her profusely and saying how much he was looking forward to the next time. Meanwhile he would practise the points she had written down. 'I will make my best,' he said.

'Do my best,' corrected Claudia. '"Do", not "make". Or you could say "I will make every effort to practise what I have learned."'

'Ah, yes, thank you.' He turned to go. 'Ciao!' he said, and with another of his attractive smiles he was gone. Claudia watched his retreating figure moving easily with a grace that highlighted the awkwardness of many English young men.

Maria arrived home from work all agog to know what had happened. On hearing Claudia's description of the Italian good looks and charming manner, Maria was full of envy, wishing she'd been there to see him.

'He sounds amazing! Next time he comes I'll tell Jennifer I'm not well, and need to have a day at home! I don't see why you should have all the fun!'

'That's strange – I thought it was you who had the fun, and I just did boring study! Anyway, my time with him is on a purely professional basis, so don't go reading anything into it.'

'Professional, my foot. As if anyone could keep their minds on professional things if he's as marvellous as you say.'

The lessons proceeded smoothly, and each time teacher and pupil became easier with each other. Whenever Stefano made a mistake he would touch her arm, throw back his head and exclaim, 'Oh, Stefano is a big fool!' He didn't mind how often she corrected him – in fact he seemed to enjoy it. She was aware that he would often touch her, in a manner that was obviously natural for him, but it slightly disconcerted her. Maria would have described it as flirty and Claudia had to admit it gave her a secret thrill. No one had ever acted like that with her before.

One day, when he was due to come, he rang to say his company wanted him for the day, so would Claudia permit him to change the time to the evening instead, as he did not want to miss out on his lesson. Claudia readily agreed.

However, when the bell rang and Maria went rushing to open the door Claudia began to regret her decision. The sight of Maria's upturned face, her eyes fixed on Stefano, and the sound of her tinkling laughter sent a cold shiver down Claudia's spine. He must have been transfixed by her looks, as he appeared to have forgotten his way to the dining-room where they normally sat.

'I know!' cried Maria excitedly, 'why don't I join you for your lesson? It will mean Stefano has to cope with both of us talking, which will make it a lot harder for him to keep up!'

Claudia was about to rebuff this idea immediately but before she could get a word out Stefano said, 'How kind that would be! But I'm afraid you will both see what a fool I am and Claudia will not be deceived any more – she will realise that I am not as clever as she thinks.'

'Come on!' Maria led the way, and soon they were all seated at the table. Maria immediately started a flow of chatter, scarcely allowing Stefano any scope for response.

'This is no good,' said Claudia tersely. 'How is my pupil supposed to learn if you don't give him a chance to get a word in edgeways, Maria?'

Maria raised her hand to her mouth in mock alarm. 'Oh my! Now you'll think I'm such an idiot, Stefano. Here I am, rambling on, forgetting it's you that should be talking! What a good thing it's Claudia who's your teacher. She's much better at being serious than I am.'

'Perhaps I should do some practice now with Claudia. But thank you for talking to me.' He rose to his feet, and bowed a little, as Maria left the room.

As soon as Stefano had left, Claudia went to find Maria and unleashed her anger. 'How dare you muscle in on my lesson! That was unforgiveable!'

Maria was unrepentant.

'Oh, what an amazing man! Those blue eyes! Those charming manners! You are a lucky so-and-so Claudia. I hope you realise how fantastic he is – or are you so devoted to your studies you don't even notice an Adonis when he's right in front of you!'

'I've told you already, I'm simply giving him lessons. Of course it doesn't escape my notice that he's very handsome, but he's paying me to teach him English, and that's what I'm doing.'

The next day Stefano rang up. His company had suggested that in order to concentrate on his language learning before he returned to Italy he could perhaps have one whole day with his tutor, visiting London, getting to know his way round, and improving his grasp of the language further. Instead of giving him an hour the following day, could she manage a day out? And if she could not spare the time, perhaps her sister might do him the honour? He added that perhaps that was not a good idea, however, as he might then be listening, rather than speaking, if Maria was with him.

Claudia was torn. She could see the sense of it. It would do him good to have a whole day – but this was the last week of her vacation, and her Finals were getting uncomfortably close. She really couldn't give up a whole day. On the other hand, she knew that if she did not agree, Maria would have no trouble thinking up some excuse to get time off work, and grab the chance of spending a day with Stefano like a shot. Common sense prevailed. She must forego the chance, but perhaps she could just not mention it to Maria.

She told Stefano that she was sorry, she could not take a day away from her studies, and her sister would be at work the next day, which was Friday.

'Then perhaps she could come with me on Sunday! I have a very good idea – when I have had my lesson in your wonderful city of London, then perhaps I could ask two lovely ladies to come to have dinner with me. Please say yes – I want to thank you for all the time you have given me.'

There was nothing for it, then, but to pass his message on to Maria, who, as Claudia had anticipated, was in a state of high excitement at the prospect. The arrangements were made, and Claudia was to meet them at seven o'clock at an Italian restaurant in Richmond.

Much to her annoyance Claudia arrived that evening to find that the other two were not yet there, and forty minutes slowly ticked by before they appeared. They came in laughing and talking, and although Stefano greeted her warmly when he saw her, Claudia sensed that there was now a familiarity between the other two which made her feel left out. She was unable to join in their chatter, and relapsed into a miserable silence, which neither of the other two appeared to notice.

Afterwards Maria came to her.

'Don't be cross, Claudia. I didn't mean to upset you. It's just that he was such fun, and so different from the boring English boys I've been out with. And you said you weren't interested in him, except professionally, so I didn't think it would matter.'

'So what happened? Where did you go? Knowing you, I wouldn't be surprised if you'd managed to wheedle a proposal of marriage out of him!'

'Don't be silly! Of course not! We just had a good time. And I did remember I was supposed to be helping him, and I showed him how to use the underground and the buses. And we walked all over the place, and sat down in the park, and I'm so tired, but it was heavenly! Dear Claudia, please say you aren't cross. He's going away very soon, so I don't suppose I'll see him any more.'

Claudia softened. Perhaps she had been rather too quick to feel jealous. Anyway, she still had one last lesson with Stefano, on Tuesday, and Maria would be safely out of harm's way.

CHAPTER 10

Stefano was his usual self when he turned up for his last lesson – smiling, gallant, and appreciative of the time Claudia had given him. She put Sunday's episode out of her mind and concentrated on making the most of this final session. There was no doubt his English had improved, but there were still many instances when it was clear that here was an Italian trying to master English.

At the end of the lesson he stood up. 'I want to say a thousand thank yous to you, Claudia. You have understand what it means to me to learn your language and you have spent much time, when I know you want really to study for your exams.'

Claudia squirmed. Had she managed to teach him anything?

Stefano continued. 'Wait here, please.' He went back into the hall, where, it seemed, he had left something. He returned carrying a large, smart carrier bag with the name Carbotti printed across it.

'I have brought you this little gift, to say thank you for all my excellent lessons. Please accept this, from me. Please.' He held out the bag to her.

Claudia opened it, and inside was a fairly large object wrapped in tissue paper. She removed this and was left holding a beautiful leather handbag of a size and quality that made the two rather tatty specimens in her cupboard look pretty pathetic.

She gasped.

'For me? This is for me?' Her fingers moved over the soft leather, feeling the texture of an object she knew was far more expensive than anything she had ever owned in her life before.

'It is for you. You have been very patient, very kind. So many stupid mistakes I know I make. You are very good to help me.'

'Oh no, you have done very well. You have been an excellent pupil. I'm sure you feel you have made progress, don't you?'

'With your help, yes, I have.'

'Oh, Stefano! I don't know how to thank you! It's an absolutely beautiful handbag. How did you manage to pick something that I would love so much? The colour is perfect, and the style – well, it's so smart. I just love it. There really was no need to give me anything – I was generously paid for the lessons, but I can't tell you how much I love it!'

Claudia was filled with a warm glow, basking in his admiration and gratitude, and thrilled by the gift which she knew was far superior to anything she would ever have bought for herself.

The next moment her blood ran cold. He was holding out another carrier bag. 'And please, give this to your very pretty sister, who was so good to come with me on Sunday, and show me London.'

It is extraordinary, thought Claudia, how one moment you can be on top of the world, and a few seconds later find yourself plummeting down to the depths.

Totally unaware of the effect of the bombshell he had just dropped, Stefano continued speaking. 'You and your sister, you have shown much kindness to a stranger, an Italian who is far from home. Please you say thank you to her, and now I say goodbye.'

He stepped forward and kissed her on both cheeks.

With very mixed feelings she watched him go. And then she had an idea. The more she thought about it the better the idea seemed. She would work out all the details of the plan she had just hatched and would put it into action as soon as she returned to Oxford.

CHAPTER 11

It was six days since Claudia had posted the letter. The lack of response was frustrating. It meant that instead of being able to give her mind fully to her carefully planned schedule of revision, she was waiting for the post daily, and rushing down to see if a letter had come for her – an unwelcome distraction in view of the proximity of her final exams, and the need for her to make one last concerted effort.

It had not occurred to her that there would be this delay. She had thought there would be a letter by return. More fool her! Why should she assume he'd be delighted with her suggestion? It had all seemed a brilliant idea when she had first devised the plan, but now she began to think she had acted very foolishly.

Then, finally, it came. She knew his handwriting – distinctly continental in its cursive, flowing style. With trembling hands she tore the envelope open and retrieved the folded sheet of paper from inside. She could not believe her eyes – he was saying everything she had hoped! He was honoured to be asked to escort her to the college Summer Ball. He would be so happy to travel to Oxford, and looked forward to seeing some of the city's famous sights, with Claudia as his guide, and then, that evening, to accompanying her to the ball.

Claudia walked on air, breathing sighs of relief, and smiling to herself. She had achieved it! For the first time in her three years up at Oxford, she was one of the lucky students who would be going to a ball. The thought of Stefano dressed in evening attire made her go weak at the knees. She knew he would look incredibly handsome, and she felt sure she would be the envy of every other female student.

A practical problem now presented itself – she had no ball gown to wear. It had seemed far too much like tempting fate to do anything about acquiring one until she had had a positive response from Stefano, and no doubt all the best ones in the 'nearly new' fashion shops would have gone. Claudia had a little money, thanks to the lessons she had given, but the frugal side of her nature would not let her spend the whole amount on one dress which, in all probability, she was only going to wear on this one occasion.

It was a glorious summer day, making the 'dreaming spires' of Oxford look more magical than ever, lit as they were by bright sunshine against a blue backdrop. If this spell of fine weather lasted until the day of the ball, Stefano would be enraptured by all he saw. How could it fail to put him in the best of moods? Dipping into her precious revision time, Claudia began a quick circuit of the shops she thought might stock dresses that had probably been worn by other students in past years, but she could find nothing. It seemed the other students had been quicker off the mark and had snapped up all the bargains! No doubt they had had their partners lined up well in advance.

Time was running out, and so was the supply of possible outlets for what she sought. She racked her brains for a fresh source – trying to think of somewhere that had eluded her so far. As she stood there mulling over her problem, she noticed an Austin Seven chug round the corner. The car was just drawing level with her when a black cat appeared out of nowhere, darted across the road, realised the car was approaching, hesitated, and then made the fatal decision to continue on its journey. There was a screech of brakes, and a dull thud. The young man who had been driving the car stepped out to investigate, a worried expression on his face. He bent down to look at the inert small body lying on the road and exclaimed, 'Holy mother! I've killed a cat!'

Claudia had run across the road to where he stood, and joined him in looking at the lifeless body.

'I saw him dash into the road in front of you. Is he …? Do you think he's dead?'

'I'm very much afraid so. I tried to stop, but there just wasn't time.'

'Poor thing,' said Claudia. 'Should we call a vet?'

'Not much use,' said the young man. 'Too late for that. I feel dreadful.'

'It's not your fault. He shouldn't have been out roaming the streets.'

'Look, there's a collar with a name tag. Perhaps it's got an address on.'

They looked closely, and sure enough the details were there. The young man squinted at the metal tag through his thick glasses.

'His name's Tiger – only his family can't spell – it's written with two gs.'

'That's not Tiger, it's Tigger,' said Claudia. 'You know, Christopher Robin, Pooh Bear, and all those characters.'

'Ah, I was a *Swallows and Amazons* boy – I think I missed out on A.A. Milne.'

He started to take off his jacket. Claudia noticed that, although the jacket was reasonably presentable, the jumper now on view had seen far better days. There were large holes in the sleeves. He saw her glance.

'Sorry,' he said. 'The jacket hides a multitude of sins, but I think Tiger's – or rather Tigger's – need is now greater than mine.'

With gentle hands he picked up the small black body and wrapped it tenderly in the jacket.

'What are you going to do now?' Claudia asked.

'I'll have to return the cat to its owner, and break the bad news. The address is only two roads away.'

'Would you like me to come with you?'

'Would you? That would give me a bit of courage.'

He smiled, and Claudia saw that, although he was far from handsome, with his bristly fair hair, freckled face and oversized ears, he had kind eyes and his smile was reassuring. Gently he laid the bundle on the back seat.

'I imagine you're a student?' he asked.

'Yes, St Hilda's, reading maths. And you?'

'Brasenose, and I've embarked on history. I'm in my second year. What year are you?'

'My third. I decided on maths, but I love history, particularly the classical period.'

'We have something in common then, apart from a dead cat. What's your name?'

'Claudia, Claudia Hansom. And yours?'

'Bernard Stubbings. My friends call me Burns – because I write poetry.'

'Really? What sort?'

'The very bad sort. Here we are.'

He drew up, and then got out to pick the cat up once more. Together they walked up to the front door. He rang the bell several times, but there was no answer.

'What do we do now?' He turned to Claudia, the worried look back on his face. 'I can't just dump the poor thing on the front doorstep. Perhaps we can get round the back.'

They found a gate to the side which was unlocked. Bernard carried the cat round to the back and laid him by the back door.

'Have you got a bit of paper? I'll have to write a note.'

Claudia fished a piece out of her handbag. He hesitated for a moment and then wrote:

'I'm so sorry, I'm afraid your cat ran out in front of my car. I couldn't stop in time. I'm really very sorry.' Then he added his name, and that he could be contacted at Brasenose College, and put the note beside the body, placing a stone on top to stop it blowing away.

'Right, that's it. I think we can go now.'

'What about your jacket?'

'It seems disrespectful, somehow, to leave the poor thing uncovered. I think I'll sacrifice it. It's the least I can do.'

They walked back to the car.

'Now, where can I drop you? Back where I found you? Or were

59

you going somewhere? I'll give you a lift if you like. It's very kind of you to have come with me. I would have felt awful doing it all on my own.'

'Actually,' Claudia replied, 'I've been trying to find a dress for our summer ball, but all the shops that sell second hand ones have none left, and I can't think of anywhere else to go. It's annoying, because I should be studying for my Finals, and I've wasted a lot of time.'

Bernard looked thoughtful. 'I know a charity shop,' he said at last, 'that I seem to remember has things like that. Would you like to try there? I could easily drop you off.'

'That would be good, if you don't mind. I'm getting a bit desperate.'

'It's the least I can do. You've been a great support to me in my hour of need.'

As they drove off Bernard remarked casually, 'I don't suppose you need a partner, for your ball, do you? I mean, if by any chance you do, I'd be pleased to …'

'Thank you, Bernard, that's very nice of you. But actually …'

'Yes, I guessed you'd have one already lined up. Oh well, I just thought I'd ask.'

What was that saying about buses? None for ages and then three come along at once? All this time up at Oxford and no one had asked her to a ball before, and now suddenly, she had two offers! For a moment Claudia regretted that she had had to turn Bernard down. She rather liked him, even if his looks left a lot to be desired. Then she thought of Stefano – charming, handsome, sophisticated Stefano – and knew there was really no contest. Still, it was a pity she had not met Bernard before. He seemed a pleasant, kind sort of man. They drew up outside the charity shop.

'Poor old Tigger didn't have much luck today, but perhaps he'll bring you some,' he said. 'I hope so. See you around!'

'Thanks, Bernard. And don't blame yourself for what's happened. It wasn't your fault.'

He nodded, and smiled once more. Then he drove off. Claudia

pushed open the shop door and went inside. The assistant who came over to see what Claudia wanted was most enthusiastic.

'How lovely! Fancy going to the summer ball! It makes me wish I were young again.'

'Yes, but I haven't been able to find anything to wear. There don't seem to be any ball gowns left anywhere – certainly nothing within my budget.'

The woman looked thoughtfully at her. 'How handy are you with a needle?'

'Quite good,' replied Claudia. 'Why do you ask?'

'Well, a rather beautiful blue dress came in a few days ago, but it has suffered a bit of damage. Goodness knows what the last person who wore it got up to! I think someone must have trodden on the hem, because it's got torn. But it might be repairable. Let's have a look at it.'

She went into a private room at the back of the shop and came back holding the dress over her arm.

Claudia gasped. The dress had style and was a beautiful shade of blue – Claudia's favourite colour. It could hardly have been more perfect. Together they studied the tear in the fabric.

'I think I could do something about that,' said Claudia. 'I feel pretty sure I could sew it up so that no one would ever know. After all, it will be dark – well, for most of the time!'

'And I think I could let you have it at a very moderate price, as you will have to work on it before it can be worn.'

It seemed it was her lucky day after all! Thrilled with her purchase Claudia carried the dress back to her room and examined it closely. It was going to take some time to do the stitching required – time which she had not bargained for. She would just have to stay up at night, or get up early in the morning. She would do whatever it took, for here was the dress she needed to make Stefano proud of her. In this dress, perhaps, even she, Claudia Hansom, could, for once, be the belle of the ball. She drew in a deep breath and started to work on it.

CHAPTER 12

Finally the day of the ball arrived, and with it an atmosphere of mounting excitement. The weather, as Claudia had hoped, was clear and bright, and the gardens were looking their colourful best. No cloud appeared on the horizon to spoil the fresh beauty of the morning.

Claudia was expecting Stefano some time in the early afternoon. He would come by train as he thought it might not be advisable to drive back after a night of 'revelry', as he put it. He would take a taxi to St Hilda's College.

Eagerly anticipating his arrival Claudia was ready in good time. She was not displeased with the reflection she saw in the mirror. Her hair which, most unusually, had benefited from a hairdresser's skills, was pleasantly curled and shiny. The blue dress, on its hanger, awaiting the evening's events, looked every bit as elegant as she had hoped. Her fellow students, unused to seeing Claudia at social events, were intrigued to see the man she had invited – especially when she volunteered that he was Italian and extremely handsome.

When he did arrive the sight of him took her breath away, and all she could think of was one of Maria's favourite words – amazing. He looked like a film star, and he was carrying a beautiful bouquet of flowers.

'Oh, Stefano! They're lovely! Thank you very much.'

'Not nearly as lovely as my partner! Claudia, I have never seen you look so beautiful. And I very much look forward to the ball.'

The evening, with all its promise of magic, was approaching, but first Claudia wanted to show her visitor a little of the glories Oxford had to offer.

'Are you tired after your journey?' she asked. 'Could we go for a walk so that I can show you some of the local sights?'

'That would be very good,' he replied. 'That I will like, and I will remember all that I see today.'

They set off from St Hilda's, and walked over Magdalen Bridge, pausing to look down on the river below where punts lazily made their slow progress through the water.

'Look! Look!' cried Stefano. 'Are they not like the gondolas in Venice? Already I feel at home!'

Continuing along the High Street they passed the glorious tower of Magdalen College and then turned right into Catte Street and Radcliffe Square, where Stefano gazed in awe at the circular, domed building known as the Radcliffe Camera. Claudia showed him the Bodleian Library on the far side of the square. Then she pointed out the University Church of St Mary the Virgin, Brasenose College and All Souls College. Stefano was clearly fascinated by it all. Using her Reader's Card, she was able to take him up to the Upper Reading Room of the Radcliffe Camera and show him views of Central Oxford.

'There's one more place I would like to show you, before we go back, as I have a surprise lined up for you a little later this afternoon and we mustn't be late.' She took him further down Catte Street where they stood before the two halves of Hertford College and the ornate aerial corridor linking them.

'There you are,' she said. 'That should make you feel even more at home. This is known as the Bridge of Sighs! Isn't it a beautiful piece of architecture?'

'It is lovely, but I think perhaps it resembles not so much the Bridge of Sighs in Venice but more the Rialto Bridge. We have a legend about our Bridge of Sighs, which I will tell you. It is said that lovers will be granted everlasting love and bliss if they kiss on a gondola at sunset under the bridge! But I do not think you could do that here, because there is no water!'

Laughing, they started to walk back to the college, where Claudia fetched a basket from her room. Then they set off again.

'Let me carry that for you. Oh, it is quite heavy! What is in this mysterious basket?'

'Be patient. You will find out very soon.'

'Where are we going?' he asked. 'You will tire me out before the ball starts!'

'I don't think so. I am going to give you a true Oxford experience.'

She led him in the direction of the river, and towards the boathouse. He looked at the boats, and saw other students propelling them along in the water with the traditional long pole.

'Is this what we are going to do?'

'Yes. Do you think you can manage?'

'It looks like a gondola, except there is no oar – only that funny long stick. Of course I can do it.'

The man in charge of the boathouse gave him a quick lesson. He showed him how to hold the pole, and feed it through his hands.

'Don't forget to pull it out of the water before your hands reach the end or you'll be in trouble. If you can't get it out in time, let go, or you'll end up in the drink as well! There's a paddle in the punt for emergencies so you can always go back for it, if you do lose it.'

In no time at all Stefano had mastered the technique and they set off, slowly winding their way along the river. They passed other punts, and Claudia, lying back in her seat, with plenty of time to appraise those in the passing craft, was in no doubt that she was being propelled along by the most handsome man on the river. She felt like a princess.

Once they had reached a quiet section, she suggested that he stop, and opening her basket, she produced two glasses, champagne and strawberries.

'I like your Oxford traditions,' observed Stefano.

They sat in the punt, the water gently lapping up against the boat, and ate and drank until the contents of the basket were gone.

'Hm,' murmured Stefano. 'I feel so happy and the evening has not started yet. Will there be more champagne?'

'Yes, and lots of other things. There will be dancing, of course, and an excellent supper. It's going to be wonderful. Thank you very much for coming, Stefano. You have made an unforgettable ending to my time at Oxford. I shall always remember today.'

'I also, I remember too. I am grateful that you ask me.'

Today was not the day for correcting errors. She was not in the mood. They returned to the college and she showed him where he could change. At long last she was ready, and as she descended the staircase she saw him waiting for her in the hall below. Again a thrill of pride shot through her – in his evening dress he looked unbelievably handsome. What had she done to deserve an evening of such heady delight? He received her with Italian gallantry, bowing and kissing her hand.

They passed through the hall to the spot where the college principal stood waiting to receive guests. Claudia presented Stefano and the principal held out her hand stiffly. On hearing the name of Claudia's guest she asked politely, 'Will you be in this country long, Mr Volpe?'

Stefano did not release her hand. Bowing slightly, he looked her straight in the eyes, his face lit up by his irresistible smile. 'I am here for two months only, thank you. And in this time Claudia has been so kind as to give me English lessons. But soon I come back to live in your lovely country.'

Finally he released the hand, and the principal, a woman of renowned scholarly attributes and usually impervious to masculine charm, was actually blushing slightly, a warm glow diffusing her cheeks.

Claudia and Stefano danced, they talked, they frequently sipped their drinks, and they danced again. The music became slower and dreamier. In the small hours of the morning they walked arm-in-arm round the garden.

'Are you tired now?' he asked.

'Oh no, I could go on for hours and hours. I don't want it ever to stop.' She smiled up at him, her eyes shining.

'Let's go for a walk,' he said and there was a note of urgency in his voice. 'I wish to walk beside that river.'

Claudia would have done anything he suggested. They set off, leaving behind the lively sounds of music and laughter, into the sharply contrasting quiet of the Cherwell river bank. The only sounds were the soft rustling of leaves and grass, disturbed by a light breeze. The trees swayed gently against a background of silvery light, as if they too had drunk of the evening's champagne. The two young people strolled in the moonlight along the river path, arms round each other's waists. Under a dark, overhanging tree he drew her close, and kissed her.

'Maybe we are not under that bridge, but tonight, bella Claudia, you are very, very beautiful, and I must kiss you,' he whispered.

'Oh, Stefano.' There could be no mistaking his meaning. Racing emotions overwhelmed her, as they slid down to the grassy ground, where she gave herself up to an unfamiliar world of sensations.

Afterwards he held her tight, kissing her hair, and murmuring how lovely she was. Idly she wondered what had happened to her blue dress, and the thought that this was how the original damage had occurred made her giggle. She was intoxicated, partly with wine, but mostly with love.

Stefano was still speaking. 'You will make very marvellous wife,' he said. 'Would you like to marry?'

Sleepily she responded, 'Yes please, darling, darling Stefano. Oh, yes, please.'

'And then you make babies, doublequick, one, two, three, four – maybe five!'

Claudia was just awake enough to object to this. 'Not yet, my dearest, not yet. I have worked so hard, I must establish my teaching career first. Plenty of time for babies later.'

Her head was resting against his shoulder, and sleep was overtaking her. She did not see his expression change.

'I think, one day, you will make very lovely wife,' he said, 'for some lucky man.'

But Claudia was asleep.

CHAPTER 13

The dream-like state Claudia now found herself in was not the best preparation for her Finals. She longed to give Maria a full account of the ball, and tell her what a wonderful partner Stefano had been. She longed to boast about the envious glances she had received from the other girls, and how even the principal had been impressed. Whether it was amazement that Claudia had produced a partner at all, or whether it was the shock of those film star looks, was difficult to tell. It had certainly been a moment of triumph.

There had been no time to write a long letter home. Better to keep her memories safely stored in her mind and wait until she saw her sister. Claudia savoured the pleasure of describing in rapturous detail all they had done during that unbelievable twenty-four hours. Well, perhaps not quite all. The last part she might skate over a little. That was something private between the two of them – something to hold in a very special place in her heart. Some things were too deep for sharing, even with Maria.

She began to apply herself to her revision. She must now make up for lost time and plan precisely how long she could afford to devote to each topic. She concentrated hard, and spent long hours at her studies, scarcely speaking to her fellow students. She knew she must be single-minded if she was to fulfil her potential. All her efforts, her hours of dedication to her work over the last three years, were about to be put to the test. If she could perform to the best of her ability she would have the distinction of being marked out for the rest of her life as an outstanding student of mathematics, and this would have a lasting effect on her career.

She closed her mind to all distractions and gave herself to this vital undertaking.

There was, however, one diversion she could not ignore. A letter arrived in that now familiar script. She tore it open – and then wished she'd taken more care to preserve the envelope. It was fairly short, but it expressed Stefano's gratitude for the honour she had done him of inviting him to accompany her to the ball, and for giving him the opportunity to make Oxford's acquaintance. He said he had loved seeing the architecture of the marvellous old buildings, declared that the river was beautiful and said he thought he had done the punting very well, like a native! Then he mentioned Claudia, saying how lovely she had looked and how much he had enjoyed dancing with her. He wished her well in her exams, told her that he would soon be returning to Italy for a short time, and signed himself 'your grateful and affectionate friend Stefano'.

A sharp pang of disappointment pierced Claudia's soul as she read the letter. Where was the warmth and affection she felt she had a right to expect? She would almost rather he hadn't written, so that she could have gone on cherishing the glow that had been inside her ever since the ball. Then she reminded herself that English was not his first language. He probably could not express his thoughts on paper as naturally as he could in speech. Yes, that was it. Feeling better, she put the letter away and returned to her studies. This did not prove as easy as she had hoped, as images kept flashing before her, and she had to deal with them firmly. In the end she managed to discipline the unruly part of her mind that wanted to linger on dark, wavy hair and warm kisses. That was a disruption to her concentration which she must subdue. Eventually she succeeded in doing so.

At last the day dawned when her Finals were to begin. She went into the exam room and found that her first paper was exactly as she had anticipated. When she got up to go three hours later she knew she had completed it satisfactorily. This helped her confidence and as she faced each successive paper it was with the knowledge that she was dealing adequately with the demands being made on her.

At last they were over, and so was her life in Oxford. All that remained was the waiting period before she would receive her results. She packed all her belongings, said goodbye to her fellow students, and left for home. Her heart lifted as she put her key into the front door. It was a Saturday so she knew her father would make a point of being at home to welcome her.

She opened the front door and called out, 'Hello, Dad!'

Hugh came hurrying into the hall to embrace her.

'Good to see you back. Well, how did it all go?'

'As well as I could have hoped, thanks. I don't think there were any major problems. Where's Maria? Is she at work? When do you think she'll be home?'

There was a silence. Hugh hesitated, and she realised he was looking strained.

'What is it?' she asked. 'What's wrong?'

'Come and sit down.'

Then he told her the news. Maria was not going to be coming home. Maria had gone. She and Stefano had been married, very hurriedly, without telling anyone, and left for Italy where they would have a honeymoon, and then go to visit his family. Stefano had asked Hugh for permission to marry his daughter, but Hugh said he would not have agreed if he had known they were going to do it so quickly and secretively.

'After all,' said Hugh, 'I know how much you would have loved to be at your sister's wedding. You and I would both have liked to witness her marriage to Stefano and I can't say how sorry I am she has done us both out of that pleasure.'

Claudia felt as though her chest would burst as the strength of her emotions threatened to overwhelm her. She did not reply.

Hugh went on, 'I'm surprised at Maria. And I must say, I'm rather disappointed in her.'

'So am I,' replied Claudia, thinking that was probably the understatement of her life.

CHAPTER 14

'How are you getting on with your job applications?'

Hugh meant well with his questions, unaware that they only exacerbated his daughter's suffering. Just at the moment, Claudia found herself unable to contemplate presenting herself at interviews and talking enthusiastically about the delights of opening young minds to the joys of mathematics.

She cursed herself for a fool for believing that Stefano would ever think of marrying her. She berated herself for allowing his sudden change of heart to drain her of all self-confidence. What difference had it actually made to her life? If you took that one day away, nothing had changed. She was now ready to proceed down the path that she had always planned out for herself. It was just that, for some inexplicable reason, it no longer held the same attractions for her.

Claudia was forced to admit to herself that the world had suddenly become a very different place. Her state of mind was the antithesis of the euphoria she had experienced throughout the day and night of the ball. Then she had been dancing on air, her spirits rising as she exhilarated in the joy and thrill of every moment. Now she felt weighed down by a burden that would not move. Each new dawn was a living nightmare, the struggle to get out of bed each morning growing worse day by day.

She went through the motions of living like an automaton. There was her immediate future that must be faced – she had to find a job. She compiled her CV, writing in the line requiring final examination results: 'Not yet available – anticipated result based on previous examinations: 1st or good 2nd Class Honours'. She bought a Times

Educational Supplement and scanned the columns for vacancies for maths teachers in the autumn term. Finding three in the locality near home, she sent for the application forms. When these arrived she sat down and painstakingly completed them, sending an accompanying letter stating why it had always been her objective to follow a career in education, specialising in teaching maths. She spoke of the pleasure to be gained from leading young minds through the processes of mathematics, helping them to reason problems out for themselves. She ended with the hope that each school would look on her application favourably, and then posted the necessary papers.

Before long she had been offered interviews by all three schools. She accepted, attended on the appropriate dates, on each occasion doing her best to persuade the interviewing panel that she possessed the qualities they sought. She hoped she was sufficiently convincing for them not to be aware of the layer of inertia just below the surface.

Believing maths teachers were in short supply she had decided not to delay her entry into the profession by taking a teaching qualification. Perhaps she had been overconfident – but she felt she knew instinctively how to put things across, and didn't think she needed to waste a whole year being told how to do it. It seemed she had convinced the interview panel that she was capable as she was offered two of the three jobs. Mechanically she wrote her letter of acceptance to the school that was nearer to her home. Without any enthusiasm, she forced herself to read the curriculum, and start some lesson plans.

Then came the day when she knew she could not go through with it. That evening, when her father was at home, she went to speak to him.

'I've changed my mind about teaching, for the time being, anyway. I'm going to have a complete break for a few months, well, until the next school year is coming up. By then I will know if it's still what I want to do.'

'What? I don't understand! Why on earth have you changed your mind?'

'I've been doing some thinking. It's just that–'

'Is this anything to do with Maria? You haven't seemed the same since you got home and found she'd gone.'

Claudia hesitated. She longed to confide in her father, but couldn't bring herself to do so. How could she tell him what she now proposed to do? Before she could say anything further Hugh spoke.

'I know you miss your sister terribly. You two were always so close. Especially after darling Mummy died. If only she were still with us! She would have known what to say to you now. I've been a useless father, I know.'

He looked so thoroughly wretched, Claudia's heart went out to him.

'Look, Dad, it's only for a year. I just want a break, to think things through.' His bewildered look told her she would have to say more. The bombshell would have to be dropped. She stumbled on, 'I have to tell you it was a dreadful shock when I found out about Maria and Stefano – that they'd married, and gone to Italy. You see, Dad, Stefano had proposed to me! You may well look stunned, but, I assure you, he did. That evening he came to Oxford for the ball … he proposed to me … I know it probably sounds absurd to you … but I'm telling you the truth … he did ask me to marry him.'

Hugh stared at her, his mouth hanging open.

'And I accepted … and now … and now I just can't carry on as if nothing has happened. I've made plans, and I want you to accept what I say. Please, Dad – you must do as I ask.'

'Oh, Claudia … I had know idea … Why didn't you tell me?'

'I couldn't … I'm sorry … It just all hurt too much. But now I know what I must do to get over it all.'

So she told him that instead of starting to teach she wanted to go away. She insisted that it was the only way she could find the inner resources to pick up her life again. During that time there were to be conditions which he must promise to respect. She would make a telephone call once a month, to assure him that she was well, provided that he made no attempt to trace her. Once the time was up she would return, and start her career. She felt fairly certain she would still want to teach, and by then she would have achieved the frame of mind to do it.

Hugh found her plans bewildering and deeply worrying. He had thought she was looking pale and unhappy … in fact, hadn't looked herself for some weeks. But he couldn't see how such a plan would result in the healing process she needed.

'How will you live? What will you do for money? Why must you go away, when I would do all I could to try and help you here? I know I've always been rather involved in my work – but now I know you need support, I really would do what I could. I can't bear to think of you in some unknown place, away from everyone you know. Without me, or Maria.'

'But that's the whole point. It's only by being among total strangers that I will be able to get back on my feet again. I need my own space so that I can come to terms with the past and start trying to face the future. I can't cope with seeing your concern because I'm looking pale, nor can I take on the responsibility of a classroom full of lively children. I've got to have some time to think so that I can work things out. I know it's a lot to ask of you, but I implore you, Dad, please trust me and accept that this is the only way. Please, please let me do it my way.'

The tears were beginning to roll down her cheeks. Hugh took her hand.

'If that's what you're sure you want, then I must abide by your wishes. You have my promise that I will observe your conditions. But in return you must grant me one thing. I want to put some money into your Post Office Account so that you can take the account book to any post office anywhere in the country and draw money out should you need it.' Seeing she was about to object he went on, 'No, don't deny me this. I shall write you a cheque straight away, and you must promise to pay it in. You don't have to use the money, if you don't need it, but I shall sleep a lot easier at night if I know you have this facility at your disposal.'

Claudia, realising it would be better to give in on this point, agreed. As she turned to go her father asked, 'When will you be going?'

'Very soon. But I won't tell you exactly when. One day you will come back from work and I shan't be here. I'd rather do it that way. I don't want any emotional goodbyes.'

Hugh wondered what 'very soon' might mean but did not have to wait long before finding out. The very next day he came back to an empty house.

CHAPTER 15

Claudia roused herself from her reveries, vexed that she had allowed her mind to drift back over the past. When she had been working there was always so much to concentrate on that she could keep her thoughts firmly under control. With leisure time on her hands it wasn't proving so easy. Surely the past was buried now? Why should these memories come back, nearly forty years after the events, to haunt her once again? Annoyed with herself she got up to make some coffee.

No sooner had she picked up the newspaper to do the crossword than her mind was off again. In those early years, when she had started teaching, letters had arrived, addressed in Maria's embellished handwriting. She had torn them up and tossed them into the waste bin.

Earlier, during her time in the wilderness, Claudia would contact her father at intervals, as she had promised. Then he would try and pass on information.

'I hear Maria and Stefano have come back to England now, and have settled in Wimbledon,' he said on one occasion.

'Stop it, Dad. I don't want to hear about them.'

But he didn't stop.

'I hear there's a child.' Claudia had banged the phone down.

Another time he told her of the letters Maria had written to him, in which she had implored him to try and heal the rift. She had said how much she missed her sister. He quoted: 'Whatever I have done, I'm willing to ask for her forgiveness – although I don't really understand why she is so against me. I knew Claudia was fond of Stefano, but I didn't think she'd ever want to marry him. He doesn't think so, either. And he swears he never offered marriage to her.'

All Claudia's emotions had risen to the surface, jangling until she could bear it no longer.

'You know nothing, Dad. You never did understand Maria. You never saw through the stories she made up. You never realised how she rewrote history to suit her purposes. Nor, for that matter, did you ever understand me! Because I sat there calmly hour after hour with my books, enjoying working out maths problems, everyone assumed I was a simply a factual person. It doesn't seem to have occurred to anyone that I might feel deeply, and suffer pain like anyone else. Well, I have to tell you that I have known the deepest, most unbearable pain a woman can ever know, and I shall never be able to forgive Maria ... never!'

'Look, Claudia, I am truly sorry. I wish you had been able to tell me. I didn't realise just how deep all this went. But isn't it time now to let these things lie where they are – in the past? What is the point of dwelling on old wounds, and as a result losing out on a family relationship that was once so good? Can't you let bygones be bygones?'

'That's the whole point! They have not gone! What happened has left a permanent mark on my life and changed the whole course of events for me. What I am now, I shall be in forty years time. Apart from my career, I have nothing to look forward to.'

'How can you be so sure of that? You can't possibly know what lies ahead! You could well meet someone far more suitable for you than Stefano would have been. You must open your heart, Claudia. You seem to have battened everything down as though no more opportunities could possibly be waiting for you.'

Claudia's voice was low, strained, and held under control only with a supreme effort.

'I told you it wasn't possible for you to understand. How can you have any concept of what it would do to me if I did allow myself the luxury of feeling emotion? I wouldn't be able to bear the consequences. Please, Dad, if you want to help me, never speak of any of this again. Allow me to decide how I must live to make my life, if not happy, at least endurable. And the only way I can do that is to cut Maria, and all she represents, out completely.'

Her father had reluctantly agreed. It meant that she did not have a great deal of communication with him. He tried to show an interest as her teaching career progressed. He rejoiced with her when she achieved the headship at Kingdown Primary School. He came to believe that she had found a level of contentment. They never had a heart-to-heart again. By the time she retired, he had died.

A sudden noise disturbed Claudia's train of thought. She realised someone was banging on the door. Composing her features into her usual fixed look that revealed nothing, she opened the door.

A woman, unknown to Claudia, stood there.

'Yes? What do you want?'

Claudia's eyes took in the woman, probably late thirties, tall and athletic in appearance, with dark hair and blue eyes that held a hint of something familiar. The woman, unfazed by the brusque, unfriendly greeting, looked straight at Claudia.

'You're Miss Hansom, aren't you?'

'Yes. Who are you?'

'I'm Fran,' she replied, 'and I'd like to talk to you. May I come in?'

CHAPTER 16

The village post office is often the hub of a small community's life, its importance going far beyond the necessary business of posting letters. It can be central to the lives of those who attend every Tuesday to draw their pension money, providing a meeting point for old friends and a place to exchange local news.

Opposite the village green in Swanton was just such an establishment, seen by the local people as vital to their well being, their lives overseen in the kindliest manner by the two caring owners, Percy and Barbie Piper. Both were trained in post office duties, but it was Barbie who usually sat behind the counter, while Percy looked after the rest of the shop, dealing with the newspapers and making sure he stocked the kind of toffees to which the rector was particularly partial.

It was Barbie who had realised, one Tuesday, that old Mrs Casey had failed to show up to collect her pension. Percy, temporarily abandoning his duties, had gone round to her cottage to investigate, but his bangs on the door and his shouts through the letterbox went unanswered. Fortunately he knew, from past experience, where the spare key lay hidden. He it was who called the ambulance, and in the nick of time – for had Mrs Casey lain there much longer she would probably have died. Now that she was getting rather muddled there were times when she forgot her insulin injection, and the result was a hypoglycaemic coma. Fortunately, on this occasion she was restored to life, and her gratitude to the watchful eyes of the Post Office team was unbounded.

Percy, an only child, had known no other life than the small shop with its post office. It had belonged to his parents when he was growing up, and he went into the business as soon as he left school. He had looked forward to doing this for as long as he could remember. From time to time he had tried to consider other types of employment, but there was nothing that really appealed to him. All he wanted to do was take his place beside his father.

He actively enjoyed the daily routines, never minding getting up early to mark up the newspapers. Never one for socialising, he found the daily contact with people in the shop sufficiently satisfying. When his parents reached retirement age he took over as if it was the most natural thing in the world. By then he was thirty, but somehow he had not got around to doing any courting. Needing to find someone to help him in the shop he put up a notice in the window: 'Wanted – lady assistant. Knowledge of post office duties an advantage but not essential.'

It so happened that a new family had come to live on the outskirts of Swanton, where a small farm had become vacant. The father, Sam Murdoch, came into the post office, and seeing the notice, had a word with Percy. It seemed he had a daughter, Barbara, who was a bookkeeper in a nearby town, but didn't like the job there very much. She was on holiday with a few friends at present, but he would mention it to her when she came back and see if she liked the idea. Percy remarked that the wages probably couldn't match what she'd been earning in the town, but that didn't seem to put the girl off. She arrived a few days later, and was keen to start. They agreed on a trial period.

Barbara quickly learned all that was necessary for running the post office, taking to the work with obvious enjoyment.

'What do you think, then, Miss Murdoch?' Percy enquired a week or two later. 'Do you think you'd like to work here?'

'Oh, yes please, Mr Piper. I love it. I do hope you'll think I'm good enough for the job.'

It wasn't only the job Percy thought she was good enough for. He suddenly found he was looking forward to her arrival each morning, and was sorry when the time came to shut up shop at the end of the day. Hesitantly, one day, he asked her to accompany him to the village barn dance. She accepted immediately. Things went on from there, and when, a little later, he asked if she would 'join the firm', as he put it, she did not hesitate at that either.

Proudly Percy watched his new wife busily fulfilling her role in the shop. How well she carried out all her duties, with her neat handwriting and tidy way of working. Her papers were organised and her money always added up at the end of the day. But what Percy enjoyed most was her interaction with their customers. She always had a cheery word for everyone, and as she became familiar with their circumstances she would add some little personal comment.

'How's that cat of yours now, Mrs Stokes? Back on her food is she?'

And Mrs Stokes would go into a long account of the pet's recovery, with Barbie making all the right noises at intervals, as though she had nothing else to do that day.

'Oh, isn't that good! You must be so pleased! Nothing like a cat for company, I always say.'

Mrs Stokes would find many reasons to come back, even if was only for a couple of stamps or a tube of pastilles, so Percy thought the chatter was probably good for business, but he didn't mind anyway. He liked seeing their mainly elderly clientele enter the shop as if it was a home from home, and he'd watch them brighten up when Barbie showed an interest in them.

The years rolled by with neither of them really noticing. Ten or more had gone since Percy had brought his new bride into the shop, and they both still loved their life – but something was missing. Percy, now in his forties, and Barbie in her late thirties, had not produced any offspring.

One evening, as they walked arm-in-arm down the country lanes and beside the river, Percy, without any premeditated thought, raised the subject.

'Pity there's no little Piper to follow us into the shop, don't you think?'

This thought had been gradually growing in Barbie's mind for some time. However hard she tried to push it away, it had kept returning unbidden.

'Perhaps it's not meant to be, Percy dear. If it's not to be for us, then we have to accept it. Some things aren't meant, I always say.'

'Seems a pity, though.' He hesitated. 'Perhaps we should have some tests, see if there's anything wrong – what do you think?'

So they approached good old Dr Flint, and underwent various tests. It became apparent that a rheumatic illness that Percy had had in his childhood had rendered him infertile.

'Oh, Barbie, I'm so sorry. What a disappointment. I had no idea.'

'It's all right, Percy. Not your fault at all. Just one of those things. Can't be helped.'

Despite the cheerful face they both put on the situation the issue nevertheless remained a sadness in their lives. Percy did some more thinking.

'I was wondering,' he said one day, over supper, 'what would you think about adopting a child?'

Barbie hadn't thought about it at all. The suggestion took her by surprise.

'Adopt a baby? Us adopt a baby? Oh, Percy, I'm not sure. I don't know what to think. I mean, it wouldn't be the same, would it?'

But the idea gradually took root in her mind, and she began to picture herself with a baby in her arms. She saw the two of them pushing the pram out on a Sunday afternoon. She saw herself bathing the little one and putting her to bed. The more she thought about it the more she realised it would bring something special into their lives. For some inexplicable reason, every time she thought about it, she saw a baby girl.

Still without giving Percy a positive answer, Barbie raised a number of issues, asking questions that taxed Percy's ingenuity to the full, but somehow he always managed to produce an answer that satisfied his wife. At least, it did for a time, until the next question had taken shape in her mind.

'We don't know anything about adopting, do we?'

'No, but Dr Flint does, that's for sure. We can ask him how to go about it.'

'Can we afford a baby? It costs a lot of money to bring up a child.'

'We'll manage, Barbie dear. The shop's not doing badly – and I have the small sum my father left me.'

'Well, suppose we did go ahead and adopt – how would we manage in the shop? I mean, I'll be pretty busy looking after a little one – so who would do the post office counter?'

'I'll do it. After all I did before you came on the scene. Then we'd have to get some help in the shop. I reckon we'd find one or two mums who'd like some part-time work – maybe share the duties and their children between them. And I'd be there to show them the ropes, or help out if they got into difficulties. What do you think?'

Barbie was impressed. Percy had obviously been giving some thought to how they could rearrange their lives around a baby.

But Barbie's last question was the hardest of all, and this time Percy had no answer ready.

'Will we be able to love the child like our own, when it isn't really our child at all?'

Percy scratched his head for inspiration, but this time it was Barbie who supplied the answer to her own question.

'We'd love her because we'd feel so sorry for her! Poor little mite! Just fancy – somewhere out there a wicked woman has abandoned her! It makes my blood boil just to think of it! How could anyone not want a lovely little baby!'

'Well, we do,' said Percy. 'That's for sure.'

'Yes,' agreed Barbie, 'that's true – so we do.'

And that, at long last, was that.

CHAPTER 17

The process on which Percy and Barbie had embarked turned out to be lengthy, laborious and, it seemed, held no guarantee of success. Dr Flint knew many of the basic facts concerning adoption and was able to point them in the right direction. He suggested that as they had always been regular in their attendance at the local anglican church it might be appropriate to approach the Church of England Adoption Society. They were fortunate to find that the Society was, at that time, open to new applications

The couple soon discovered that there were numerous forms to fill in, interviews to attend, and many weeks of waiting when nothing happened. It was hard on the nerves, now that they had committed themselves to the idea, and sometimes it was Percy who became despondent, and sometimes Barbie.

'Perhaps it's all too much for us,' said Percy one day, when they had both rushed to pick up the post, and there was still nothing from the Adoption Society. 'Perhaps we should have accepted that having a child is just not for us.'

'Don't lose hope, Percy. That's not like you. We must just keep smiling. It'll be all right, you'll see.'

Then, a few days later, the letter came. The Society had accepted them as prospective parents and would let them know when a suitable baby had become available. Percy and Barbie were overcome with joy. In a surprisingly short time another letter came. The Society knew of a baby that was to be handed over for adoption in March, and provided all went well then they suggested the Pipers prepare themselves for an arrival in April.

There were three months to wait. It proved to be an enormously exciting time, and there was so much to do – a nursery to prepare, helpers to find for the shop, equipment to be bought – all the paraphernalia a baby requires. But everything was in place in good time, and then it was just a matter of waiting.

At long last two proud parents stood either side of the cot, gazing at its tiny occupant, speechless with wonder. For her part the baby gazed back, her deep blue eyes mirroring the adoration bestowed upon her by the two mesmerised adults. She gazed at her new parents, her eyes unblinking and steady.

'She's so tiny!' gasped Percy. 'How can she be so small and yet so perfect!'

'She's beautiful! Oh Percy, isn't she beautiful?' Tears were rolling down Barbie's cheeks. She was consumed by the rush of love that swept through her body as she realised that this tiny infant was now her daughter. The baby seemed to approve of what she saw, too, as she gurgled happily. The mutual admiration continued for some time.

Then suddenly the little face began to pucker, the body trembled and sobs gained in crescendo until the whole tiny being was transformed into a seething cauldron of misery vociferously expressed.

'Whatever do we do now?' Percy, alarmed, felt helpless at the sight of such tragic emotion. 'Should we feed her?'

'I don't think it's the right time.' They had been given a sheet of the baby's daily routine and advised to stick to it, as this would provide continuity.

Barbie hesitated for a moment, then bent down and picked the child up out of the cot. Holding the baby against her, with her left arm bearing the baby's weight, her right hand caressed the little back with an expert touch that surprised herself, let alone Percy. Miraculously the sobs began to lose their power, and after a few snuffling noises peace descended once more.

'There, all she needed was a cuddle.' Barbie walked up and down, talking softly and soothingly to the little bundle that was now apparently enjoying a deep sleep.

'You're a wonder, Barbie! You knew just what to do. How did you know that?'

'Don't know,' admitted Barbie. 'Just felt right to do it, somehow. I tell you what, Percy. We should use her name, so she gets used to hearing it. The name's written on this wrist band, and we saw it on the birth certificate – it's Francesca.'

'That's a bit of a mouthful. Can't we change it?'

'Oh no!' Barbie looked shocked. 'That's her given name – the name her mother gave her – we mustn't change it.'

'I think we can. It's not written in stone. After all, we're her parents now, so we can call her what we want.'

'I don't know so much, Percy. I really don't think we should change it. It's as if … oh, I can't explain it, but it's like a trust … the woman who bore her named her, and even if she has upped and left, leaving the child behind, I still wouldn't feel right changing it.'

'Just as you like, Barbie. In any case, we can always shorten it. There's nothing to say we can't do that. Perhaps we'll call her Frannie, or Fran. I wonder what her surname was, before it got changed to Piper. We don't know, do we?'

'No, we don't. The Society told us, didn't they, that it's usual in these cases to use the shortened form of birth certificate, so the parents' names are not shown, only the adoptive parents' names.'

'I bet her real parents weren't married,' muttered Percy.

'Poor little mite. What a start in life! Never mind, she's all respectable now, and that's all there is to it. She'll never know how her life began. All she needs to know is that she belongs to Mr and Mrs Piper, and now she's in a good home and she'll be loved.'

'Yes,' agreed Percy, knowing that was what Barbie needed to hear. But silently he wondered if the tiny scrap now fast asleep on his wife's shoulder ought to be told about her origins, some time. Ah well, that thought could be shelved for a very long time.

CHAPTER 18

Still waiting for her fifth birthday Fran had not yet started 'big school', with the result that she had to be content with a local nursery school. She was already finding this did little to stretch her enquiring mind and longed for the promotion that would come the following September. Finally the all important milestone arrived. Very early one March morning an excited little girl opened the bedroom window, calling out to anyone who might happen to be passing, 'I'm five!'

Skipping up and down eagerly Fran went off to Oakdene Nursery School, looking forward to the birthday cake she had been promised that evening. Barbie had decided they would wait until Saturday afternoon for a party, so that Percy could be there to enjoy it with them. He was loath to miss any of the excitement where his small daughter was concerned.

To try and make the day an especially happy one, Barbie took Fran to the park on the way home, so that she could play on the swings. Fran loved this and would fearlessly swing daringly high, until Barbie's nerves were in shreds. On the way to the play area they passed a grassy patch interspersed with flower beds.

'What does that notice say?' asked Fran, bending down to look.

'It says we must keep off the grass.'

'Why do we have to keep off it, Mummy?'

'Because, darling, if you run all over it and trample it under your feet the grass would probably wither and die.'

'But it looks so strong – I didn't think if I just walked on it that I would hurt it.'

'It's not as tough as it looks. Under that surface, where you can't see, there are some tender young shoots. Some people might have great big boots, and the poor little shoots would get broken when those big boots trod on them.'

Fran looked at the grass thoughtfully. The next moment she put her foot out and stood with one shoe on the grass.

'Fran! What are you doing? It's not like you to be naughty!'

'I'm not going to trample on it … I just wanted to see what happened if I stood on it gently, and look, it's perfectly all right!'

'Maybe, but you can't see the damage. That goes on under the surface, and it will only show after a time. That's why we mustn't walk on it.'

'Well, if I did jump on it and break the young shoots, would they ever grow back again?'

'I don't know, Fran, dear. I think it would probably need someone, like one of these clever gardeners, to look after it very carefully, and then perhaps, after a time, it might recover. But it's best not to hurt it in the first place, so let's do as they say, and stay on the path. Come on, let's go to the swings!'

'Okay!'

Fran ran ahead to the play area, and jumped on a swing. She showed no fear, and her legs, already unusually long for her age, swung to and fro energetically, driving the swing higher and higher.

'Not so high!' cried Barbie. 'I don't want you to fall off, not today of all days!'

Fran obediently slowed the swing down. A mother was passing, pushing a toddler in a pushchair.

'Hello!' Fran called out. 'I'm five today!'

The woman stopped. Happy to enter into the spirit of the occasion she registered immense surprise. 'Five! Are you really? Well, I never, how very grown up you are. Fancy you being five!'

'How old's your little girl?' Barbie felt the conversation shouldn't be entirely one way.

'She's not two yet. Next month she will be.' Turning to Fran again she said, 'Have a lovely birthday. It's so exciting, being five.' She smiled and continued on her way.

Enjoying whizzing down the slide as fast as she could Fran noticed a policeman approaching. As he came up she announced once more the all-consuming piece of information. The policeman came to a standstill in front of her, feet planted firmly apart, hands on his hips.

'Do you mean to tell me that you're five? I don't believe it.'

'Yes, I am! I am! I'm five.'

'Goodness me. I must make a note of this.' He withdrew a small notebook from his breast pocket, flipped open the cover, and felt around for his pencil. He started writing, and then looked up.

'I've written here that the little girl on the slide is five. But my sergeant will want to have a name for the records, so what's your name, little girl?'

'It's Fran.'

'Fran,' he repeated, writing laboriously.

'Well, it's Francesca, really.'

'Francesca Really.' He continued writing.

'No, it's just Francesca. Not Really.'

'I think you're having me on, young lady. Is it Francesca Really or isn't it?

'It is and it isn't. It's Francesca. Not Really. Really isn't my name.'

'Oh, I think I'm beginning to see. So if it's not Really what is it?'

'It's Piper. That's my surname – I'm Francesca Piper.'

'Gotcha,' said the policeman. 'I think I've written it down right now. Well, I'm very pleased to make your acquaintance, Francesca Piper. I must congratulate you on having achieved your fifth birthday, and I should like to convey, on behalf of my sergeant and all the lads at the station, our very best wishes on this special occasion.' He touched his helmet, and went on his way.

Fran went and sat on the seat by Barbie, laughing.

'Wasn't he a funny man? I do like having birthdays. Everyone talks to you!'

Barbie put her arm round the child. Perhaps she could seize the moment.

'Your daddy and I are enjoying your birthday as much as you are. We are so happy to have our little girl. And you're all the more special because we chose you. The thing is, dear, Daddy and I found we couldn't have a baby of our own, so instead we chose one, and we chose you. And we're very happy that we did.'

Fran thought for a bit. 'Where did you choose me from? Is there a shop that has babies?'

'No, not a shop. There's a very special home where they look after the babies who don't have a mummy. Then when a mummy comes along who doesn't have a baby, they let you choose. And so everyone's happy.'

'Why did you choose me?'

'You were so pretty, and we just knew we could love you and love you.'

Fran didn't reply. Her attention was distracted by an elderly lady approaching with a small dog.

'I'm five,' she announced, anxious not to miss an opportunity.

The elderly lady's expression conveyed the requisite pleasure and surprise. 'Look at that,' she said to her dog. 'This little girl is five!'

Since the dog failed to respond Fran asked, 'What's your dog's name?'

'Sugar,' replied her owner. 'I called her Sugar, because when I went to choose her I thought she looked so sweet. She was only a little puppy then.'

'My Mummy chose me. She didn't have me, she chose me.'

'Then aren't you the lucky one! Just like my Sugar. She's lucky, too. You have a nice birthday, now.' The lady moved on, and left Barbie marvelling at the kindness and understanding of total strangers.

When they got home they put the cake on the table with its five candles, and blew up some balloons, in readiness for Percy's arrival. Soon he came whistling up to the front door.

'Look at that wonderful cake! Barbie, you're a genius, to be sure.

Now, I wonder how many candles there are! Let's count them, and then we can light them – and then we'll all have a piece of this lovely cake!'

Percy would much have preferred a helping of Barbie's steak and kidney pie and mash, or sausages and chips, but nobly he managed to wolf down a large portion of very sweet cake instead, with the promise of a proper supper later.

When Fran had gone to bed that night Barbie told Percy how she had raised the subject of the adoption, and about the conversations in the park. Together they chuckled over the policeman, and jointly delighted in the fact that breaking the news had gone so smoothly.

For so it seemed to the doting parents. But they were not yet fully acquainted with their daughter's probing mind, nor her need to explore and test out all she was told. Fran may have appeared to accept the information easily at the time, but from now on the question of her origins would absorb her innermost thoughts. The more she allowed her mind to dwell on it, the more she realised that she couldn't have been told the whole story. Important facts were missing, leaving gaps she would become desperate to fill. Gradually questions began to take shape in her mind – questions that, before long, were going to cause considerable disquiet in the Piper household. Questions that, despite Fran's best efforts, would continue to remain unanswered.

CHAPTER 19

'Goodness me, Fran! I don't know! You'll have to ask your father when he comes in.'

Barbie, an excellent book keeper, and capable of carrying out duties at the post office counter meticulously, found herself floored by the things Fran wanted to know. She had just been putting her daughter's tea on the table one day when Fran asked another of her many questions.

'How do the stars stay up in the sky? Why don't they fall down?'

Percy, when he came home, did his best with it, although not at all confident of the answer he supplied.

The questions soon became more searching, leaving both her parents floundering.

'Who told the people in foreign countries, like France and Italy, that they mustn't speak English?'

'How did they find out which berries were poisonous to eat?'

Fran's teachers were pleased with her from the beginning, knowing she would do well although it soon became clear that, whereas numbers presented no problems to her at all, words sometimes had a way of causing her to stumble. She came home frustrated one day and demanded to know, 'Who decided the right way to spell words? Why don't they get spelt the way they sound?'

Then came the inevitable question, just as they had settled down one evening – Percy with his newspaper and Barbie with her sewing.

'Mummy, how do you make babies?'

Percy spluttered and buried his head deeper in the newspaper. Barbie, fearful he might start rambling on about storks and gooseberry bushes, decided to take the bull by the horns.

'It all begins when a daddy and mummy love each other and decide they want children of their very own.'

She went on to describe how the daddy planted a seed into the mummy, where she cared for it until it had grown into a lovely baby, strong enough to come out of the mummy's tummy and join the family.

Fran seemed satisfied with the answer, and Barbie breathed a sigh of relief. A few evenings later, however, it became clear that the child's thinking had moved on.

'You know you said I was specially chosen, because you and Daddy couldn't make babies – well where did I come from before that?'

Barbie had known the question would have to be faced at some time, but she wasn't prepared for it quite so soon. She thought for a moment before replying.

'There was a mummy who grew you in her tummy, but she wasn't able to look after you, and she wanted you to have a home where there would be a mummy and daddy who would love you very much, and give you a proper home – and when we saw you we knew you were the little girl we wanted.'

'But why couldn't that mummy look after me?'

Barbie began to get flustered.

'We don't know dear, and as we'll never know it's better to forget about it. Just remember how much Daddy and I love you.'

'I know you do – I know you love me lots.'

Hoping that was the end of it Barbie stood up indicating it was time for bed. Fran, however, hadn't finished.

'I just wondered who the mummy was, and there must have been a daddy, too, mustn't there?'

Seeing Barbie looking tearful Percy tried to take over.

'It's like Mummy says – it's better not to think about it. Your home is here with us, and we'll always look after you – that's for sure.'

Fran was perplexed. She had the feeling that something from her past was being concealed from her, and, young though she was, she realised that when she tried to explore her history her parents became distressed. She did not want to upset them – and yet she needed to know. There was a piece missing from the jigsaw puzzle and she had a strong urge to find it.

'It's like I always say, dear,' said Barbie, who had recovered herself by now, 'when one door closes, another opens. Well, there's a door that's closed behind you now, but our door opened just when you needed it and that's all that matters. Now promise me you won't worry about these things any more. Come here and give Mummy a nice big kiss!'

Fran obediently did so.

'Well, that's that question laid to rest,' said Percy optimistically, when Fran had left the room.

Disappointed with her lack of progress Fran nevertheless realised that she wasn't going to be able to pursue her enquiries – but the question wouldn't go away. Her strong spirit and enquiring mind didn't much like the idea of doors being closed to her. She made a mental note that one day, when the time was right, she was going to do everything she could to open it and find out just what lay behind.

CHAPTER 20

'Mum! Dad! I need some help with my homework!'

Barbie and Percy were surprised to hear this request from Fran, now nine years old, as she normally got straight down to her projects without requiring any assistance from them. This was just as well since they freely admitted she had already outstripped their academic abilities in most areas. Barbie had undoubted capabilities when it came to post office matters and Percy, for his part, was quick at mental arithmetic, rarely making a mistake when giving change to customers. But as they had both left school at the earliest opportunity and knew their particular areas of expertise were limited, it was a relief to find that their little girl rarely referred any school problems to them.

On this occasion, however, the class had been told that they would need to co-opt help from their parents, who would have the information required. Fran produced a large sheet of paper on which, at the bottom, was written her own name, in a box.

'We have to build a family tree. Mrs Seymour showed us how, only she said we would need to sit down with our parents, who would probably have to find certificates, and photos to help fill it in.'

'Goodness,' said Barbie. 'That's quite a task. Not sure I remember too clearly who my ancestors were.'

'How far is it supposed to go back?' asked Percy. 'I haven't much knowledge, either.'

'Mrs Seymour said it didn't matter. She said some parents might only know one or two generations, while others might be able to go back several. She said she just wanted us to learn how to build it, and never mind if it wasn't very big. She said she didn't want a whole lot of angry parents at the school door on Monday morning because they had spent every minute of the weekend trying to find out the names of all their aunts and uncles!'

'I tell you what,' said Percy, 'we'll sit down with you on Saturday evening, after the shop's shut, and see what photos and papers we can find. Then on Sunday we'll devote the whole day to it. How would that be?'

'I don't know that I'm going to be much help,' worried Barbie. 'I've gone quite blank trying to think of people.'

'It's all right,' said Fran. 'It doesn't matter if we don't have too many people on it. As long as I can build it up a bit, so I can show Mrs Seymour I know how to do it. Thanks, Mum and Dad.'

When Saturday evening came they spread out on the dining table all the certificates and photo albums they could lay their hands on, although Percy carefully omitted Fran's short birth certificate which he had filed away. Then they got side-tracked as they opened the old albums and started laughing at some of the pictures.

'Look at my mother sitting in a deckchair on the beach!' cried Barbie. 'Her dress is down to her ankles and she's got a hat on!'

'Who's that strange looking man with the wing collar, smoking a pipe?' Percy got quite excited looking back at the memorabilia they had produced. 'I tell you what, we made a mistake not writing down the names of people at the time – you think you'll always remember them, but you don't.'

'Well, let's make a start.' Fran was eager to get on with it. 'First I'll draw a vertical line above my name, and then a horizontal line, with two small vertical ones above that, and I'll put you two down.'

'Only you must put my maiden name down,' said Barbie. 'You know what that was, don't you Fran, dear?'

'Yes, it was Murdoch. And I know Grandpa is Sam Murdoch, and I know Auntie June is your sister, and Grandpa's other daughter.'

'That's right. And we can put in Grandma's name, which was Doris. See, we're gradually getting it done. Shame we never see

Grandpa now – he's got so ill it isn't possible.' Barbie skirted round the fact that poor Grandpa had Alzheimer's Disease to such an advanced degree that he didn't know anyone, and it would have been too distressing to take Fran to see him.

'You don't have any brothers or sisters, do you Daddy? You're like me, an only child, aren't you?'

'That's right, but we can fill in the names of my parents. Then we'll see if we can do anything on the line above.'

Slowly they began to fill it in. They got to their own grandparents, and after much discussion they thought they had correctly remembered how many offspring each had produced, and the names, although they weren't too sure.

'I suppose it doesn't really matter too much,' said Percy. 'After all Mrs Seymour won't know if we've got it right or not.'

The finished chart looked quite impressive in the end, although it was clear that neither family had been large, with Percy not having any siblings, and Barbie having just the one sister. However, by the time they had gone back two generations it seemed the productivity levels were higher.

'There,' said Barbie. 'That's very nice, dear. You can go back to school on Monday feeling we've done a good job.'

Fran was silent. Percy sensed that she was wrestling with something and feared he probably knew what it was. 'What is it, Fran dear?' he asked.

'This isn't right, is it?'

'What do you mean dear?' asked Barbie, innocently. 'What's not right?'

'Well,' said Fran, 'this isn't my family tree. It's yours, and Daddy's, but it isn't mine. Those aren't my ancestors.'

Percy stepped in quickly. 'Well yes, they are. As you know, you are ours by adoption. It was legally done, so everything is legally the same for you as for us. This is your family just the same.'

'But they aren't …' Fran struggled to find the word, 'they aren't the people I descended from. They aren't my blood relations.'

'It doesn't make any difference.' Barbie was beginning to get agitated. 'They're all your ancestors, like Daddy says.'

'It makes a difference to me,' said Fran obstinately. 'I'm going to draw my own family tree.'

She took another sheet of paper – a smaller one this time – and wrote her name in a box at the bottom. Then she drew a vertical line and put a horizontal line across with two small vertical ones on top. On these she put two large question marks.

'There,' she said, 'I've done it. That's my family tree.'

Barbie began to cry. 'Why do you have to think like this, Fran? Haven't we been good parents to you? Haven't we loved you from the day you came to us? Why can't you just accept us and forget that there was anyone else?'

'Because I can't forget! I can't! And you shouldn't ask me to.'

With that Fran grabbed the two family trees from the table and went up to her bedroom, slamming the door behind her.

Percy went upstairs to speak to her. She had obviously been crying. He begged her to come back downstairs and make her peace with Barbie, who was sobbing her heart out. Fran hated upsetting her mother, but there was something inside her that could not let the matter rest.

'Why can't Mummy understand, Daddy? I love her very, very much, but I can't help it, I can't just put out of my mind what happened to me. I know that there were two people, who I don't know anything about, who made me. And it's so cross-making that I don't know who they are, and I'm not allowed to try and find out. But even if I think about it sometimes it doesn't change anything with you and Mummy – I love you as my Mummy and Daddy – why can't Mummy understand that?'

'I don't know, Fran, but the fact is that she sees it as a kind of disloyalty, and whatever you or I say we can't seem to change that. I'm going to ask you to do something. It's something grownups sometimes do for the sake of the people they love. Could you pretend a little? Could you tell Mummy you really have put all those past events that you don't know about out of your head? It would make her so happy.'

'You mean lie?'

'It's called a white lie. It's only done because you don't want to hurt someone who's important to you. So it's not really lying. You're doing it because you want to be kind.'

Fran nodded. 'I will, as long as you understand how I feel. I need to be honest with someone.'

Percy nodded.

'I do understand. I know it must be difficult for you, but you'd make Mummy so happy, that's for sure.'

Fran smiled at him gratefully, returned to the living room and kissed her mother. She said dutifully that she was sorry she had caused her unhappiness and promised she would not think about it any more from now on. Percy, standing behind her, saw she had crossed her fingers behind her back.

The next day she came back from school saying they had had lots of fun in class comparing their family trees. One or two, apparently, had gone back several generations, and all the children thought their parents had enjoyed the trip down memory lane.

Later, when Barbie took some clean clothes up to Fran's bedroom to put them away, she noticed a piece of paper tightly screwed into a ball, lying in the waste paper bin. Out of curiosity she picked it up and opened it. It was Fran's family tree – the second one, with the two question marks.

CHAPTER 21

At eighteen years of age Fran left school, her exams now all behind her. To celebrate the start of this new phase in their lives Fran and her two best friends, Jill and Bunty, decided to spend a few days exploring attractive coastal villages and bays in south east Cornwall. Jill's parents had kindly loaned their car for the occasion, so that they could have a little celebration. Jill was the only licensed driver amongst them, but with the confidence of youth she happily undertook to do all the driving. Little did Fran know that one particular day of that holiday would be etched indelibly on her mind.

It was a beautiful summer day when the friends set out in a little Morris Minor on their long journey to the West Country. The three of them had been firm friends at school, the bond they had formed during those formative years being a strong one. They might all have been on the point of entering the adult world, but the girlish giggling and peals of laughter that enlivened their journey rather seemed to belie the fact.

Jill was the creative one, instantly making up stories about everyone they passed on their way.

'You see that man and woman parked at the side of the road? There must be a reason why they aren't getting on with their journey. I think they're having a heart to heart. They've probably run away together and now they're not so sure about it, or one of them isn't. I bet they've left their poor spouses at home wondering where on earth they are. One way or another there's trouble ahead!'

'Really, Jill! Whatever will you think of next? I suppose you've got an explanation for those two men trying to flag down a lift?

'Certainly. They've committed a bank robbery in the town we just passed through, but their getaway car's broken down and now they're desperate to leave the scene of their crime.'

'Stop it, Jill! You'll have us believing every word you say!'

Fran was the logical one who had worked out their itinerary, and knew exactly how much the few days were likely to cost them. Bunty was happy to go along with the other two – she lacked ideas of her own but was always easy company.

It took many hours to reach Fowey, but Fran had allowed for several stops on the way, and the girls were still in high spirits when they finally pulled into the bustling resort and found the bed and breakfast place Fran had booked. After a meal provided by their landlady and hungrily devoured by the weary travellers, all the girls were glad to call it a day and wait for the next day to dawn.

Early the next morning they made their plans. They hoped to explore much of the area on foot, walking along coastal paths and following trails to see some of the glorious sights this part of the country afforded. One attraction was the Llanteglos Parish Church where the author Daphne Du Maurier had married the dashing Grenadier, Major Frederick Browning, on 19 July 1932.

'Oh, how romantic!' sighed Jill. 'I just love her books!'

'I'd like to go coastal walking, so we catch sight of some of the marvellous bays and coves round here,' said Fran. 'Shall we get the ferry across to Polruan, and then walk over the headland past Washing Rocks and Blackbottle Rock, where we'll be able to see Lantic Bay? Then we can go inland to the church. How does that sound?'

They all agreed it sounded wonderful, and with rucksacks full of supplies, plus, at Fran's suggestion, a bathing costume and small towel each, just in case they wanted to take a dip, they set off. There was nothing that could possibly dampen their spirits, the weather being everything they could have wished for – beautiful, warm July sunshine beamed down on them. It seemed they had certainly struck lucky where the weather was concerned.

They were young and full of spirit, so it mattered little that the going was fairly tough. Finally they drew up at the point where they could look down on Lantic Bay. For once they fell silent.

'It's just amazing!' Bunty broke the silence.

'Let's go down to the sea!'

Fran was excited at the thought of standing on that deserted beach, and perhaps dipping her toes into the swirling surf.

'If we go down, we'll have to climb up again,' remarked Jill.

'I know, but it'll be worth it. Look, there's no one in sight, and we can walk on the pebbles, and there's a lovely sandy spot. Oh, do say you'll come!'

With the impulsiveness of youth they immediately set off, picking their way down the cliff path that led to the beach.

'I thought you said it was deserted! Look, there are two people over by the rocks,' Jill pointed out.

'And no doubt you're going to tell us exactly who they are, and what they're doing there,' remarked Bunty.

'The young lad is rather handsome, with that dark hair, and fine build. He's with an older woman – and I don't honestly think she can be cradle-snatching to quite that extent. Reluctantly, even I have to admit he's too young for that, so she must be his mother.'

'So what's a fine young man like that doing going on holiday with his mum?'

'He'd normally be with his pals, but his mother's just been through a tough time – either she's been very ill, or her husband is horribly cruel to her. Yes, that's probably it – I expect he beats her, and she's had to get away. So the son, who is very kind, and extremely attached to his mother, decided to take her away for a few days so she can forget it all and absorb some of nature's soothing balm from this secluded place.'

'I'm so hot!' Fran had got tired of the make-believe. 'Who's for a dip?'

She started to peel off her clothes and, hiding behind her towel, managed to wriggle into her swimming costume.

'It looks awfully rough.' Jill's voice echoed the doubt Bunty was feeling. 'Do you think we should?'

'Come on!' cried Fran. 'It'll be wonderful, you'll see!'

The others followed her example, and soon, shrieking girlishly, they all ran to the water's edge. Jill and Bunty dipped their toes in, but when a large wave broke around them they ran back screaming.

'It's so cold! I'm not going in – it's too rough and cold!' said Bunty.

'Nor am I, 'agreed Jill.

But Fran didn't hear them. She was fighting her way through the waves as they crashed around her, until she got to quieter waters where she could swim. Her strong, athletic body could be seen plying a path towards the mouth of the bay.

'I don't like the look of this,' muttered Jill. 'She's going a long way out.'

'We'd better shout at her to come back.' Bunty was equally worried.

So they shouted at the top of their voices, but Fran did not hear. Exhilarating in the sensations of the water surrounding her body and her movements through it she was lost to all else. At last, remembering she had persuaded her companions to come in for a swim, she turned to see where they were.

What she saw shocked her. She was much further out than she had intended. She saw her friends at the water's edge, jumping up and down and gesticulating. Then she saw that the other two people on the beach had also come down to watch.

She lifted her arm and waved, to show she was aware it was time she came back, and struck out for the shore. She was a strong swimmer, but despite her decisive movements she knew she wasn't gaining much ground. Once more she put her face down into the water and this time made a superhuman effort. Rhythmically she lifted each arm in turn to take another stroke, kicking her legs with all her strength and turning her head to gasp for breath. Then she looked up – and saw that the beach was still no nearer. In fact it seemed even further away.

'Dear God,' she thought, I can't get back. 'I'm getting weaker, and all the time the current is pulling me further away from the shore.'

She knew she needed to keep trying, but for a moment she couldn't do it any more. All her resources seemed to have drained out of her. Powerless, she was beginning to slide under the water.

No! No! She would never give in. Desperately she fought her way back to the surface. Panic-stricken, she struggled to get back into the rhythm of swimming.

Then she saw him! With masterful strokes that broke through the water, travelling at speed towards her was the young man who had been on the beach. The next moment he had grabbed hold of her.

'I'm going to swim on my front,' he said. 'I want you to hang on to my shoulders, and we'll do the breaststroke kick together.'

She clutched hold of him the way he had instructed her to and tried to get the timing right so that her movements fitted in with his. Together they fought the current. Instead of attempting to go straight towards the shore he took off in a direction parallel to it until the swimming became easier. Then he began to cut a diagonal line in towards the beach. At last they were really making headway. Fran could see that the distance between them and dry land was narrowing.

All her strength had drained out of her by the time they finally stumbled out of the water and up onto the beach. Fran collapsed onto the sand, gasping for breath and shivering. Her friends, their faces white with anxiety, brought their towels and putting them round Fran began to rub her, trying to get her warm and dry.

The older woman approached, bringing the boy's clothes. She knelt down beside him, fussing over him. He had stripped to his underpants for the swim, and as he didn't have a towel the girls offered one of theirs. The boy started to pull on his clothes.

Despite the heat Fran was still shivering. She turned to speak to the strangers.

'I don't know how to thank you. I thought this was going to be my last day ... I couldn't seem to swim back.'

'It's okay. The current here's pretty deceptive.'

The boy spoke gruffly, as he struggled into his socks. Then he pulled his trainers towards him and began to lace them up.

'I'm so sorry for causing you all that trouble. I should never have been so pig-headed.'

He shook his head. 'It doesn't matter. I'm glad I managed to bring you back.'

'I'm more glad than I can say. What's your name? You were absolutely wonderful. You've saved my life. Are you a trained lifesaver?'

'I did a course recently. Didn't know it would come in useful so soon!'

Then he grinned, and it was a lovely, heart-warming grin. Fran, who had been feeling frightened and miserable, and thoroughly ashamed of herself, felt this young man's smile begin to dispel her wretchedness.

'Please tell me your name.'

He stood up, now fully dressed.

'It's Timothy', he said. 'My friends call me Tim. This is my mother.'

'Please forgive me,' Fran said, tuning to the older woman. 'You must have been going through agonies. You have a son to be very proud of.'

The woman had seemed aloof up to this point, giving Fran the distinct feeling that she didn't want to speak to her. This was very understandable, in view of the fact that she had just put this stranger's son in danger by her foolish actions. But at last the woman smiled, and her whole face softened.

'I am. Very proud of him, for all sorts of reasons. Fortunately all has ended well. I'm glad you're safe. Come on, Tim. Let's get back.'

They turned to go. Fran watched their retreating backs. She saw that the young lad, who had streaked through the water with the grace of a dolphin, walked on land with an awkward, uneven gait. Something about his shoes, when he had been putting them on, had caught her attention and now she realised what it was. The heels were of a different height, the left one being higher than the right.

She was silent as she watched mother and son walk away. Then she turned to her companions.

'Come on – let's go and find that church. I think I need to say a prayer.'

CHAPTER 22

The three friends had returned to Fowey and were sitting in a pub consuming their evening meal. The laughter that had characterised their holiday earlier was missing. Conversation was desultory, soon drying up altogether.

'Let's clear the air,' said Fran, her tone matter-of-fact. 'I want to say that I'm very sorry for what I put you through today. I know I should never have tried to swim out as far as I did.'

'I'm furious with you,' said Jill. 'We shouted at you to come back, and you took no notice!'

'I was so frightened,' added Bunty.

Fran looked at the strained faces of her friends and felt ashamed. She knew she could be headstrong and determined – Barbie and Percy had told her often enough. It was one thing if her obstinacy didn't harm anyone else, but a very different matter if it caused her friends to suffer. She sighed.

'It was exciting, swimming against the waves. And the noise of the water was so loud I didn't hear your shouts. Believe you me, when I turned and saw how far out I'd swum, I was pretty scared. Then I saw you jumping up and down on the beach, and I fought to get back, but the current was too strong.'

'Those other people came to watch,' said Jill. 'The lad started pulling off his clothes, and the mother tried to stop him. She begged him not to go. She said better one life lost than two. She actually said that!'

'Now I feel worse than ever.' Fran hung her head.

'The lad was determined. He took no notice of his mother and started to plunge into the waves. We thought we ought to speak to her, because we felt, well, kind of responsible. So we said how brave he was.'

'What did she say?'

'She said of course he would go, she knew that, despite anything she might say. She said swimming was the thing he was most good at, and it must have seemed hard that she had tried to stop him, but he was all she had left in the world now.'

'Oh dear! I feel terrible about the whole episode.' Fran's remorse was plain to see.

'Then let's forget it,' said Bunty. 'Let's pretend it never happened.'

'That's no good, because it did happen. I was idiot enough to let it happen. But it's made me think, and I want to say one or two things, if you'll let me.'

The friends nodded, so Fran went on.

'It concentrates the mind wonderfully when you think you are about to drown. I had got to the point where I was completely exhausted. I couldn't raise the energy to move my arms and legs even one more time, and the water was closing over my head. Then somehow a voice inside me told me not to let go, to try once more, and fight. So I fought. I managed to surface – and that's when I saw him, coming towards me. And in those moments I knew what really mattered to me, what I needed to go on living for.'

'Which was?' prompted Jill.

'I couldn't let my parents down – they had given me so much. I couldn't make them endure a terrible tragedy. Then I thought about my friends, especially you two. We've been together since secondary school, in our tight little group, keeping out the classroom bullies and fending off the cutting remarks of teachers.'

'All for one and one for all!' Jill tried to lighten it.

'Exactly so. I realised I was lucky to have friends like you, and if I got back I wanted to say – don't let's ever lose touch. No matter where life leads us, whatever husbands or family come along – let's always be there for each other.'

'A pact!' cried Bunty. 'Should we seal it in blood?'

'Not me!' Jill was the most squeamish of the three. 'Anyhow, that's all understood. So is that it?'

'Not quite.' Fran was looking more thoughtful than ever. 'Do you remember me telling you, a long time ago, that I was adopted?'

'Yes, I think so.' Jill answered, and Bunty nodded. 'But so what? You've got lovely parents now, you said so yourself.'

'I know I have and I've been extraordinarily lucky. But neither of you can understand how that feels. You belong to your parents in every sense of the word. I don't, in the same way, because somewhere out there a man and a woman exist who are my real parents, my birth parents. And not knowing who they are or anything about them makes me feel that I don't really know who I am.'

'I can't really see that it matters.' Bunty looked puzzled. 'Would knowing make any difference to you?'

'I think I can understand what Fran means. I can't fully, because, fortunately, I'm not in that position.'

'I feel sort of in limbo, kind of stateless. You see, I've absolutely no family of my own. We were talking just now about making a blood pact. Don't you see – I've no blood relative, anywhere on this earth, that I know about. And yet they are around, somewhere.'

'You might, perhaps, rub shoulders with one, and never know they were your relation,' said Jill thoughtfully.

'Yes, I might. Wouldn't that be a strange coincidence! And it makes me feel I never want to have children of my own, because they would be just as much in the dark about my side of the family as I am. And it would hurt them, as it hurts me.'

'So what are you planning to do about it?'

'I made a resolve, that if I did get back to dry land, then one day, when the time was right, I would start searching.'

'When would the time be right? What's wrong with now?' Bunty liked to get on with things.

'Because it would upset my adoptive parents dreadfully. When I was first told that I was adopted – or "specially chosen" as my mother put it – I was quite young, so of course I started to ask questions. And even at that tender age I realised that Mummy was terrified that if I found my birth mother she might be displaced. Some time later I tried bringing the subject up again, and she got so distressed that I promised I would put it out of my mind. I haven't ever mentioned it to her since, but of course I can't forget – it's too much a part of who I am. But I vowed I would wait until my dear mother has passed on, and then I shall set about it with a vengeance.'

'Don't you think it might be too late then? By the time Barbie dies, your real mother might have died as well.'

'That's true, and it's a risk I must take. But I'm guessing that my real mother was quite young – that was probably why she couldn't keep her baby – and Barbie was relatively old to be a mother, so there's a chance. And it's a chance I have to take.'

'How strange it will be, if you do find her. Do you think you will instantly love each other?'

'I'd have to get to know her, of course, but I think I'd immediately experience the feeling of connection. I long for that sense of having someone who's truly mine – who is a part of me, and I'm a part of her. Please don't ever pass this on to anyone, but the truth is I don't really feel I belong to my parents – dear though they are to me. I'm different from them, I have different abilities. Once I knew I had it in me to go on to further education I also realised that I'd left them behind completely. They are both lovely people and greatly respected in the village – but far more goes on in my head than I can ever share with them. What I long for is to find that person with whom I can have a real empathy. And one day, I will. I promise you, I will! I dream constantly about it, and after what happened yesterday I am more determined than ever to make it happen. And when it does, when I find my birth mother... I just know... it will be wonderful!'

CHAPTER 23

Driving through the open countryside Fran struggled to raise her spirits. Everywhere around her looked beautiful in the spring sunshine. After so much rain the fields were thickly carpeted with grass, and 'England's green and pleasant land' was a sight for sore eyes – especially for someone who spent her working life in London and lived on its outskirts.

She was ashamed of her bad temper. It was just that all her friends had gone for a weekend down to the Dorset coast. They had rented a little cottage and would have a wonderful time socialising, possibly doing some boating, eating at picturesque pubs, and generally have the fun that young people enjoy. What's more, among them was a certain John Peters, who had begun to pay Fran some marked attention. She was hardly smitten by him – he didn't seem to have the initiative and drive she looked for in a male companion – but at thirty years of age, when you lacked anything approaching a boyfriend, you welcomed signs of interest, initially, anyhow.

Well, she was committed to going home for Barbie's birthday, and she knew that her presence at the tea party would make the event for her parents. She had a birthday cake in the boot of her car on which, written in icing sugar, the words 'Happy 70th birthday, Barbie' were emblazoned. When she thought of her parents and all the love with which they had enveloped her all her life, she knew there was no place for resentment, and started to look forward to seeing them.

It was just that, at the age she now was, it seemed appropriate to draw the conclusion that a single life was going to be her lot, and she knew this was probably her fault. The fierce independence of spirit that characterised her was off-putting to the male sex, and usually frightened any boyfriends away in a matter of weeks. She wondered why she had to be quite so self-protective, and guessed that it had a lot to do with her origins. If you did not know who you really were you needed to cling on to what little identity you did have. Oh well, she'd probably hate sharing her life with anyone, anyway.

Deep in her musings she became aware that the car was making some odd noises and proceeding rather jerkily. Then the engine cut right out. She managed to pull in to the side of the road and tried to restart it, but without success. Just what she needed! A breakdown on a country lane surrounded by fields and not a house in sight. She got out and looked up and down the road – perhaps she could flag down a passing car – but there wasn't a single one to be seen. The only sign of life was a small herd of cows in the nearby field who were sufficiently interested to come up to the wire fence to find out if there was a little bit of excitement taking place on the other side.

'Stop looking at me!' said Fran. 'If you can't help, just go away and let me think what to do. Haven't you got lives of your own? How can I come up with an idea if you're just going to stand and stare at me!'

The cows' unblinking gaze did not waver as they solemnly continued to chew their cud. Once more she scanned the empty road in both directions, ready to stop any approaching car, but again there was nothing in sight. She was just thinking she was going to have to set off to try and find some sign of habitation when over the brow of the hill there appeared a tiny yellow dot. Fascinated, Fran watched as the dot grew bigger in size, until it finally was transformed before her eyes into the smallest car she had ever seen – more like a Noddy car than a real one. It drew up behind her and out climbed a large man, his face covered in a bushy moustache and beard, but his eyes, which she could see, looked kind.

'It appears we have a maiden in distress.'

'I'm afraid my car cut out on me, and I can't get it going. It would happen miles away from anywhere. There isn't even a house to be seen – only these stupid cows.'

'I don't suppose they've come up with any useful suggestions? No, well, perhaps we'd better have a look under the bonnet.'

'Would you really? I'm so sorry to be a nuisance.'

'Not at all. I like looking at car engines, although I'm rather more conversant with old ones than modern ones.'

'What's your car then? How old is it?'

'It's an Austin Nippy. It was born in 1936 and it likes going for spins along country roads.'

'It looks so small, you'd think other drivers wouldn't see it.'

'They don't always, but fortunately I can see them. I'm Nigel, by the way.'

'I'm Fran, and I'm very grateful to you.'

By now he had taken several things out of the engine, looked at them and put them back, while Fran stood anxiously by. Then he had a go at starting it, and the engine fired into life.

'Oh!' cried Fran. 'How clever of you! Thank you so much. What was it?'

'There was a short in the electrical circuit, but I think I've got rid of it. Still, I'd get a garage to check it over as soon as you can. How far are you going?'

'I've got about another half an hour to do – it's my mother's birthday – I've got her cake in the back of my car. She'd have been so disappointed if I hadn't made it.'

'Well I've got a thermos of tea – we could have had our own tea party. You can have a cup now, if you like.'

He went over to his car and from the back picked up a thermos flask which he held out to her. It was covered in greasy marks.

'Perhaps I'll forgo the pleasure – anyway, I've no knife to cut the cake.'

'I've got a couple of screwdrivers and a pair of pliers. I expect we could manage. Still, I'm sure your mother's tea is preferable. Mind if I follow you a little way? Just want to make sure your car's functioning properly now.'

'Would you? That would be very kind. And look, why don't you come in and have some birthday cake with us? I know my parents would be delighted.'

'I'm not exactly dressed for the occasion.' He was wearing trousers that had seen better days, and an old jacket – but mercifully his clothes did not seem to be covered in oil.

'You look fine,' she said. 'It's only going to be us. Just a family tea party. Will you be able to keep up with me?'

'I will ignore that remark, and put it down to ignorance,' he replied. 'Off you go.'

She set off, and saw that the yellow car was indeed keeping up with her, although the driver was maintaining a respectful distance. This meant that when another car did catch them up it would pop into the gap, so that she had to pull in to let it go by – otherwise she couldn't see the yellow car at all. Half an hour later they both duly arrived, and parked outside the cottage.

Fran received a rapturous welcome, and when the greetings were over she introduced Nigel. He had been hanging back respectfully but now he came forward smiling as Fran explained what had happened on her journey. Her parents immediately turned the warmth of their welcome on him, as Fran had known they would, and expressed their thanks for his roadside rescue.

'Think nothing of it,' he replied. 'I make a point of coming to the assistance of, on average, about one damsel per week. But they don't all take me to birthday parties.'

'I wonder,' said Percy tentatively, when they had eaten lots of cake and drunk numerous cups of tea, 'I wonder if I could have a look at your car? It's a Nippy, you said? The first car I ever owned was an Austin Seven.'

'In comparison with the standard Austin Seven the Nippy, as you probably know, has an uprated engine. Fran was surprised that I could keep up with her.'

'It did seem to go fast for such a small car,' said Fran.

'Yes, on a good day and with a following wind, it can make 60 mph or more. The only problem is stopping.'

'Why? Don't the brakes work?'

'Not as effectively as those in your modern vehicle. But you have to admit it's a lot more fun. I wonder if the ladies would mind if I took Percy out for a little spin?'

'Would you?' Percy was beaming from ear to ear.

'Providing you bring him back safely,' said Fran.

'Oh dear, yes!' Barbie was looking distinctly worried. 'Please go slowly, won't you and make sure he fastens his seat belt.'

'There's a slight problem with that,' admitted Nigel. 'There aren't any.'

'You'll have the police after you!' Barbie's fears were mounting.

'Not at all – you see they're not a legal requirement on a car of this age. But never you fear – I'll have him back safe and sound, and all in one piece, in twenty minutes, if that's acceptable.'

Percy went off looking like the cat who has found the cream. The two women couldn't help laughing at his boyish enthusiasm, and went to the window to watch. While Percy had a door that opened on his side so that the passenger could get in, the driver, it appeared, had no such luxury and was forced to climb into his seat. With a number of splutters and bangs the car drove away, leaving Barbie and Fran to enjoy a little time of being together and catching up on news. Then the loud bangs and splutters could be heard once more, heralding the men's return.

'Wonderful!' cried Percy. 'Absolutely wonderful! Takes you back. Upon my soul, that's for sure – it certainly takes you back.'

'I hope you didn't get cold, dear, with it being all open like that.'

'Nonsense, my love, it's a beautiful warm day.'

'I suppose you can only take it out in the good weather?' asked Fran.

'There is a cover you can put up,' replied Nigel. 'The only thing is …'

'I knew there'd be a "but",' said Fran.

'Well, the only trouble is that whoever designed the cover forgot that you don't just need to look ahead – from time to time you need to be able to see out of the side windows as well. You can't do that, when the cover's on.'

At last it was time to go. Fran was delighted to see her parents looking so happy, and although Barbie was now frail, Percy, at seventy-five, looked fit enough. It had been a good afternoon. She was pleased she had come.

As they went out to their cars Nigel said, 'I do hope that was all right, I mean taking your father out in the car. Your mother might have preferred him not to go, as it was her birthday, and you had come to be with them.'

Fran, touched by the thoughtfulness, assured him that Barbie had been quite happy about it.

'To tell you the truth,' she said, 'I didn't much want to come today because my friends have all gone off for a weekend down to the coast. But actually, it's turned out to be a lot of fun.'

'That's good,' he said. 'I'm glad. I shall drive behind you some of the way, until I need to turn off, after about three quarters of hour. By then we should be fairly sure that your car will behave until you get back.'

'You don't need to follow me now. I'm sure I'll be fine.'

'Oh,' he said, 'are we having our first argument? I do hope so.'

'Why?' Fran was puzzled. 'I don't understand. Why would you want to argue with me?'

'Believe me, I don't. But if it's our first, that implies I'll see you again to have another.'

Fran smiled. 'That was the most oblique chat up line I've ever heard.'

'I was just wondering,' he said, 'if your friends are still away, whether you might like, that is, I don't know how you'd feel about having a ride in this tomorrow? But you'd probably hate it. Never mind, it was only an idea.'

Without giving her a chance to answer he climbed back into his car, and they set off. The journey went without a hitch, and Fran couldn't help smiling whenever she looked in her rear mirror and caught sight of the yellow car, because in some strange way it appeared to be smiling at her. They reached the point where they would be going their separate ways.

He honked his horn and pulled over to the side of the road. Fran stopped also. Nigel appeared at her window.

'Perhaps you would be kind enough to give me your telephone number? Then I can ring later, and make sure you've arrived home safely.'

'What if I haven't?'

He thought for a minute.

'Then don't answer the phone.'

He ran back to his car with the piece of paper containing her telephone number, climbed in and started up again. They moved off, and Fran saw him wave just before the Nippy moved out of range of her rear view window. She waved back, laughing to herself, and continued on her way home. Feeling certain she'd hear from him later she found she was rather looking forward to speaking to him again.

CHAPTER 24

Fran had been married to Nigel for eight years when she heard the news that Barbie was fading fast and wasn't expected to live much longer. Immediately she asked Nigel if he would come with her as she went down to the care home where Barbie had been living for the past six months to pay what would probably be her last visit. She knew he would not demur – he had turned out to be a kind, gentle man, and beneath the joking exterior there was a surprising sensitivity to her needs and to those of other people, so that she blessed the day when their paths had accidentally crossed.

She knew she had this fighting spirit, which probably meant she wasn't the easiest person to live with. It wasn't always easy living with herself. Nigel gave her all the freedom she needed and made few demands – other than that she kept the fridge loaded with cheese and pickle, so that he could make his daily sandwiches. She did her best to enter into his world of old cars and engines, often going for rides with him in the Nippy, which she never came to love, as he did – it was frankly rather a nerve-racking ride – but she enjoyed being out with him. Meanwhile she pursued her career in accountancy, achieving a position with a London firm of high repute. She found her job satisfying, and enjoyed the challenge of it as she had to hold her own against the bright young men there.

There was one issue in the marriage which could not be resolved. They were both getting on in years, and she knew Nigel would have liked a child before it was too late. In many ways Fran would have liked one too, but there was one insurmountable barrier. She had broached the subject, only two weeks previously, when it had been a beautiful weekend, and they had gone out for a picnic.

'You must think I'm very selfish, letting my baggage get in the way of something so important.'

'I don't see it as selfishness. I see it as a total impasse until the basic issue has been explored, and in some way sorted out.'

'You're so understanding, as always, which makes me feel worse than ever.'

'Just see if you can put it into words – that way perhaps we might see a way through, or if not that, at least perhaps a beginning. You see, it's not just the question of a child. It's really about you, and your "baggage" as you put it. I can hardly live with you as your husband without being aware that there is something gnawing away at you. For your sake I should like to see you being able to deal with that. So let's take it out and have a look at it.'

They were sitting on a rug at the edge of a grassy field, their picnic spread out before them. There was little sign of life, other than a few insects who were taking rather too much interest in their sandwiches. Nigel knew some lovely spots where you could wander away from the bustle of city life. Fran always found her spirits lifted and refreshed when they had been out for one of their 'little jaunts', as Nigel called them.

If there could be a better time or place to open her heart, it would be difficult to imagine it. Even so Fran had to think hard. It wasn't easy to express her feelings, but she knew she owed it to her husband.

'I would love to have a child so much – I can't tell you – but I can't bear to inflict on that child the feeling of being in limbo that I have always lived with. When you don't know who you are, you feel … this is the bit that's so hard to describe … that you don't belong anywhere or to anyone. No matter how brilliant your adoptive parents have been, the feeling is still there. You can keep it submerged, and lead a normal life, but it never leaves you. It comes up and hits you at the most unexpected times. I don't want my child to have to go through that.'

'You don't think it would be a little bit different, in that our child would know his parents? And the relatives on my side of the family, such as they are, especially those who aren't behind bars, are an open book. It's only your side that is missing.'

'Of course you are right. I know you are. But there'd still be that whole area where I wouldn't be able to answer any questions.'

'I do see that.'

'Do you know, when I was about nine, my school gave us the task of producing family trees. We had to ask our parents to help us, and go through old family albums – that kind of thing.'

'Oh dear, I see big problems ahead.'

'Exactly so. We sat down together and spent a whole day working on it, and when it was finished, instead of being delighted, I argued that it wasn't right, and I drew another, and all it had on it was my name and two big question marks!'

'I bet that went down well!'

'Poor Barbie was dreadfully upset, and Dad made me promise that in future I'd say I wasn't thinking about it any more, even if I was. That was quite a burden to put on a small girl! And at that tender age I simply couldn't understand why my mother got so distressed at the thought of me having a natural mother. Of course, as I grew older, I was able to see it from her point of view. I realised she thought I might feel I belonged to my natural mother more than I did to her. As she and Dad had always been so wonderful to me, I simply couldn't do that to them, so I resolved to wait until they were in a place where it wouldn't trouble them any more.'

'Well, you lost Percy last year with his heart attack, and now Barbie is frail and confused, and unlikely to know anything about it – so I suggest you start making some enquiries. The sooner you lay this ghost, the better I think things will be for you.'

'Oh Nigel – do you really think it would be all right to start the search now?'

'Yes, I do. After all, I'm sorry to say that I think, for Barbie, it will only be a matter of weeks now.'

Nigel had been right. Barbie's time was running out fast. Having gone down to be with her, Fran sat at her bedside, holding her hand, but Barbie did not open her eyes. Something told Fran not to go away, so she went and found Nigel, who was giving his car a polish, and told him that she wanted to stay on. He told her not to worry – there was nothing he needed to get back for and he was perfectly happy to wait.

Thanking her lucky stars that she had such a supportive husband, Fran went back inside. Barbie's breathing had changed, and she was now struggling to draw breaths. The nurse came and said gently that she thought they wouldn't have long to wait. Fran sat quietly and watched as the miracle happened – the opposite of a new life coming but a miracle just the same – the moment when an old life goes, leaving behind all suffering, and entering a welcome state of peace. She kissed her mother tenderly, tears running down her face.

'Thank you, dearest Mummy, for everything you did for me, and for all the love you gave me,' she whispered. 'You've been the best mother in the world, and I shall never forget you.'

Then they went back home and there, on the doormat, was a letter. The search agency she had contacted believed they had traced her natural mother. If she telephoned they would provide details so that she could go and visit.

'Oh Nigel!' breathed Fran. 'This is the moment I have been waiting for. This is what I have been longing for, all my life. I can't believe it has come at last – and I'm terrified!'

'Try to take it slowly,' advised Nigel. 'She may not immediately be receptive to you.'

'I know. I know I mustn't expect too much at the outset. But I am just desperate to go and see her, and find out what she's like – this woman who gave birth to me almost forty years ago. Oh Nigel, now it's got to this point, I'm so scared, but I'm so happy too. At long last, everything I've been longing for is about to happen!'

Nigel smiled, hoping, for his wife's sake, the moment was going to be all she had anticipated. But he said nothing.

CHAPTER 25

'Get out of my flat! Get out – and don't ever come back!'

Claudia had risen from her chair, her white face taut with anger, her whole body trembling. Fran didn't move. She remained seated and looked steadily at the furious woman in front of her.

'How dare you think you can come waltzing back here after forty years and expect to be received like an honoured guest! How dare you assume I'll be glad to see you! I've told you to go, so do it. Now!'

Still Fran didn't move. Claudia's stiff stance began to loosen. Her body was shaking uncontrollably. She fell back into her chair, put her head in her hands, and sobbed – great heart-broken sobs. The pain that seared through her chest was a reminder of the torture she had experienced forty years ago. First there had been that dreadful day when she had signed the papers agreeing to hand her child over to the Adoption Society. Then the moment when she had walked out of the hospital alone, leaving her baby behind – a moment that was etched indelibly in her memory. She had cried for a week before she had taken control of herself and vowed she would never allow herself to think about that day again. From the moment she had made her resolve she had kept a watertight control over all her emotions so that they were untouchable by any other human being – or so she thought.

'I know it's a terrible shock for you' said Fran, gently. 'I've thought for a long time about whether I should write in advance, but I decided not to do that as you might well have refused to meet me and then my bridges would have been burned for all time. But I can't tell you for how long I have wanted to contact you – I've longed to know who my birth mother was, and–'

'I know. You wanted to know why some terrible woman left you to the tender mercies of an adoption society and abandoned you without a thought. Well, now you know what that woman is like – an embittered spinster, who lives by herself with only her cat for company, who has no life now that her career is over, and no friends. The only acquaintances are the school colleagues who, for years, made fun of me behind my back. So now you know, go away and leave me in peace. I don't want to know anything about you, and I don't want you to know any more about me.'

The sobbing had ceased and a hard, set look had taken over. It was the sort of look her colleagues knew so well. It was the look that said, 'Keep your distance. Don't think you can invade my personal territory. We communicate strictly for business reasons, and then we part. Don't ever overstep the mark.' It was a look that had daunted all who worked with her over the years. Now the look was directed at Fran, but Fran did not flinch.

'I am not asking you to tell me my background at this stage, although obviously I am curious both about you, and about my father. I understand that you don't want to know anything about me. I just want to say that I had a very happy home. I grew up with two of the kindest people it is possible to imagine. But the older I grew the more I realised that somehow I did not fit with them. I knew I belonged in a different setting. I was anxious to leave home and get more education and training, so that I could have something of a profession, rather than just a job. I'm not sure now that I have fulfilled my potential, but I am satisfied that I have achieved something worthwhile. Now I've seen you I am beginning to understand these feelings that puzzled and bothered me so much when I was growing up.'

'I'm glad your problem has been solved.' The icy sarcasm was blatant. 'So now you can go back to wherever you came from feeling comfortable about yourself and forget you ever contacted me. I mean it. I don't want to see you again. I don't want to know any more about you. I washed my hands of you when you were born and I knew, that day, that I never wanted to have anything further to do with you.'

Claudia stood up once more, making it clear that the conversation was over. Fran started to say something, thought better of it, and decided she should leave. What did one say in these circumstances? 'It was nice meeting you' hardly seemed appropriate. Should she offer to shake hands? Her mind whirring she stumbled towards the front door. Unable to bring herself to look back she opened it and walked through.

As she left she thought she heard a strange, strangled noise behind her. Driving home that noise kept echoing through her mind. Her jangling emotions made it difficult for her to concentrate on her journey. Nor could she see clearly through her tears.

CHAPTER 26

The front door slammed shut with a ferocity that shook the house. The next moment the lounge door was flung open. Nigel, who had been absorbed in a technical manual, looked up to see Fran standing there, her face white and tense, her body shaking with emotion.

'She's horrible! Horrible! Horrible! Horrible! And I hate her!' Fran threw herself down into an armchair and burst into tears.

'It didn't go too well then?'

Nigel came over to sit on the arm of his wife's chair, and took her hand.

'Poor darling,' he said gently. 'Want to tell me about it?'

'No. I don't want to talk about it – not now. Not ever! I don't even want to think about it. She told me to get out – so I did. Oh, Nigel! I've made the most dreadful mistake.'

The weeping was gaining momentum. Nigel was silent.

Then Fran suddenly stood up.

'I'm going out for a walk,' she said. 'Don't come. I want to be by myself. Please just leave me alone.'

She was gone for two hours. Nigel waited patiently, worrying, but knowing it would do no good to try and find her. Eventually Fran returned.

'I want to say two things,' she announced. 'First, I'm very sorry I was bad-tempered with you, Nigel. I didn't mean to take it out on you. Secondly, I made a bad mistake in trying to make contact and that's all there is to it.'

'How about dining out?' suggested Nigel.

'No, sorry, Thanks, but I'm not hungry and I'm not in the mood.'

'Not even for a special meal at Luigi's?'

Fran hesitated. Luigi's was their favourite restaurant. Perhaps a relaxing evening there would help to take her mind off things.

'We wouldn't get a table at this short notice, would we?'

'We already have a table. I've booked it. You have half an hour to wash and brush up, so get started. Senor Luigi awaits us.'

Fran smiled. 'You're so good to me. What would I do without you?'

'Go and get ready,' he said.

They had reached the coffee stage before anything relevant to the issue was mentioned. The candle flame flickered over the bright red checked tablecloth. They had enjoyed a delectable meal and Fran had drunk two glasses of excellent wine. Finally Nigel raised the topic.

'So what are you going to do now?'

'Forget the whole thing.'

'What's happened to Fran the Fighter – that persistent woman who never gives up?'

'She's disappeared off the scene. In her place you see Fran the Fool – the complete idiot who's been living a dream. Well, reality has now dawned with blinding force. I know you had reservations about my going in search of my natural mother – and you've been proved right.'

'If I had reservations it was only because I was afraid you might not get the reception you hoped for. I didn't want you to get hurt.'

'Well, as you saw, I did get hurt, dreadfully.' Fran's eyes became moist. Nigel put his large hand across the table and grasped Fran's in his.

'Let's look at it from Claudia's point of view. She gave up her baby almost forty years ago – we don't know why, nor do we know what that did to her. I'm not a woman, as you well know, so I can't put myself in her place, but I imagine that's a pretty traumatic experience for any mother.'

'I'm sure it is – so you'd think she might be pleased that I came to find her. But she clearly couldn't bear to see me. She didn't want to have anything to do with me.'

'Think of the shock it must have been for her to have you turn up, out of the blue, on her doorstep. You'd been planning this moment for years. You'd been lying awake at night thinking about it. She knew nothing of the way you'd been building your hopes up for this meeting. Just suddenly, one day, there you were – the baby she never watched grow up.'

'Perhaps I should have warned her. It was silly, I know, but I believed, when we met, that there'd be something there – right from the start. I thought … I thought when she opened the door, I'd recognise her! Doesn't that sound stupid!'

Nigel squeezed her hand.

'Not stupid, my darling. Just optimistic, perhaps idealistic. That's what I love about you – always believing everything will turn out well in the end. Always concentrating on the positive. Never accepting defeat.'

'I know what you're saying. I should have another try.'

'That's up to you.'

'Perhaps, if she's had time to get over the shock, it might be better next time.'

'Who knows?'

'Do you know what I love about you? You never try to stop me doing anything, even if you think it might be unwise. You're so supportive, no matter what foolish course of action I decide on.'

'So what have you decided?'

'I'll have another go. I'm not going to give up yet.'

'That's my girl,' said Nigel.

CHAPTER 27

'Oh, it's you. I suppose you'd better come in.'

Claudia's greeting was marginally better than the first time.

As they went into the lounge Fran noticed that Claudia seemed distracted. She appeared to have no intention of starting a conversation and kept looking round the room. She ignored Fran's presence, as if her mind was absorbed with some problem.

'What is it? What are you looking for?'

'My cat, Socrates. I can't think why he isn't here – he's usually back by this time. I haven't seen him since breakfast.'

As she spoke there was a scrabbling noise at the cat flap. Socrates, who usually leaped nimbly through, scarcely touching the edges, was having difficulty making his entrance. Both women moved towards the kitchen and watched a bedraggled black cat, eyes staring, body trembling, heave his frame through the flap and land in a heap on the kitchen floor. He was immediately violently sick.

'I must get him to the vet.'

Claudia looked distraught. Fetching a basket she picked the cat up and laid him gently inside, on a blanket.

'I've got my car outside,' said Fran. 'May I give you a lift?'

'That would be a help. It's two buses, you see, and it can take an hour if there's a long wait.'

It only took fifteen minutes by car. They went to the reception desk, Claudia holding the basket containing its precious treasure. At the desk they waited for some attention. It was at least thirty seconds since they had presented themselves and the receptionist had still not taken her eyes from the computer. Claudia, out of her mind with worry, found the delay intolerable.

'Kindly fetch the vet immediately. This cat is very sick – he may be dying.'

'He has a client in with him at the moment. Would you please take a seat?'

'I will not take a seat until you inform the vet that Miss Hansom is here with Socrates, who is in an extremely bad condition. I need him to be told straight away – before you do anything else on that computer!'

The girl finally raised her eyes from the screen, a hostile look on her face. She was clearly about to refuse Claudia's request.

'It would be so helpful if you would just tell him,' interposed Fran, 'so that he understands the urgency. We would be so grateful.'

Claudia was on the point of telling her to keep out of it when the girl nodded and went to open the surgery door, speaking quietly to the vet. Whatever she said proved effective because he could be heard apologising to his client and came out. He took one look at the basket and its occupant. Socrates lay there listlessly, his normally bright, intelligent eyes glazed and uncomprehending. The vet took the basket from Claudia, promising to examine the cat in the next few minutes.

They went and sat down. Suddenly Claudia wondered what on earth she was doing sitting beside this woman who claimed to be her daughter. How had it happened? She had done her best to send Fran packing, once and for all, but here she was, back again. Under other circumstances Claudia would have made sure it was a very short visit, but she had not been able to resist the offer of a lift to the vet's surgery, since it was obviously going to save a lot of time. It was the sensible thing to do, for Socrates' sake. She didn't mean Fran to come in with her, but somehow it had happened.

Those words were still echoing through her mind: 'I have very good reasons for believing that you are my birth mother.' The shockwaves that had flooded through her whole body had almost engulfed her. For forty years she had tried to suppress the knowledge that somewhere out there was the woman who had been her baby – hers and Stefano's – and the pain she had felt when she gave the child up was buried deep inside her, never to be revisited.

Those floodgates must not be opened. She must put a stop to it as soon as possible, and now was as good a time as any. She turned to say this to Fran, but at that moment the vet appeared and came over to speak to her.

'I'm sorry, Miss Hansom, I'm afraid your cat is very ill indeed. He seems to have eaten something poisonous. I'm going to try and wash his stomach out but I'm not very hopeful.'

'How long will it take?' Claudia, used to being in control, was outwardly composed.

'I'm not sure – half an hour or so. Do you want to wait or shall I ring you at home?'

'I'll wait.' Claudia was decisive. She turned to her companion.

'It was kind of you to accompany me here.' Somehow she couldn't bring herself to use this woman's name – the name she had lovingly chosen such a long time ago. 'However, I'm going to sit and wait, so I'm sure you want to go now. No doubt someone will be expecting you.'

'I'll wait with you, if you'll allow me to.' Laying a gentle but strong hand on Claudia's Fran felt an involuntary shudder pass through the older woman's body. She wondered how long it had been since Claudia had experienced any physical contact with another human being. Then the older woman snatched her hand away.

'There's absolutely no reason why you should. My cat and I are of no concern to you. I'm quite sure you don't want to be bothered with our little troubles. Please leave me in peace. I'd really rather be alone.'

Fran stood up.

'Are you sure you wouldn't like me to wait until … Well, until there's some news? I have no issue with the time.'

'There's no need.' Suddenly the thought of being alone with a dead Socrates was overwhelming. 'Well, perhaps …just until …'

Then the vet was standing in front of them again. Claudia rose to her feet.

'I'm so sorry, Miss Hansom. It was too late. The poison had got into his bloodstream. I'm sorry to tell you that he's died. Do you want me to see to the disposal, or do you want to take him away?'

'I'll take him.' The voice was low, controlled, expressionless.

'Wait here, please.'

'Oh, Claudia,' whispered Fran gently. 'I'm so sorry.'

Somehow they moved towards each other, and the next moment Fran had both her arms round the older woman who was sobbing on her shoulder. Claudia only allowed it to happen for a few seconds, then she moved away and began to scrabble through her bag. Silently Fran produced a man's large handkerchief which she passed to Claudia who accepted it, dabbed at her eyes, blew her nose, and then handed it back.

'You keep it. They're so much more practical than tissues – I always carry one. Are you going to bury him in your garden? I'll come and help you.'

'I really don't want to involve you – but I don't think I can do it by myself, and I do want him at home.'

'With a little plaque, to mark the spot.'

'Yes, then I'll have a reminder.'

Now completely covered by a blanket, Socrates' body lay in the basket for the homeward journey. Neither of the women spoke.

Back at her home Claudia found a trowel and selected a spot. She began to dig, but her hands were unsteady, and she was finding it difficult.

'May I help?' Fran took the trowel, and with her strong hands had soon managed to scoop out a hole big enough to accommodate the cat's body.

Claudia laid Socrates to rest. Shovelling the earth back on top of him was the worst part of it. She was unable to prevent tears rolling down her cheeks once more. Fran helped her smooth over the top of the grave.

'What about the plaque?'

'I'd like to think about it, and do that by myself.'

Fran nodded.

'I'll go now,' she said. 'I'm so sorry, but thank you for letting me share it with you.'

Claudia walked with her to the front door.

Fran smiled at her and then turned to go. Claudia said nothing. Fran walked as far as the gate, and was just going through when she heard her name. She turned.

'Thank you.'

Fran smiled, nodded, and was gone.

CHAPTER 28

Clutching the large bouquet of flowers that had just been delivered she withdrew the card nestling in the foliage and read:

'To Claudia. I'm so sorry that you've been subjected to two dreadful shocks recently – first my visit, and then poor Socrates' illness and death. Fran.'

Receiving the flowers was another disturbing experience – for some reason it brought back memories of that bouquet in Oxford … well, she wasn't going to think about that.

But she did have to think about Fran's visit. Still reeling from the loss of her cat, and hating the emptiness in her flat, she knew she was in no state to tackle the issue, but she couldn't just ignore it. It was clear Fran wasn't simply going to go away, now she had made the contact. The trouble was her arrival had lifted the lid on all the memories so that they came flooding back, and with them the pain.

With startling clarity Claudia saw her twenty-one year old self bending over the cot, touching the tiny hand and feeling those little fingers grasping hers. Suffocated by searing emotions she had wrenched the tiny fingers away, turned her back on her baby and walked out of the hospital. Once again she experienced the pain of the razor-sharp sword that had pierced her heart, inflicting a penetrating wound so excruciating that she instinctively knew she would never recover.

At first she had done nothing but lie on her bed and give vent to deep, anguished sobs that brought no relief but could not be controlled. Emotionally drained and weak from lack of food, she had summoned all her resources and made a resolve. She would pick up the threads of her life again, and embark on the career for which she had prepared herself – but never would she allow herself to feel anything for another human being again. Such vulnerability must be avoided at all costs.

Ten years ago she had admitted Socrates into her life. That had been a difficult decision initially, but soon it was hard to tell who was looking after whom. Socrates was born with an intuition and wisdom far above the normal level for cats, Claudia believed. She had almost lost sight of his true nature, so that it was only when someone else used the term when referring to him, that she remembered he was a cat.

Gradually she allowed herself to draw comfort from his presence and pleasure in his companionship. She realised now that she had lost sight of that resolve to shut everyone out, and had allowed herself to love – and once again she was denied the object of her affection. For a second time the punishment was being meted out to her – she must endure the intense pain of loss.

So what should she do about Fran? There was no easy way of getting rid of her – that had been obvious yesterday. She had lost count of the number of times she had told her to leave, and somehow it hadn't happened.

Did she want her to go? It was a simple decision really – nothing more than a mathematical equation. Put the pluses on one side and the minuses on the other, and see which side held the higher number.

She'd start with the plus side. Here was the opportunity to have someone of significance in her life. (Was that actually a plus, or a minus?) There might be someone around if she was ill, or who could perhaps help her tackle things that were beyond her. (Definitely a plus – although in fact she was never ill, and she'd managed everything herself up to now, so she probably didn't need anyone.) She could make the acquaintance of the daughter she had lost so long ago. (Did she want to? It had all been buried for so long, what was the point of raking it up now?)

It was time for the minuses. Seeing Fran would awaken memories she had refused to allow to surface for almost forty years. (No doubt which side of the line that was.) This woman might make demands on her. She might be jogged out of the quiet existence she had managed to establish. She might be required to connect with her emotions again. She might have to become a human being once more!

No! No! No! It couldn't be done. She was too old, too tired, too set in her ways to change now. She had kept people at a distance all her life – how could she let anyone get close to her now? Sleeping dogs must be left to lie – there would be hell to pay if they were disturbed. She would resolve now, once and for all, that she would never allow this woman anywhere near her again.

The decision was made. She turned to pick up her latest library book and started to read. Then into her mind flooded the memory of how, the previous day, in the midst of her pain, she had laid her head on that broad shoulder and felt the strong arms encompass her. Resolutely, she turned her attention to the architectural relics of ancient Greece.

CHAPTER 29

Claudia's telephone rang.

'I've got two tickets for a West End show this afternoon.'

'Why are you telling me?'

'I would like you to come with me.'

'I never go to shows.'

'You never go to the theatre?'

'Yes … to see something serious … not to a show.'

The last word was spoken with a withering sarcasm that might have daunted a less stout heart.

'You'll love this – I know you will.'

'What sort of a show is it?'

'It's a musical.'

'A musical!' Again that scathing tone. 'If you had suggested a classical concert I might have been interested.'

'We'll meet in the foyer – it's the Prince of Wales Theatre – and a matinee performance so you won't be late back. I'm going to be in the office that morning – doing some overtime – so it would work out well to meet you there. I'll be waiting for you.'

'Then you'll be wasting your time. I won't be coming.'

'See you there.'

No you won't, thought Claudia. Did this woman ever take no for an answer? It was quite ridiculous to expect her to go to a show – and a musical of all things! The telephone rang again.

'I forgot to tell you what it was.'

'That's immaterial, since I shan't be coming.'

'It's a great show – everyone's raving about it. It's *Mamma Mia*.'

'Fran! Is this your idea of a joke?'

'I'll be waiting.'

Saturday was three days away. She would simply put the whole conversation out of her mind. For the next two days she concentrated on not thinking about it. Claudia Hansom was known for her determination – any course of action she had decided would be advantageous to her school usually took place. It was a brave colleague who tried to oppose her. It had happened, once or twice. Poor Rita Worthington, who had been the English teacher at the time, had wanted to stage a drama production that Claudia considered totally unsuitable. She could see Rita standing in her office now.

'But really, Miss Hansom, the children would so enjoy dressing up as animals. It would release their inner spirit and help them to express themselves without the inhibitions they experience when playing the parts of humans. The very fact that we wouldn't see their faces would enable them to feel they were free – free as the air – an empowering and enriching opportunity that may not come their way again.'

What rubbish! What words to use where eight- and nine-year olds were concerned! Miss Worthington had gone away with her tail between her legs, and had left the school a few months later. Her letter of resignation had stated that it seemed fruitless to produce ideas of her own and she felt her opportunities to enhance the children's self expression were being limited.

It was proving difficult to fill her mind with other matters. The house seemed so empty without Socrates. Somehow, with him in his usual place, she had been able to take an interest in various projects. Without his presence it was hard to summon up the motivation – even her latest book on the classical ruins to be seen in northern Africa failed to inspire. With an effort she attempted to lose herself in its pages and congratulated herself that there was nothing else on her mind now to distract her from reading.

Why was it, then, that when Saturday came, she found herself watching the clock? Why did she go to the wardrobe to see if there was something suitable to wear? The light grey suit was not too formal – with a cream blouse it might do. She put it on. Then she picked up her handbag.

On the underground train she worked out why she was going. It certainly wasn't to see the show – it was out of curiosity to see if Fran really would turn up. Perhaps she would take someone else, to use the tickets. Claudia would try and position herself where she could just peep round the corner – and then she'd withdraw.

Her plan was foiled because Fran was waiting on the pavement outside, and spotted Claudia as soon as she crossed the road from Piccadilly station. She showed no surprise whatever.

'We're in the circle. They're good seats.' Only three rows from the front, the seats gave them an excellent view of the stage.

'I've ordered some drinks for the interval.'

Claudia couldn't contain herself.

'You did that before I came? How could you, when I gave you so little encouragement?'

'That's something of an understatement. But Nigel says I'm a very positive person – always expecting things to go well. Like when I started looking for you – I knew I'd find you in the end. And I was prepared to give it as long as it took.'

'Who's Nigel?'

'My husband.'

'You're married!' Claudia was astonished.

'Why shouldn't I be?'

'But you are in full-time employment and you don't wear a ring.'

Fran was secretly pleased Claudia had taken enough interest to notice.

'Lots of married women work – and I don't like being forced to wear a badge of office.'

Claudia was silent. This news disturbed her, although she had no idea why it should.

'Nigel and I have a very good relationship – we are both

independent people and need our own space. He knew I wanted to pursue a career and was inclined to do my own thing now and again, and I knew his hobby would absorb a lot of his time. He's a bit of an eccentric, really.'

'What does he do?'

'Basically he's an engineer. That's what he does for a living. But he's a bit older than me, and he can afford to arrange some free time so that he can indulge in his chief joy in life – getting his hands thoroughly immersed in engine oil, and accumulating oily rags. He loves fiddling with old engines and trying to make them work.'

'Where does he do all this?'

'In his workshop, which is supposed to be our garage. He has been known to buy a bag of rusty bits for £5 and fifteen years later there is a gleaming, apparently brand new, Douglas motorcycle – every detail authentically reproduced.'

The overture was starting. There was no escape now. The curtain lifted revealing white walls against a dazzling blue background, invoking a Greek atmosphere of warmth and happiness. As the story unfolded the music swelled, filling the auditorium. The catchy rhythms captivated the audience, setting feet tapping and hands clapping, until finally people were standing, waving their arms, and dancing in uninhibited abandon.

Claudia, embarrassed initially, found her foot beginning to move, despite her best endeavours to keep it stationary. Fran did not stand, but clapped enthusiastically, swaying from side to side in her seat. Suddenly Claudia found tears beginning to roll down her cheeks. How ridiculous! Whatever was happening to her?

Nearly two and a half hours later Claudia, bewildered by the sensations that had flooded through her, followed Fran out of the theatre.

'I thought we'd go for a bite of supper – I know a good place only five minutes away.'

'I suppose you booked that too.'

'Actually, no – I didn't think it would be too full at this time.'

A hand under Claudia's elbow guided her at what seemed almost a running speed, and soon she found herself sitting opposite Fran in a pleasant Italian restaurant.

'Won't Nigel be expecting you back?'

'No – I told him to look after himself – he'll probably make an enormous cheese and pickle sandwich and eat it in the workshop. No doubt the bread and his hands will absorb black oil in the same proportions.'

While musing over the menu Claudia remarked, 'What an idiotic plot that was.'

Fran smiled. 'I saw your foot tapping, so don't pretend to be an old grump.'

'I can see this was all part of your plan. The significance of the title scarcely escapes my notice.'

'I didn't think it would – you're too much of a cute cookie.'

Claudia grimaced. 'What's wrong with using the Queen's English?'

'Nothing at all. The Queen's welcome to it – but if you're going to associate with me you might have to get used to something a little less formal.'

'I can't think why you've been so persistent – first I'm a "grump", then I'm too correct for you. Let's face facts – we have very little in common.'

'I think we have something so big in common I can't ignore it. Anyway …' Fran's face softened, and her voice was gentle, 'I knew when I set out to look for you that I wasn't going to find "the perfect mother" at the end of the trail. Which is just as well, because I'm hardly the perfect daughter. I knew I'd probably find someone who bore the scars of past sorrows. Well, in my own way, I've had a struggle over the years too, coming to terms with not knowing who I am. And now I've found you, I want to get to know you, and I'm not going to let you get away easily.'

Claudia lowered her head. She fought to allow herself to speak from the heart. It was so hard, after all these years of suppressing her emotions.

'You'll have to give me time – I think I'm probably a terrible disappointment. And I know if we go on seeing each other you're going to want me to answer the other question.'

'Which is …?'

'You know very well what it is – the same question Sophie, in that stupid musical, was asking.'

Fran nodded.

'I realise going back over the past will be painful, but the question isn't going to go away. Of course I want to know who my father was, and what happened to him. I'm not looking for a relationship with him – it is enough that I have found you, but I am looking for information. I'm not asking you now, but, Claudia, I need to know. I really do need to know.'

CHAPTER 30

They were driving through the Sussex countryside. It was a crisp, autumn morning and as they crossed the open heath of Ashdown Forest, with its waving bracken, the view was beautiful – marred only by an incongruous ice cream van parked in the lay by.

'Fancy an ice cream?' asked Fran.

'Certainly not.'

'That's just as well as we will shortly be arriving at our coffee stop.'

'As usual you've got this all mapped out, haven't you!'

'Some forethought is necessary when taking out a retired head teacher – who, as it happens, is my mother.'

They drew up outside a pretty tea room.

'Where's this?' Claudia looked round, admiring the setting, and enjoying the homely atmosphere inside.

'The Duddleswell Tea Rooms. Would you like coffee? I don't know enough about your tastes yet.'

'A cup of coffee would be most acceptable, thank you.'

'I have just spotted the most beautiful apple pie,' remarked Fran, 'which is a pity because we can't have any. It would spoil our lunch.'

'Needless to say, that's all arranged.'

'Certainly, and it's not a secret. We are lunching at the Grand Hotel in Eastbourne.'

'Oh Fran, you are spoiling me. I'm not used to anyone taking me out to lovely places.'

'Then you'd better start getting used to it. I'm enjoying spoiling you, as you put it.'

An hour or so after the coffee stop they were driving along by the seafront in Eastbourne. Fran guided the car into the car park in front of the imposing white building of the Grand Hotel. As they approached the door, a uniformed doorman in top hat greeted them deferentially and wished them a very pleasant afternoon.

Claudia, impressed by the opulent entry hall, allowed Fran to guide her towards the restaurant. The lunch was ridiculously expensive – Claudia caught sight of the bill at the end – but she found she was experiencing a thrill sitting at the table covered with a white, starched tablecloth and gleaming silver, being served efficiently by polite waiting staff quietly going about their task of bringing beautifully presented dishes to the diners. And opposite her was this bright young woman – a companion anyone would feel proud to be with. She began to pat at her hair, suddenly feeling distinctly dowdy.

'You should have warned me we were coming to such a high class establishment. I would have tried to dress up rather more. Not that I've got much in the way of smart clothes – I've never needed them.'

'You look fine – but I'll tell what we'll do another time. We'll go to town and frequent some good department stores, and find you something to wear that's a bit different from your current range.'

'That's a polite way of saying I need some clothes that don't make me look like a retired head teacher.'

'Perhaps. Anyway, it's a good excuse to go shopping – it will be fun if you'll let me help you choose.'

'I'd like that – I've rarely looked beyond grey or black suits. Well, I have had the occasional beige one.'

'Oh, that's a relief!'

Fran smiled, and Claudia found she was actually enjoying the teasing.

'Now we need to walk that down. I know it's a bit blowy, but are you game for a turn along the promenade?'

Fran took Claudia's arm to guide her across the wide road between the hotel and the seafront. When they reached the promenade she didn't release it. They walked in companionable silence. Then Claudia spoke.

'Your father was Italian.'

Why on earth did she say that? The remark seemed to come from nowhere. Perhaps she felt she owed Fran something for generously providing this enjoyable day.

The younger woman did not turn or register surprise.

'How did you meet him?'

There was no escape. Now she must embark on the story. The waves were rolling in towards the shore and noisily breaking into white foam particles as the two women continued towards Beachy Head, with Claudia desperately trying to marshal her thoughts into some sort of order. How could she give a coherent account of what had happened some forty years previously – in such a way that her daughter would understand? It suddenly seemed the most important thing in the world that Fran did not think she had been casually abandoned to her fate.

'It was my father who brought him into our home. It seemed that Stefano was to be working in England and was looking for some English lessons. My father thought it would be a bit of pocket money for me, and useful teaching experience. I was in my last year at university, and about to embark on a teaching career, you see.'

Claudia went on to describe Stefano's charming manners and good looks, to which she had steadfastly remained immune during the lessons, concentrating only on the task in hand.

'But my sister thought he was amazing – she couldn't take her eyes off him when she saw him. She–'

'You have a sister?' Fran could not help interrupting. This piece of information was news to her.

'Yes, a younger sister, called Maria. She was everything I was not – pretty, flighty, interested only in boys and having fun with her friends. She considered further education to be a pure waste of time and energy. I did get rather annoyed at the interest she took in him – after all he was mine in the sense that I had the responsibility of helping him. She should have kept out of the way, and not distracted him.'

When she recounted the events of the summer ball Claudia's eyes glowed as she described the excitement of dressing up in a ball gown, Stefano's breathtaking appearance in his evening clothes, the way he had been the envy of the other students, attracting all eyes as they danced together, and how marvellous that had made her feel.

Then her mood changed and her voice became sombre. The final walk in the moonlight had to be faced, and put into words.

'What happened was all right because he proposed to me that night, and I accepted. Even all these years later I can remember it as if it were yesterday. I was so happy, I could hardly contain myself. I hugged the knowledge of it to myself and felt it bubbling up inside during the next few days – and then his letter arrived, thanking me for inviting him to the ball. It wasn't at all what I expected from my fiancé – it was stiff and formal and I cried over it. Then I persuaded myself that perhaps he couldn't manage to express himself in writing, so I wrote back – a loving, heartfelt reply, but there was no response! Little did I know he had already married Maria and left for Italy. And then, worst of all, I found I was pregnant!'

Claudia heard Fran draw a sharp breath. Determinedly, she went on to describe her decision to delay her teaching career, and go away by herself so that no one would ever know about the baby. She had made all the arrangements for adoption, and then waited for her time to come.

'You were born in a small maternity hospital in Gloucestershire. My beautiful baby daughter whom I held in my arms for four days. Then I had to leave the hospital – I had signed all the papers. They said I should leave my baby there, and when I had gone the adoption society would come and collect her. So I packed my few things, and then I left. I walked out of that place without a backward glance. I knew if I looked back I would be lost, so I just walked out. And I left my baby – my beautiful little girl – I left her behind. I never saw her again!'

Claudia's shoulders were now heaving, the tears running down her face.

'I'm so sorry, Fran. I'm so terribly sorry. Please say you don't blame me. I didn't know what else to do!'

Fran said nothing, but her arm was round her mother's shoulders, grasping her firmly.

'The torture of giving up your baby – oh, Fran, there's nothing in this life worse than that! There are no words for how much it hurt. I went back to the tiny room that had been my home, threw myself on the bed and howled like a wounded animal. For several days I howled – the pain was so excruciating I couldn't stop. I don't know how long it was – I couldn't eat, or think, or sleep. At last I knew I couldn't go on like that. So the resolve came to put everything in the past behind me and start a new life. I worked out how I would manage it – I would never, ever, let anyone get close to me again – I would keep everyone at arm's length. I had let myself love, and the result had been an anguish so unbearable it could not be endured. And the people I loved had betrayed me, and left me. So I would draw a firm line between me and my sister, and in fact all members of society – I would function as a teacher and become a good one – I would reach the higher levels of my profession and run a first class educational establishment – and no one, no one at all, would ever be able to get near enough to hurt me again.'

'Thank you for telling me,' said Fran in a hoarse voice. 'I know that cost you a great deal, but I'm so glad to have heard it all. I can't tell you how glad.'

Then she squeezed Claudia's arm before releasing her hold on it. 'Tell you what! Race you to that small shelter!'

'Oh no, I can't run – not possibly!'

But Fran had set off and streaked towards her goal with effortless power. Claudia took a deep breath and began an awkward, clumsy movement that gradually speeded up to a kind of running step. Meanwhile Fran had reached the finishing line and turned to look back. She laughed as she saw Claudia coming towards her and held out her arms. Claudia laughed too, and when she finally drew level with Fran she fell into the outstretched arms.

'Well done!' cried Fran. 'See – you made it! I knew you could do it.'

Claudia straightened up, patting her hair which had blown in the wind, and tried to regain her breath.

'I don't know when I last tried to run! But you challenged me – as you have done ever since you arrived on the scene – and I decided I wasn't going let you get away if I could possibly help it.'

'Good,' replied Fran. 'I'm glad about that. Very, very glad.' She reached for Claudia's hand, but instead of holding it, she wrapped her fingers round one of Claudia's, gripping it tightly. 'Believe you me,' she added, 'no one is going to separate us now.'

Together they walked back to the car.

CHAPTER 31

'Now it's your turn.'

They were sitting in a coffee shop, in Oxford Street, with several large carrier bags propped against their chairs. Tired out after searching rail after rail of possible items of clothing for Claudia, but flushed with success, they were having a break and enjoying a reviving cup of coffee.

'I'm so glad you picked that royal blue jumper, and the scarf sets it off to perfection. You look really good in blue.' Fran appeared not to have heard Claudia's remark.

'You don't think it's a bit bright?' Claudia found it hard to relinquish the grey tones of the past.

'I like the fact that it's bright. At last you're going to wear something really interesting and attractive.'

'When I first saw it I thought I could wear it with a grey skirt.'

'Why doesn't that surprise me?'

'Then you got me trying on those black trousers. I hadn't realised how comfortable trousers were.'

'And very smart they look too. What's more, you can wear them with pride. You don't stick out in any of the wrong places. And that stylish jacket – what a change from your previous "uniform" ones. I'd take you anywhere in that – it looks really nice on you.'

Claudia blushed. She'd never had anyone comment on her looks, not since … well, it was a nice feeling. 'Thank you for your help,' she said. 'I would never have made those choices without your kindly persuasion. Fran …'

'Yes?'

'There are things I need to know. I've bared my soul to you. I risked hurting you when I told you how I had left you behind in the hospital. I was so frightened I might lose you.'

'Would that have mattered?'

'I don't think I could have endured it a second time.' Claudia stared at the cup of coffee. 'And since then I've done some more thinking. I want to know why you came looking for me, and why you have been so persistent, in the face of no encouragement whatsoever. If you could live happily without me for almost forty years, why did it suddenly become important to you to find me?'

'That's just it.' It was Fran's turn to become pensive. 'I didn't exactly "live happily", as you put it. I was well cared for by my adoptive parents, and no child could have had more love lavished on it. I know that, and for that very reason I've been puzzled by this insistent voice inside me that kept wondering who I was really was. You see, I knew I didn't really fit in that home. Dear, dear people as they were, my parents lived in a tiny world that was quite enough for them – but it wasn't for me. When I became curious about things, and started asking questions, they couldn't answer me. When I grew up and began to achieve academically, I knew I had left them far behind. It was something they couldn't possibly share. Dear Barbie, with her clichés which she brought out on every occasion – she didn't know how to voice an original thought. And Percy was such a thoroughly good, kind man, but could never see beyond the immediate horizon. The older I grew, the more the conviction came to me that out there, somewhere, was the person who could tell me where I came from and why I am like I am, with these dark physical features and a brain that is never still.'

'So why did you leave it until now?'

'Barbie was very secure in her home, and with her little family, but there was one thought that tormented her. It was that I might not be satisfied with her as a parent and would go looking for my birth mother. She was convinced that if I found my natural mother I would no longer belong to her. So I made her a promise – and it was a very hard one, at the time. I promised her and Percy that I would never do that. I felt they deserved my loyalty, because they had done so much for me, and the last thing I wanted to do was to hurt them. So I have waited until they both died before starting my quest.'

'Did you forget the idea, while they were alive, or did you always cherish the notion that one day you would go looking?'

'Something happened to me one day – an incident that was very nearly the end of me. It was a long time ago now, in fact when I had just left school – but when I thought I was going to drown I suddenly knew with startling clarity that I didn't want to die before I had found out. That day decided me, but I never told Barbie and Percy. I simply buried it until such time as I knew I could openly start the search.'

'Oh, Fran – you nearly drowned? What a dreadful thought! To think you might have died! To think … well, it doesn't bear thinking about. Whatever happened?'

'Ah,' said Fran. 'That's another story. Are you sitting comfortably?'

Then she embarked on an account of that day on the beach at Lantic Bay, painting a vivid description of the current that dragged her out, and the waves closing over her head. And she spoke of the boy who swam out to rescue her – a boy who wore odd shoes, with one heel higher than the other.

CHAPTER 32

Could there be anywhere more romantic for a honeymoon than Venice? Or any husband more handsome than Stefano? Maria stretched out in the huge bed, a contented smile on her face, her body enjoying the sensations of luxury and of being pampered. From the whirlwind wedding to the arrival at the Cipriani Hotel every moment had been full of excitement.

As for Stefano, wouldn't any woman give all she had to claim such a prize? Wherever they went Maria was conscious of female eyes attracted immediately, enviously watching this handsome Italian go by with a pretty young woman on his arm. And what a night it had been! Italians certainly made the most wonderful lovers. Admittedly Maria's experience of this was limited to one particular Italian – in fact, to one particular man, if the truth were to be told – but Stefano had been everything a young girl could want, charming, complimentary, gentle, lavishing words and deeds of love upon her until she felt she might burst with happiness.

Was it all a dream? It had happened so suddenly – Stefano proposing, then saying he wanted to marry quick, quick, with a special licence, and off to Venice for their honeymoon. The world in which she found herself now was full of dreamlike qualities far removed from reality. Take the Cipriani Hotel, for example, on the tip of Giudecca Island, with its luxurious accommodation and attentive service, an oasis of calm away from the bustle of tourists in the Piazza San Marco. Despite its proximity to Venice – a mere four minute boat ride away from its own private jetty in the heart of the town – the hotel provided a seclusion that offered protection and peace. Their bedroom, a room full of elegance and grace, adorned with opulent furnishings, had picture windows down to the floor and a private balcony that ran the full length of the room. Here they could sit and have their breakfast, brought to them by immaculate waiters, and watch the boats going by. Then there were the amazing views over the lagoon, with the Doge's Palace on one side and the church of San Giorgio Maggiore on the other.

Maria sighed. It was all too good to be true. Her only regret was that none of her family had been at the wedding. She had begged Stefano to wait a few more days until Claudia had returned from Oxford, and then she could have had both her father and sister there to witness the most important day of her life. But Stefano had insisted that it was to be very private, just the two of them, and then they would go straight off to Venice for their honeymoon. It seemed he had urgent business to attend to back in Italy, but there was just time to fit in the honeymoon, and then he would take her to meet his family. His mother and father would be in raptures, Stefano assured her, when he produced their pretty, young English daughter-in-law.

It was sad that her family could not have been included, but Maria had put that behind her now as she savoured the sheer joy of sitting in the romantic garden of the hotel, with its cypress, pomegranate and hanging maple trees, and its lavender bushes. Here, Stefano assured her, she could write letters on the hotel notepaper telling her family all that had happened. He was so certain that this would make up for any disappointment they may have felt at missing the ceremony that Maria was swayed, and spent the first morning composing separate letters to Claudia and Hugh. The things she wanted to say to her sister were, of course, quite different from the factual account she wrote for her father. Claudia would revel in hearing all the intimate details about her wedding and honeymoon, and would share her joy as she described how marvellous Stefano was. She just knew Claudia was going to love every word she wrote. For once she did not have to add any embellishments of her own – reality provided all the romance she could possibly want.

Stefano was busy making telephone calls, but when he had finished, and they had had lunch, they would take the boat and make that spectacular ride across the lagoon, where she would see all the famous sights. What an advantage to have such a guide! Stefano knew how to lead her through the labyrinthine passages of Venice, stopping so that she could enjoy an espresso, or make a purchase at some of the interesting and unusual shops. Maria decided she would buy a piece of Murano glass for Claudia. She felt sure she would love it. She would appreciate how special it was, with its elegant design and glorious ruby colour. But before they returned to their island haven, Stefano had a few more surprises lined up for her. She began to realise why he had been busy using the telephone.

First they would have a drink at Florian's, and as they sat there looking out onto the famous Piazza, they could imagine past figures such as Dickens and Byron patronising the café. Secretly, Maria thought Claudia would have lapped up all that history with rather more appreciation than she did, but her ignorance in that department was amply compensated for by her appreciation of a very fine man when she saw one, and there was the very finest of them all sitting right opposite her, gazing into her eyes and making her go weak at the knees. Oh, to share all this with Claudia! She couldn't wait.

'When shall we go back to England, Stefano?' she asked.

'Is my little bird tired of her nest in Italy already? Perhaps she has grown weary of her new husband!'

'Oh no, I didn't mean that! It's all absolutely wonderful here. I'm so happy and I love every moment of it. What's more I can't get enough of my amazing, handsome husband!' She reached across the table and took his hand. 'It's just that I wondered what our plans were, that's all, because I'm longing to tell Claudia all the amazing things we've done.'

'I have a little business I must see to first, in my home town, so we can stay with my family for a few days. But let us enjoy our time here, and forget the future. That will come soon enough. For this evening, I have some very special plans for you!'

He was looking deep into her eyes, and all her sense of excited anticipation returned. She pushed aside any fears of what was to come.

'Tell me!' she cried, eagerly.

'First we have the lovely romantic dinner at the Ristorante Masaniello – this is to be found in the Campo Santo Stefano – so how could we go anywhere else? And then I have booked a private ride in a gondola – just for two, through the little canals of Venice, by moonlight!'

Maria told herself she would never forget that evening. She felt sure she would repeat it to the point of tedium to her children and grandchildren. Dining on delicious Neopolitan cuisine in a fantastic atmosphere, blue oil lamps illuminating each table, sitting opposite her amazing husband, was little short of paradise. But there was more to come!

After a stroll to pick up their gondola at Bacino Orseolo, they settled themselves on plush red cushions in an ornately decorated black gondola with its crescent-shaped hull and metal nose. Their gondolier in his traditional black trousers, striped shirt and straight-brimmed straw hat with its red sash, took his place at the rear, and, using his single oar, skilfully negotiated them down small but enchanting canals, such as the Rio del Palazzo, where they went under the Bridge of Sighs. Just as the bridge was overhead Stefano kissed Maria tenderly. She looked at him in surprise. Stefano smiled.

'We have a legend in our country that lovers who kiss here, under this bridge, while they are on a gondola, will be granted everlasting love and bliss. So, my bella Maria, I kiss you, and you will see, this legend will come true for us!'

Stefano decided it was politic to leave out the fact that it was supposed to be at sunset, since this had been several hours earlier, and the impact of his words would have been spoiled. Why do anything tonight to upset Maria? She looked so completely happy.

Their journey continued along small canals and then out into the Grand Canal where they passed under the famous Rialto Bridge. For much of the time their gondolier had been adding to the delight of their journey with renditions of *O Sole Mio* and other Italian love songs, in a powerful tenor voice.

Maria nestled close against Stefano and felt his strong arm around her. She closed her eyes for a minute, thinking perhaps she could make this moment last for ever, but then opened them quickly, not wanting to lose a single sensation that she could absorb.

'This reminds me of punting in Oxford,' remarked Stefano. 'This gondola is not so different from the punt. Only there you must use the pole, not the oar, so I like more our gondolas, I think.'

'You took Claudia punting, didn't you?'

For a moment a pang of jealousy had shot through Maria, threatening to destroy the sense of well-being that had been paramount in her all day. Quickly she reminded herself that it was she, Maria, who had received Stefano's proposal of marriage, not Claudia, and the disturbing feeling began to abate.

'Oh, Maria – you must not mind that I went with Claudia to her summer ball! I wanted to thank her for her patience when she gave such a stupid man some English lessons. I had no plans to marry her, and I'm sure she did not want to have me – for she wants to be a teacher, spending her days in a room full of children, who will be much better pupils than Stefano was! That is what Claudia wants.'

Maria reprimanded herself for letting a negative thought threaten to spoil this perfect day. It was just as Stefano had said – she was the lucky one who had received his proposal of marriage, not Claudia. Of course Stefano was completely trustworthy! How silly of her to doubt for one single moment. She would never let such thoughts trouble her again.

As Stefano helped her out of the gondola and guided her back to the jetty for their short trip back to the hotel Maria felt wrapped in warmth and happiness. She sighed contentedly, confident that these sensations would last for ever. She and her friends had dreamed of romance – but here she was living it out in a way that exceeded all her girlish hopes and expectations.

That night was a night of tenderness and passion, with very little time for sleep. In the morning she woke to the realisation that Stefano was shaking her.

'Wake up, Maria. It is time for us to go. Today we have a journey to make. Now we leave this hotel and you will be so happy, for we are going to meet my family!'

CHAPTER 33

'Suppose they don't like me, Stefano?'

Anxiety had gripped Maria as they drove westward in their hired car towards Milan, where Stefano had been brought up.

'Of course they will like you – they will love you *molto molto*! They will think you *bellissima*!'

'They might much rather you'd married an Italian girl. I'm sure you must have met lots of lovely ones – Italy seems to be full of beautiful girls.'

'Bella, they will look at you and think Stefano has found himself the loveliest little wife. Come, smile, Maria – your Stefano does not like to see your face full of frown.'

He reached across and squeezed her hand.

Maria relaxed. Of course it would be all right. Hadn't Stefano shown her just how much he loved her? So how could anything spoil things now?

'Tell me about your family. Who is living in your family home?'

'There's my mother and father, of course – their names are Giulia and Gino. Then I have two brothers – Daniele and Enzo, and four sisters – Luisa, Isabella, Susanna and Carmela. I am the oldest, and the next is twenty-four, down to the baby, Carmela, who is twelve. Daniele has a wife, Vittoria, and Luisa has a husband, Tristano. Then there are many cousins and friends, so we are always a big crowd, and it is hard to know who is actually living there.'

'Goodness, it sounds quite a houseful!'

Maria could not help contrasting it with her own quiet home, with just her father, always absorbed in his work, and Claudia, up at

Oxford for much of the time. She used to bring friends home occasionally, but because the house did not have a lively feel the friends often preferred to congregate somewhere else.

She couldn't help feeling nervous as they drew up outside a large house on the outskirts of Milan. Stefano tooted the horn and out flew a stream of people, headed by a plump middle-aged woman, with young men and girls all shouting and laughing, following behind.

Giulia had her arms outstretched and Stefano, who had leapt out of the car, was immediately enveloped. 'Come, Mamma!' he cried. 'Come and meet Maria!'

Now it was Maria's turn to be clasped against the ample bosom whilst an outpouring of Italian, which she could not understand, went on all round her.

'Mamma and Papa think you are beautiful!' Stefano was bursting with pride. 'Come, we go in the house – they will bring our things for us.'

As they walked towards the entrance the others all crowded round excitedly. At the back of them all Maria caught sight of a young girl, perhaps about seventeen, holding a small baby in her arms. Her quiet demeanour and sad expression contrasted noticeably with the smiling faces all round her.

There were more exchanges between Stefano and his family, and he introduced them all to her, one by one, except for the girl with the baby. They all embraced her warmly – especially the two young men – and then Stefano said his mother would bring some refreshments. Later they would have dinner.

After they had been plied with reviving drinks and tasty delicacies, Stefano, accompanied by Giulia and several of the girls, led her up to their bedroom. At last the door was shut and they were alone.

Without thinking, Maria asked, 'Stefano, who was the girl with the baby?'

His face momentarily lost its engaging smile. Then he replied, casually, 'That's Rosa, the servant girl. She helps Mamma with the housework.'

'That must be difficult, if she has to look after a baby. Whose is it?'

'He belongs to a cousin, but she has been very ill, so Rosa helps look after him. She is very good with him, and he is no trouble. He is a very fine boy – his name is Carlo. Perhaps you might like to help with him while you are here.'

'I don't know anything about babies!' Maria was alarmed at the thought.' I wouldn't have any idea what to do!'

'It is no matter – you will soon learn – they will show you. Imagine taking him out for walks! You will look so beautiful, everyone will stop you, pretending to admire the baby – but really they want to talk to you!'

'You really are incorrigible!'

But he had made her laugh, and she forgot her anxieties, about the baby, at least. She still felt apprehensive at the thought of being among this large family, all jabbering away in their own language while she would have no idea what they were saying, and be unable to join in. She tried to express this to Stefano, asking him not to leave her there on her own.

'I must work,' he said, 'and sometimes I will take you with me, when it is suitable, but sometimes not. Then Mamma or one of the girls will look after you, so do not worry. Now we will unpack, and then we can get ready for dinner. But first, I must welcome my wife to my home.'

Smiling, she allowed him to lead her over to the bed. This was more like it. Her fears suddenly melted away and she began to feel that she could be happy here. After all, it wouldn't be for long – soon they would be going back to England – to their own home. She would see her own family, and everything would be wonderful.

'Oh, Stefano …' she murmured, as he made her feel very welcome indeed.

CHAPTER 34

Maria was surprised to find that they stayed over four weeks in Milan – far longer than she had anticipated. At first she felt ill at ease. It was disturbing to be surrounded by so many people, all trying to be kind to her, but with whom communication was impossible. For some reason they thought that if they shouted, or said things several times over, she would grasp what they were saying – but, of course, she couldn't. Stefano tried to teach her some basic words and phrases, such as si, no, (at least that was easy), grazie, buon giorno and quanto costa? – which was all very well but as she couldn't understand what was said to her, she didn't know what the right replies were.

Gradually she got used to the atmosphere, realising they were all doing their best to be friendly. They kept greeting her enthusiastically, and hugging her at the least excuse – especially Gino and the boys – so that after a little while she began to feel slightly more comfortable. The house was full of life, with people milling round all the time, and voices that never seemed to stop calling out and laughing. Everyone smiled frequently, at least in her presence, but behind the scenes she sometimes overheard verbal spats – usually involving Stefano and his mother, or one of the boys. Once, it was Gino's turn. As head of the household he never lost an opportunity to embrace her, to make her feel welcome, and he was holding her rather tightly when Giulia had walked in. Maria appreciated his friendly overtures, but possibly Giulia did not, as raised voices could be heard for some time afterwards.

Since the rest of the family were going overboard to please her, it was rather marked that the one person who rarely smiled or took any more notice of her than necessary, was Rosa. The poor girl looked white and strained, kept mostly in the background, and showed no particular interest in Maria. But once or twice, when Maria came upon Rosa unexpectedly, she noticed that when she was playing with little Carlo her face was wreathed in smiles.

It was strange the way they seemed to think she would delight in spending time looking after the baby. Rosa had obviously been instructed to bring him frequently for her to see and admire. Maria, who had had no practice in clucking over babies, didn't know how to start. Anyhow, why should she? He was nothing to her, and soon she would be leaving him behind, so why get excited about him?

At first Stefano took Maria out with him when he went on his business trips. She enjoyed this, as they would travel through attractive countryside, her new husband being an attentive and charming escort. Although she had to wait while he made his visits, he would treat her to lunch in some delightful bistro, keeping her amused with stories about his childhood, or describing aspects of his family life. Sometimes he would become more serious and talk a little of the life they would have back in England. He planned to settle in the Wimbledon area, since travel would be easy from there to various places that he would need to visit. He would find a fine house to rent – somewhere she would enjoy living – and they would set up a real family home for themselves. Soon, he said, he hoped they would fill it with a family of their own.

Maria smiled, saying nothing. She had kept a secret from Stefano. As soon as she knew she was going to be married she had visited her doctor and started to take a contraceptive pill. Knowing Stefano to have a Catholic background, she was well aware he might disapprove – but at eighteen years of age, what did she know about looking after children? The last thing in the world she wanted was to be saddled with a baby while she was so young – plenty of time for that in the future. The present was the time to have lots of fun with her new husband, and not get tied down with responsibilities. Young as she was, she instinctively knew this information was better kept to herself, and she was always careful to keep the pills hidden.

Once when they were having lunch together she said, 'Stefano, tell me about Rosa. How long has she been with the family? And why does she look pale and miserable all the time?'

'Oh, now, bella, don't you concern your head about her. She's only the kitchen maid!'

He had laughed, and quickly turned the subject to a different topic.

At the beginning Maria had three full days out on the road with Stefano, but on the fourth she was brought back home at the end of the morning, as apparently the afternoon's visit would not have been of any interest. After that she found she was sometimes left at home in the morning, possibly being picked up at lunch time. On these occasions Giulia would suggest she might like to fill in the time by taking Carlo in his pushchair for a walk in the park. Rosa came with her, initially, to show her where to go, but once she knew the route she was encouraged to take him out by herself. Fortunately, for the most part, he was a placid baby, but the third time she took him out he suddenly started to scream. Alarmed, Maria turned round and ran all the way back.

'Rosa!' she called, the minute she got into the house, 'take Carlo, please! He's making a terrible noise and I can't stop him!'

Rosa might not have understood the words but she knew what to do, picking the screaming baby up and clasping him in her arms. Immediately the noise subsided.

Sometimes Maria would be taken to the dress shops with some of the girls, who would draw her attention to items of clothing they thought would suit her. Such forays into the world of Italian fashions were far more to her taste than taking Carlo out, and Maria would get excited by the beautiful designs held up for her to admire. If she looked doubtful, the sisters would immediately put it back and find a replacement, chattering away among themselves as they did so. Stefano had generously given her a sizeable sum of money, so she was able to buy if something appealed to her, and many of the clothes did. Her sound dress sense told her that they were good quality and she always knew if something was right for her. She began to wonder whether her suitcase would contain all these purchases.

Most of all she liked going out with the youngest girl, Carmela. These occasions were quieter and rather enjoyable as the young girl loved trying out a few English words, and teaching Maria some Italian ones. Finding they had a wavelength where they were comfortable in each other's presence, Maria was not daunted by her and could relax.

She missed her father and Claudia more as each day went by. She frequently wrote long letters to each of them, and eagerly watched for the postman to come – but there were never any letters for her. Finally she asked if she might be allowed to telephone. Gino showed her how to put a call through to England and having dialled her father's number she waited with bated breath. As the telephone began to ring she pictured Claudia, or her father, hurrying into the hall to pick it up. But although she held on for a long time no one answered, that evening or any other evening. It was puzzling and rather worrying.

Maria found she was spending more and more time with Carlo. Gradually she got over her apprehension and became a little more used to him. His tiny hands and feet were adorable, and if he had been a girl she would have loved dressing him in beautiful baby clothes. As she became more used to him she was encouraged to take part in his activities. She learned how to give him a bottle, and help with his bath. She supposed they were trying to prepare her for when she produced her own child, but she wanted to say that at the moment she really would have preferred not be so involved with him. She did not like the assumption that she would be embarking on having babies to look after so soon after the marriage. Somehow everyone seemed to expect it of her, and she did not know how to express her objections. Stefano was no help – he just said she made such a good little mother, so why not?

She began to ask when they would be leaving. Stefano said he thought they would be ready very soon, perhaps the following week. After a few more days he said he had arranged flights for the next day. Maria was delighted, seeing no reason to hide her feelings. After all, they must realise that by now she was getting homesick.

That evening she went to the kitchen for a drink and saw the maid, Rosa, sitting at the table with her head in her hands, weeping copiously.

CHAPTER 35

At last the day had arrived! Maria could not contain her excitement at the thought of returning to England, and to her family. Suddenly the past four or five weeks shrank in her mind, and all that mattered was today's journey. Just a short flight – then they'd be in familiar surroundings once again.

She had been disappointed by the lack of contact from Hugh and Claudia despite all her full and enthusiastic letters, but eventually a letter had arrived from her father, just as she despaired of ever getting one. He said he was sorry he had not written before but he had been working hard, and had been getting home late. Maria supposed that explained why he had not been there when she'd telephoned, but she was surprised by the brevity of his letter. He said he would give her all the news in person, and was looking forward to seeing them both very soon. He did not mention Claudia, which Maria thought distinctly odd, but there was no point in bothering about that now – perhaps this very day she would be able to pay them a visit! She would try and get Stefano to agree, but she wouldn't mention it until they were on the plane. After all, he had to say goodbye to his family in a few minutes and fly to a country that was not his own.

The luggage was rather a problem. It seemed to have doubled, if not trebled, since they came out. She had to admit she was returning with rather more than she had brought, having succumbed to the purchase of some tempting clothes in the shops. It was all the girls' fault really – her sisters-in-law had kept persuading her that she would look lovely in various outfits, and she knew for a fact they were right. She'd had to buy an extra bag to accommodate those things, but it wasn't just that. Stefano had assembled a number of large boxes – samples for his business, apparently – which had to be taken on the flight. It was clear they would have to pay an excess fee.

The car was outside and the boys carried all their cases and boxes out of the house. Everyone was shouting at each other as usual, while Giulia was sobbing and declaiming loudly that she was going to miss her baby. Gino kept hugging Maria, saying what a pretty girl she was and how lucky his son was to have such a bride. As always, Rosa stood in the background holding Carlo. She looked more miserable than ever – tears rolling down her cheeks. Carlo, dressed in new clothes and wrapped in an enormous blanket, looked for all the world as if he were about to embark on an expedition.

The moment came to get into the car, which was piled high with luggage – there was so much that the back seat was obscured from view. Everyone crowded round Maria to give her a last embrace, while Stefano was hugging all the members of his family and exclaiming over them. The girls held the door open for her, standing close against the car, urging her to get in. Stefano reached forward to start the engine but just before its noise drowned everything else Maria thought she heard the sound of hysterical crying. She tried to look, but could not see through the throng of people waving and shouting. But as the car rounded the corner she caught sight of Rosa, her head in her hands, obviously in great distress. Maria wondered if it was the thought of Stefano going away.

As they drove to the airport where they would return the hired car, Stefano kept up a barrage of chatter, ranging from how much all the members of his family loved her, and how they were going to miss her now, to the beauties of his country, its landscape, its food, and its wine.

'Better than your sausage and mash, yes? Ah, you English, you not know how to cook. Here in Italy we make the lovely pasta, and the fish, that is divine!'

A noise caught Maria's attention – she couldn't make out what it was. It sounded a bit like a snuffle. She looked round, but couldn't see anything past the boxes piled up on the floor. Meanwhile Stefano was off again.

'What you think of the fine baby, Carlo? Very handsome boy – he will grow to be big, strong man, he make his parents very proud of him. I see you take care of him very good, look after him like you were his mother. I think you make excellent mother.'

There was that sound again. Puzzled, Maria tried to look behind once more, twisting round in her seat to see what it was.

'You like to have baby to look after? Stefano like to see you looking after …'

This time there was no mistaking the noise – it was a baby's cry.

'Stefano! What on earth …!'

'Do not worry, bella, we have Carlo in the car.'

'What do you mean? Why have we got him?

'We take him …'

'Take him where? Tell me, Stefano! Where are we taking him? Are we taking him back to his mother?'

'He will come to England with us. Carlo wants to be an Englishman!'

'I don't understand – is his mother in England? I thought you said–'

'Maria, bella, now you will be his mother, because he will come and live with us. And very beautiful mother–'

'Don't you start that again! You expect me to look after him? But I've told you, I don't know anything about babies, and I'm not interested in them. I'm only eighteen – you know that – and I want to have fun with you, when you're not working. I don't want to be tied down by a baby!'

By now Maria was beside herself with anxiety and resentment.

'Please, Maria, do not shout – you will frighten baby Carlo!'

Sure enough the child was crying loudly.

'What about me being frightened? How dare you trick me into

this! Give me one good reason why I should look after this baby! I won't do it, I tell you. I won't!'

'I give you good reason,' responded Stefano, quietly. 'You look after Carlo, because you are now my wife, and Carlo, he is my son.'

CHAPTER 36

The flight back to England was a nightmare. It was clear that flying was not one of Carlo's favourite occupations. The plane, poised at the start of the runway, began to rev up its engines and hurtle forward. The louder the plane's engines screamed, the shriller the crescendo of noise Carlo emitted, until it seemed impossible one so small could produce such a cacophony of sound. Airborne, the plane's uproar suddenly decreased, but that had no effect on Carlo who remained intent on producing the maximum possible uproar.

'Stop that child crying!' ordered Stefano.

Maria turned to look at him, astonished.

'How on earth do you expect me to do that? I told you I know nothing about babies – nasty, noisy things!'

'Haven't you learned anything from the last few weeks?'

So that was it. That was why they had lingered in Milan all that time. She had been supposed to absorb the intricacies of childcare, in preparation for taking full responsibility for this bellowing brat. As things began to fall into place with uncomfortable clarity she saw how naïve she had been. There was still one aspect of the whole sordid story that kept nagging at her – just at present she couldn't concentrate enough to think out clearly what it was – but much of what had happened over the last few weeks was beginning to make sense.

She realised that Stefano, who was going to be living and working in England, had decided to find an English wife who wouldn't know anything about his circumstances back home – someone who would be seduced by his Italian charm. Once he had found a suitable candidate for the role, he would woo the lady with soft words and compliments so that she became putty in his hands.

Then he would rush her into marriage, give her a short but extremely sweet honeymoon, finally bringing her to his family where she would be swept up in the atmosphere of their lively ménage, and the baby would go almost unnoticed.

That was why he wasn't interested in Claudia. He would have realised that she would have been far too clever to be taken in by any of his plans, and he would not have been able to mould her as he had Maria. So he had settled on the unintelligent sister, who questioned nothing, and took everything at face value. Well, she may not have been the brightest that ever lived, but she knew she was pretty, and that would certainly have appealed to him. He undoubtedly appreciated an attractive girl, and no one in their right mind would actually describe Claudia as pretty, even if she could look quite nice sometimes.

She had fallen easily into every one of his traps, and had ended up, as he had intended, in Milan. Now she knew why she had found herself so often in Carlo's company – at first with Rosa, or one of the sisters, and then by herself. Stefano had hoped that just as she had fallen for him she would also fall in love with this helpless infant, and all her maternal instincts would come to the fore. He had hoped she would get involved in Carlo's daily routine, until it became second nature to her to feed, and bathe him, and see to the other disgusting necessities of caring for babies. Well, thought Maria, he had misjudged his new wife. She wasn't going to be pushed around like that! Anyway, she had her own ideas about married life, and they didn't include babies for some time yet.

It was hard to think at all with this bundle of rage on her lap, his sole purpose being to shriek incessantly, his tiny body contorted with the agonising emotion to which he gave vent in uncontrollable sobs.

'You do something!' she said to Stefano. "You take him – he might calm down then.'

'I can't. I'm a man,' he replied, as though that explained

everything. 'Holy Mother, think of something, Maria, before the whole plane riots!'

A stewardess appeared in the aisle.

'Would you like a bottle heated, madam?' she asked.

The warm bottle was brought and Maria stuck it into his mouth. Carlo sucked enthusiastically as though he hadn't had a feed for days, and the noise subsided.

Maria breathed a sigh of relief. Perhaps that was all you had to do every time he cried – just jam a bottle into his mouth. At least she knew how to do that, thanks to Rosa's tuition.

Rosa. An image of that poor girl flooded back into Maria's mind. Suddenly, while everything was peaceful, temporarily, at least, she realised what it was that had been nagging at her. It was that other screaming she had heard when they were driving away, with Maria innocently unaware of the extra passenger in the car. She may not have known that Carlo was coming too, but the others all did. This was obviously part of the plot – that they would take him back with them to England. How she had been manipulated!

She tried to think what had been said about the mother – some cousin, who did not live in Milan, and who was too ill to look after her own baby. She remembered asking questions about this woman, but no one had ever answered her clearly. Well, this was as good a time as any.

'Stefano, there is something I need to know. After all, I'm your wife and I think I have a right to be informed. You have told me that Carlo is your son – so who is the mother? You said it was a cousin, so why didn't you marry her, instead of me? After all, if she was ill, and she was having your baby, shouldn't you be with her, helping her?'

'Shush, we cannot talk like this on a crowded plane.'

'We can, and we will. You have been deceitful, and tricked me into doing something you knew I would refuse if you had asked me outright. You have taken it for granted that I will look after your son, so I have a right to know, and if you don't tell me I shall stand in the aisle and shout out that this baby is not mine! I shall say I have had

170

him foisted on me by a cruel husband. I don't care what anyone thinks!'

She started to undo her seatbelt, and despite the difficulty of having Carlo on her lap, she managed to pull herself up. Stefano grabbed her and pulled her back down.

'Sit down, you little fool. Do not play the idiot.' Then his voice became calmer, and he began to speak more gently.

'I give you bad time, I know. But you must believe, I wanted you for my wife. You are my bella, my tresore.'

Maria cut to the chase.

'Never mind all that. Just tell me the facts. I want to know. I have a right to know.'

He hesitated, and as he fumbled for words she realised she could place those heartbroken cries. The scene came back to her. They were all crowding round the car, blocking her view of the back. Someone must have taken the baby and put him in his little cot on the back seat. Someone had taken him out of the arms of …

'You don't have to tell me.' Her tone was icy. 'I know.'

He nodded. 'Si,' he said. 'The mother is Rosa.'

Carlo, having drained his bottle in a few hungry gulps, decided to start yelling again.

CHAPTER 37

It was three whole days before Maria found the opportunity to visit her family. She had hoped, before they left, that as soon as the plane had landed and they had picked up a hired car, they could drive to her home, which really wouldn't have been much of a detour while en route from Heathrow to Wimbledon. Then she could have basked in the familiarity of her own people – her father and sister – and proudly shown off her handsome husband.

She had not counted on the presence of a baby. Carlo changed everything. His needs were now paramount, and he set about disrupting just about every area of Maria's life while still managing to look beguilingly innocent.

Weren't babies supposed to sleep at night? Carlo had apparently come into the world ignorant of this piece of vital information. To be fair, he did sleep for the first few hours after he was put down. Peacefully slumbering, with a butter-wouldn't-melt-in-his-mouth look on his face, he waited contentedly for that moment when Maria, exhausted from all the ministrations he had demanded during the day, had finally sunk into a deep slumber. Then he started, rending the air with screams that were impossible to ignore. The first night Stefano nudged Maria, telling her to go to him.

'Go yourself!' retorted Maria. 'He's your son! Yours and Rosa's!'

With a big sigh, he heaved himself out of bed, picked the child up, and sang Italian lullabies in a gentle tenor voice. This apparently appealed to Carlo, as he soon became sleepy and succumbed obligingly to being returned to his cot.

Sometimes Stefano was not willing to help, refusing to budge and claiming in a martyred tone that he had a long day's work ahead of him. Maria, unable to stand the noise, would have to respond to the incessant bellows, but her attempts at pacifying him were not successful until she hit on the method that had proved, temporarily at least, to work on the plane. So what if the advice had been to feed him at regular times? If a bottle was going to pacify him, and allow her to get back to sleep, a bottle he was going to have. Her night's sleep was just as important as Stefano's.

As she cradled the baby who was eagerly devouring his milk, she thought over the shattering events of the past few days. It had been a double shock, discovering about the child's parents. First Maria had had to swallow the unpalatable truth that Stefano already had a child, and when she had managed to accept that, she was hit by the bombshell of the mother's identity.

'Rosa!' she had shrieked, when he had told her. 'How could you, Stefano! How could you!'

'Shush, don't make the big fussing. Everyone look at you!'

'How could you have … have … with Rosa!'

'She always had big thing for me. She used to follow me about the house, eyes like puppy dog. Silly little girl, I gave her what she asked for.'

'You gave her a baby – and then you took him away!'

Was this the gallant, handsome Italian who had swept her off her feet with his loving words? It was horrible to hear him talking like that. Poor Rosa, to have fallen for the oldest son, been landed with an illegitimate baby, and then have the boy snatched out of her arms. No wonder the girl had seemed sulky in Maria's presence. She had known Maria was being trained up to usurp her rightful place as Carlo's mother. No wonder she had been reduced to hysterical sobbing as the car drove away.

Now she, Maria, had been landed with Carlo, and what she resented above all was the way everyone assumed that, as Stefano's wife, she would take on the maternal role without a qualm. Well, two could play at this game. If Stefano was going to throw these things at her and expect her to comply, then he would quickly find out that she, too, could make her demands. Whether he liked it or not, she was going to visit her father and sister. She would go on Saturday, when he would be at home. She was surely entitled to a few hours of freedom.

To her surprise Stefano did not demur. He agreed to stay at home and look after Carlo so that she could go on her own, if she promised to be back in the afternoon. Maria, who not very long ago had looked forward to taking Stefano home as her new husband, now relished the prospect of having some time alone with her family. She would have promised anything for the chance to get away briefly so she could visit them.

She arrived at the familiar front door. As she rang the bell she was so excited she thought her heart would burst. At last she would see the two people she loved most in the world – apart from Stefano, of course – once again.

Her father was ready for her, as she had telephoned the previous evening to say she would be coming. He beamed at the sight of her and embraced her warmly.

'Good to see you – you're looking well. How's Stefano? I was surprised you said you were coming without him.'

'He's a bit tied up.'

How was she going to explain about Carlo? She couldn't make up her mind whether to keep quiet about the whole thing, or to tell it in all its unpleasant detail. After all, they would be bound to know soon. It could hardly be kept a secret.

'Come and have some coffee. I'm not much of a cook, as you know, but there are some sandwiches.'

He led the way into the lounge. Maria looked around, surprised that Claudia hadn't come to the door to greet her. She went into the lounge after her father, but there was no sign of her sister there, either.

'Where's Claudia?'

'She's not here … she's … she's gone away.'

'What do you mean – gone away? Gone where? And why didn't she write to me?'

'Look, Maria, this is very hard for me.' Hugh's hesitation was beginning to worry Maria.

'You didn't write much to me either,' she said. 'You just said "all news when we meet". Dad, I can't tell you how much I've been longing to come back and see you both. I felt so lonely, at times, being left with Stefano's family, all jabbering away in Italian and I couldn't understand a word!'

'I will tell you the news here, but first I want to hear about yourself. How is my little girl? I can't think of you as a married woman! I must say, Maria, I'm sorry you did everything so suddenly – without giving any of your relatives the chance to attend the wedding.'

Maria tried to explain. She said it had been Stefano who had wanted it all to happen quickly – he had been so passionate, demanding that they must marry instantly – and that it could only be fitted in with his work commitments if they married straight away, and then rushed off to Venice for their honeymoon.

'That was just amazing! So romantic! Oh Dad, I've been longing to tell you and Claudia all about it – and now she's not here!'

Then she told him how they had travelled to Milan, to stay with his family, and while they were there he had been working, and spent much time going off on business trips during the day.

'Were the family kind to you?'

'Yes, I suppose they were. But it's awfully difficult when you can't follow what they're saying, or tell them anything yourself.' She hesitated, unsure whether to say any more about her time there, but she was anxious to return to the subject of her sister. 'So where is Claudia?' she asked again.

Hugh sighed. 'What I have to say is very hard. I love you both, and don't want to take sides.'

'Sides? Why should there be sides?'

'I'll come straight out with it, Maria. Claudia believes that Stefano had asked her to marry him, and she had accepted his proposal. That was when he went to Oxford to accompany her to the ball. She thinks that, after that had happened, you took him away from her, while she was still up at Oxford.'

'Stefano proposed to Claudia! That's not possible. He didn't ever want to marry her! He said she was a very good teacher, and he liked her, but I know for sure he never wanted to marry her!'

'How can you be so certain? Claudia was utterly convinced they were engaged.'

'Engaged! There's no way that could have happened! I know that for a fact – because … because ….' It was all going to have to come out. 'Because there's a baby, and I only found out afterwards that the reason he wanted to marry so quickly was so that he could bring his son to England, where he's going to be working, and this way he's got a ready-made mother for Carlo.'

'A baby! I don't understand. If it's his son, then who's the mother?'

'The kitchen maid,' Maria replied bitterly.

CHAPTER 38

Gradually Maria resigned herself to the duties of motherhood. When the weather permitted she would push Carlo up to Wimbledon Common, finding that several young mothers congregated there. She began to get to know some of them, and life became more sociable.

As for her feelings towards Carlo, slowly but surely they altered. It was hard to resist his smiles, and she enjoyed playing with him as he became more responsive. She was intrigued by each new stage in his development. When he could sit up he seemed more like a human being, and thank goodness he did soon learn to settle at night, which in itself made her feel more kindly disposed towards him. Gradually her resentment faded.

Seeing her caring for his son with genuine warmth, Stefano was less edgy and slipped back into the role of adoring husband, most of the time anyway. She had hit the depths during the first days back in England, trying to come to terms with all that had happened. Now she felt she was picking up again, and life was becoming happier in many ways. But one wound continued to gnaw away at her, its pain never diminishing.

Those words still rang in her ears – the words Claudia had spoken to Hugh the last time he had seen her. He had passed them on, during that first visit Maria had made, because she had been unable to grasp the extent of Claudia's hostile feelings. When Hugh told her Claudia had gone away for a whole year she had said, 'Claudia doesn't mean it, I'm sure. She won't stay away all that time! Why should she? She'll soon be back, and when she does come, please tell her I'm longing to see her.'

'It's no good hoping, Maria. Claudia said she could only cope by cutting you out of her life completely. I can't pretend to understand it. Her hurt seems to have gone very deep – I was extremely worried about her when she was on the point of going away – she looked so pale and tired. I'm worried about her now, but I don't know where she is and there's nothing I can do. And I'm afraid you will have to accept what she has said.'

Cut her out of her life! Maria still couldn't believe her sister had said that. Well, she wasn't going to accept it. She would write, and she would keep on writing, and one day, she was quite sure, Claudia would write back. Claudia surely wouldn't stay away very long. Fancy going off so secretively! What a strange thing to do.

So every few weeks Maria wrote. She sent the letters to her father, just in case Claudia had come back, or in case he knew where she was. She did not hear back, but she went on writing. Each time she said how much she missed her sister, and hoped they would soon be in touch again. She went on writing all that year.

At last a letter came from her father. He reported that Claudia had returned, looking thin and pale. That she had pursued teaching posts in various parts of the country and settled on a school in a large suburban town, but he was not at liberty to tell her where, and that she was as adamant as ever in her refusal to be in contact with Maria. He said he had passed Maria's letters on to Claudia, and subsequently found them torn up, unopened, in the waste bin.

Maria had felt deeply hurt when she learned that her sister had returned but still did not wish to see her. She wept bitterly when she learned of the fate of her letters. Hugh went on to say that he had begged Claudia to relent, telling her how upset Maria was, and how she longed for the rift to be healed. But he was extremely sorry to have to report that he could see no change in her attitude. It pained him greatly to have his two daughters at odds with each other, but he couldn't see what else he could do.

Finally he said he was more worried about Claudia now than when she first went away. Her physical condition may have been reasonably satisfactory – although she was very thin and pale – but her face had settled into a hard expression, and she never smiled. He wished he had happier news to send, but there it was. He added that Claudia had seemed to take it particularly hard when he had mentioned baby Carlo.

Maria sobbed her misery out to Stefano. He tried to comfort her, maintaining, as before, that he had never proposed to Claudia. He said he could not understand how she had got hold of the idea.

One special day Carlo brought joy to them both. He did what every baby is expected to do, and yet, when they do, it is a miracle. He stood up and walked – first with a few, tottering steps, and then with such confidence he virtually ran across the room.

'My son moves with the skill of a great footballer!' cried Stefano.

From then on he took pleasure in playing ball games with Carlo, much to the delight of his small son. They would go out together into the garden and squeals of mirth soon filled the air.

'See, bella! See how good he is. When he grows up, he will play for his country! Everyone will be so proud of him, you will see.'

Carlo continued to grow big and strong, and at five years of age was already a handsome, athletic little boy. That was when Maria realised that at long last a child of her own was on the way.

CHAPTER 39

When Maria gave birth to a baby boy Stefano was moved to tears. He cradled the new arrival in his arms, his face the picture of fatherly pride.

'Now we have the start of a football team! Two fine boys in our family now!'

There was a little conflict over the name. For some reason Maria wanted to call the new baby Timothy. She couldn't explain why, but she had set her heart on it. It was not a name that appealed to Stefano, having no Italian undertones, but he was so overjoyed to have been presented with a second son that he gave in easily.

Carlo was fascinated by his small brother, although disappointed initially that the new arrival lacked any mobility skills. But he was assured by a doting father that very soon Timothy would be running round, and they would all have a game together. Every day Carlo would enquire hopefully if Tim – as they all called him – was ready to play football yet. It was disappointing that there seemed to be little change in his small brother since the previous day, but Carlo remained optimistic that Tim would be replete with football skills any day now.

Fortunately this sad lack did not detract from Carlo's pride in the new arrival. He boasted to his friends that he had 'a very fine brother', his status as the firstborn giving him a sense of superiority.

It was now six years since they had settled in Wimbledon. Carlo had started school and Timothy, who had just reached his first birthday, was an easy-going little chap who smiled frequently. He had not yet learned to stand up and walk, but he had discovered a method of moving that achieved his purposes amazingly fast. With a strange, crab-like motion he shifted himself along while in a sitting position, his bottom sliding across the floor as he propelled himself with his hands. He was quite satisfied with this, and even though Stefano tried to encourage him to stand up, he simply grinned, sat back down, and took off on his current quest.

One day Stefano came back from work to find a letter from his mother waiting for him. He was shaken by its contents, exclaiming loudly as he came to tell Maria. The news was not good. His father had had a heart attack, and was seriously ill.

'We must go to Milano, we must visit him, before it is too late! We must all go, so that my father can see his very fine grandsons. This is what he wants, I know.'

Stefano had been back to Italy several times on business trips, but he had never suggested that Maria should accompany him. Sometimes he had gone for only a few days, and sometimes for a week or more. Maria accepted that this was a necessary part of his business, and rather enjoyed the peaceful times while he was away.

Now, as she thought about going back to Italy, she was not at all sure she wanted to go. Memories of those difficult days with his family had not completely faded, and she remembered how much she had hated not being able to understand what everyone was saying. Stefano, however, was adamant. They must all go, and they must go very soon.

Carlo, at six years of age, revelled in the experience of the flight. He sat bolt upright on his seat, craned his neck to see all he could out of the window and asked interminable questions.

But if Carlo had now shed his dislike of flying, the same could hardly be said of Timothy. He screamed loudly as the plane took off, vividly reminding Maria of that nightmare flight six years ago when she had found herself saddled with a baby. As the journey proceeded Timothy squirmed on Maria's lap, his usual happy face the picture of misery.

Stefano ignored him, as much as he was able, turning his attention to Carlo, pointing out all that was happening as they flew through the skies. When the stewardesses came round Carlo beamed at them, charming them into producing extra treats for him.

Maria did her best to calm her distressed younger son, but although his loud cries died down, he continued to sob quietly against her shoulder. The flight was mercifully only two hours and soon they were coming in to land. As the plane began to swoop down onto the runway Timothy's churning stomach erupted and he vomited down the front of Maria's blouse.

'Pooh!' cried Stefano. 'Stinky, stinky! Now my family meet us and we are stinky, stinky!'

The stewardess did her best to help. She came with a damp cloth and dabbed at the soiled areas, removing some of the worst of the vomit.

'I'll go into the cloakroom when we're in the airport,' said Maria. 'I expect I can sponge us both down so it won't smell.'

Giulia and Carmela were there to meet them. There was a noisy and emotional reunion with Stefano. Maria waited until it was over, standing back with Carlo, and holding Timothy, who had rediscovered his smile, in her arms. Giulia looked older and her hair was greyer, but the surprise for Maria was Carmela, now a beautiful young woman. Mother and daughter enveloped Maria in a warm welcome, exclaimed over Carlo and finally turned their attention to Timothy, cooing over him and generally making a fuss the way women do of babies.

Stefano was now conversing in Italian, but Maria heard the names of the boys being used, and from the look on Stefano's face, knew he was expressing fatherly pride in Carlo; but she also saw the disdain when he mentioned Timothy. She knew, in his father's eyes, poor Tim had rather blotted his copybook on the journey.

As soon as they had arrived at the family home Stefano went racing upstairs to see his father. Giulia suggested to Maria that she might like to have some time to wash and change and see to Timothy before paying her visit to the old man. Obviously the odour was still clinging to their clothes!

Meanwhile Stefano could be heard calling Carlo. Maria wished she could be there when Carlo was presented to his grandfather, but she accepted that Stefano did things his own way.

Finally it was her turn. With Timothy in her arms she was ushered into Gino's bedroom. The old man cried out with pleasure at the sight of them. He insisted on clasping Maria tightly against him, a rather awkward manoeuvre as she was still holding the child. The sick man appeared to be captivated by his new grandson, who smiled benignly as the old man went into an outpouring of rapturous praise.

Once again it was Carmela who was Maria's greatest comfort and ally. Now a college student, she had time to spend at home, and as her English had greatly improved, she was by far the most fluent in the family. This helped Maria to feel less isolated.

Stefano announced that he would be taking everyone out to lunch the next day, but after that he would need to do one or two business visits. Maria was a little surprised – she had thought he would want to spend the maximum possible time with his father, but he explained that it was necessary, while he was in the country, to attend some meetings, and in any case, his father would be easily tired if he stayed with him too much.

The first time he went on a business trip he said a colleague would be picking him up from the house. Maria happened to be upstairs at the time, and looking out of a front window, saw that a flamboyant, open-topped sports car was parked outside. Stefano came running upstairs to embrace her.

'You will be happy here, Maria! My family, they look after you and give you good time. Ciao!'

He kissed her warmly, and was gone. As the car drove away Maria saw long, flowing hair blowing in the wind. She asked Carmela if she knew who this colleague was.

'That is Valeria De Luca. She work in the same business as Stefano. She is … how you say … representative?'

'Does she live near here? Is she married?'

'I not know.'

Maria wasn't sure which of her questions was being answered. 'Where are they going today? Do you know that?' Was she imagining it, or was Carmela slightly ill at ease?

The young woman shrugged. 'I not know. Stefano not say. He say they have important meeting.'

That evening the car could be heard zooming up to the front door and Stefano was deposited on the doorstep. He came bounding inside in high spirits, calling for Maria and his sons. Giulia came running to greet him also, so that the conversation was in Italian, and once again Maria was lost, unable to pick up anything from the fast flow of words.

It appeared that the next day they were to have another family day. A picnic was prepared, and apart from Gino, who had a nurse to care for him, everyone piled into the large family car. Both boys loved this, especially as a football was brought and an impromptu game took place in the field between father and son. Timothy chuckled at the sight of it, eagerly watching his older brother dive for balls, and laughing heartily when his father fell into a patch of rough growth. He tried to crawl towards them to join in, but Maria held tightly on to him.

That evening Stefano said that this time his business required him to travel far, and he would have to stay in a hotel for the night. Maria, her suspicions already aroused, felt her blood run cold. The next morning he said he must prepare the things he needed for the meeting, and pack them in a small suitcase. He must also take a few clothes and other necessities. Singing loudly, he busied himself putting together what he needed. He was about to take the case downstairs when his mother came to say Gino was anxious to see him before he left. He went to his father, leaving the case on the bed. Maria eyed it, just for a moment, and then, without hesitating any further, opened it.

There were no business papers inside. Pyjamas and clean underwear were neatly arranged. Something made Maria reach in and lift the clothes. Underneath them was a packet of condoms. She shut the case swiftly as she heard Stefano returning.

'I am sorry I am leaving you for two whole days! You look after my very fine sons and soon I am returning!'

He gave her a hearty embrace and a long kiss, ran downstairs to the front door where the sports car was just arriving, and leapt in. He turned to wave and was gone.

For the rest of the time they were in Italy Maria went through the motions, longing for the day when they would return home. She believed she would feel more comfortable once she was on her own territory.

After an emotional farewell they were driven to the airport, with Stefano loudly bewailing the fact that he would never see his father again. Queuing at the check-in desk they looked up at the sound of a commotion. A woman was running across the departures hall, shouting. It was Valeria.

'Wait here!' said Stefano, sharply.

He ran across the floor towards her. Maria couldn't help wondering if they would throw themselves at each other, arms outstretched, as happened in the old movies. But they stopped short of this.

Watching as the two of them exchanged a few words Maria clearly saw a letter being passed to Stefano, which he quickly slipped into his pocket. Then she saw him give the woman an Italian kiss on both cheeks, after which he returned to his family, looking rather sheepish.

'Unfinished business?' murmured Maria.

Unaware of the barb in the phrase Stefano nodded solemnly. 'She brought an important message. She arrived just in time!'

'How fortunate.'

On the return journey Timothy was much calmer. Perhaps he, too, was glad to be going home. He sat on Maria's lap, and in a few minutes had gone to sleep, his head resting on her shoulder.

Maria hid her face against her sleeping son and wept silently. She wept for the way her innocence and trust, eroded by the hard school of experience, had given way to cynicism and bitterness. And she wept for the loss of a sister who used to be there for her, her comforter in times of depair, her support when she felt uncertain, her guide, always ready to advise during the difficulties of adolescence, and her best friend.

CHAPTER 40

In time Timothy did grow, his development mirroring all the natural stages of progress that Carlo had achieved, except that he omitted crawling. He was quite satisfied with his action of sliding on his bottom.

He did not stand as early as Carlo had done. But eventually the day came when he did pull himself up to his feet. Maria gasped with delight, heaping praise on him. He was the cleverest little boy who had ever lived! Grinning, Timothy set off across the room. He did not move with the same easy grace that had been natural to Carlo. There was a strange lurching, that did not stop him walking, but his steps were uneven.

Throughout the day, while Stefano was at work, Maria watched Timothy, willing him to get the hang of it properly before his father returned home, but the movement remained clumsy. She heard the key in the lock.

Maria called out, 'Look, Stefano! Tim's walking now!' Summoning all her acting skills, she was careful to portray nothing but pride, but as Stefano watched, he began to frown.

'What's the matter with the boy? Why does he walk like that?'

They took him to the doctor, who referred them to a specialist. The diagnosis was that the left leg was slightly shorter than the right.

'That cannot be!' Stefano was angry. 'How can he be in the football team if he cannot run like all the other boys?'

The specialist thought he must be trying to make a joke of it, until he saw the father's face.

'I'm sorry, Mr Volpe, but your son has a shortened limb. He will never walk quite normally, but there are things we can do to improve the situation.'

'What can you do?'

Maria knew she must keep calm – one of them had to.

'There's an operation, which may help, but how much we shan't know until after we have carried it out. He will probably always have a slight limp.'

'Then operate, man, and make sure it is good! No son of mine is going to walk up down, up down like that. Do you want all the other boys to laugh at him?'

The specialist ignored Stefano and spoke to Maria.

'He will also need to wear a tailor-made shoe that is built up at the heel. This will go some way towards helping his step become more even.'

Maria was not altogether happy about the operation, but Stefano insisted. She found it difficult to stand by while her small son was wheeled into the operating theatre.

Once Timothy had recuperated he began to walk again. Stefano watched anxiously, and threw up his hands in despair when the uneven movement, although perhaps marginally improved, was still noticeable. He stormed out, railing about incompetent medical nincompoops who did not know how to do their job. Maria took Timothy in her arms and clasped him tightly, telling him what a wonderful little boy he was.

She took him to be measured for his special shoe. Once this had been procured, and Timothy had become accustomed to walking in his new shoes, the limp was less noticeable – but it was still there.

Carlo, watching all the proceedings, accepted without question that his brother could not run as easily as he could. He knew he himself was the apple of his father's eye, and could do no wrong. His self-confidence was high, and he enjoyed outdoor pursuits. Academically he was not an achiever, but his physical prowess was known among his peers and admired throughout the school. Maria was delighted to find that he was patient with his small brother, and did not tease him – at least not about the way he walked.

Stefano found it impossible to accept the situation. He would praise Carlo to the skies, but took little notice of his younger son. If he did speak to him, it was usually to mock him, or belittle him.

Timothy learned to keep out of his father's way. It was enough that his mother adored him, and his brother would, from time to time, play with him. Despite his problems he was a happy child, without any malice. When he first went to school the other children simply accepted him, and the way he was. His good nature made him popular, and it wasn't until he was older that he came face to face with the spiteful bullying which can make a child's life wretched. He put up with demeaning remarks without retaliation. No one ever poked fun at Timothy if his elder brother was around.

Timothy found there were two things he could do well – the second one, in particular, raised his status in the eyes of his peers. He excelled in the classroom, having a mind that mopped up facts easily. He mastered new subjects without any great effort, consistently turning in work of a high standard. But what made him admired by his school mates was his prowess in the swimming pool. Tall and strong for his age, he could streak through the water at an amazing speed. Soon he was winning all the races, was much in demand when teams for inter-school competitions were being selected, and his cupboard of trophies grew fuller each year.

This talent helped to improve his standing slightly in his father's eyes, but it was still clear that Stefano considered him a disappointment. As Carlo was no mean swimmer himself, Maria was delighted to find a pastime in which they could participate on almost equal terms, and it was difficult to appreciate, seeing them both in the water, that Timothy was five years younger.

When Carlo was eighteen he left school and applied to join the army. Maria was not happy about this, but it was what he had set his heart on doing, and he did look marvellous in the uniform.

'What if there's a war?' Maria couldn't help worrying.

'Have no fear. My Carlo is indestructible. He will defeat the enemy, no problem, and come home victorious, you'll see.'

Carlo had just finished his training at Pirbright when Mrs Thatcher announced that England was at war with Argentina over the Falklands Islands.

CHAPTER 41

Maria, Stefano, and thirteen-year old Timothy were among the crowds who waved and cheered as the taskforce left for the Falkland Islands. Carlo waved back, smiling broadly and looking immensely proud and very handsome in his uniform. At eighteen years of age Carlo found the prospect of going to war exciting. He set off without a moment's anxiety.

Of the 255 casualties of the war, one of the youngest was Private Carlo Volpe of 3 Battalion, the Parachute Regiment. It happened on the night of 11 June during the battle for Mount Longden. The authorities, naturally, greatly regretted the loss.

Stefano was devastated by the news, immediately storming out of the house. Timothy, overwhelmed by his own grief, nevertheless did what he could to comfort his distraught mother. Late that night Stefano returned highly inebriated, and the shouting began. Maria, who was sobbing herself to sleep, was now subjected to a barrage of angry questions.

'Why this happen to Carlo? Why my very fine son have to be killed? Tell me that, huh! Tell me, woman – why my Carlo? Why?'

Maria tried to pull the covers over her head to blot out the rage that was directed at her. But Stefano was not going to stop.

'My son, my lovely son is dead. How could he die? Carlo was strong! Carlo run like the wind! Why should he die? Now what have I got left? Only hop hop hoppy, with his up down, up down. What use is he?'

Maria could keep quiet no longer. 'Stop it, Stefano, stop it! How dare you ridicule Tim like that? He's been the bravest of boys! When have you ever heard him complain? You have taunted him, and ridiculed him, and he has taken it, without trying to hit back. He's endured bullying at school without getting bitter. It's about time you started to praise him, instead of humiliating him.'

'You stupid woman. You never see how fine Carlo was. Because Carlo not your boy, you make mother's boy of namby pamby Timothy! He is like very small mouse out in the fields, for people to tread on. My Carlo – he was a roaring lion!'

Timothy, downstairs, hearing every word Stefano shouted, put his hands over his ears, unable to bear the onslaught on his mother. And what was that about Carlo not being Maria's son? Whatever did that mean? Accustomed to his father's frequent taunts, he had learned to shrug them off. But perhaps there was more reason for the way his father treated him than he realised. And if Carlo was not his mother's son, whose son was he?

Soon after that the physical abuse started. To begin with, Stefano carefully limited it to the times when he and Maria were alone in the house. Timothy would come home to find his mother with a bruised face and arms. Alarmed, he would enquire the cause, initially naively accepting her stories of having fallen down the stairs, or perhaps that she had unwittingly walked into an open cupboard door.

Then Stefano grew more drunk and more reckless, so that Timothy, back from swimming, heard the sound of blows and his mother's screams and pleadings. He rushed upstairs but the bedroom door was locked. Without hesitation he kicked it open. Never would he forget the scene that met his eyes – his mother cowering in a corner, Stefano wielding a cricket bat, lifting it up to bring it down with force once again. Grabbing hold of Stefano from behind and wresting the bat from his hands, Timothy threw his father down on the floor. Stefano tried to get up, but with his fist Timothy knocked him flat again. Stefano, in his drunken rage, lacking the control to outsmart his son, started to plead for mercy.

'Get out of the bedroom,' commanded Timothy, 'and never, ever raise your hand to my mother again. What has she ever done to hurt you? I know how much she loved Carlo – don't you think she's suffering over his death every bit as much as you?'

The next day Stefano left the house. He took his most important possessions with him and never returned. To help his mother recuperate, Timothy decided it would be a good idea if they went away for few days. It was still summer holiday time, and perhaps, away from it all, she would open up to him. He may only have been thirteen, but he was emotionally mature for his age and there were questions he wanted to ask. They spent a few days in Cornwall, enjoying driving along the coast, visiting the picturesque bays. During that time Maria told him as much of the story as she thought appropriate.

A pleasant phase superseded those dreadful times. Maria regained her strength and found the confidence to take a job in a local shop selling women's clothing. She enjoyed this, as she could easily combine it with running the home for the two of them. Timothy worked hard at school and achieved good marks in his examinations. Although the pain of loss would never disappear, this was a time of peace and contentment for them both.

The years passed and Timothy, who had decided on a legal profession, left school to begin his training to be a solicitor. When he qualified he found a firm to join in London, where his career started to flourish. All this time he continued to live with Maria. Although he had a good social life, and kept up his competitive swimming, he showed no sign of settling down with a partner. There were plenty of girl friends, but they never seemed to last very long.

'If you don't move out by the time you're thirty,' said Maria one day, 'I shall kick you out.'

Secretly, she was in no hurry for him to leave – he was never any trouble and she enjoyed his company – but she knew it was something he needed to do. Timothy was in no hurry to leave either, as the arrangement left him in a position to put some money in savings, even after he had passed on a generous proportion of his salary every month.

Then something happened to delay these plans. He noticed that his mother grew weary more often, and lacked the energy to do very much. She changed her job to part time – fortunately, since her father had died and left her a capital sum, she did not need to earn – but even then she began to telephone the shop with various excuses. In the end it seemed best from everyone's point of view if she left. Timothy insisted that she went to see the doctor. After blood tests had been carried out, she was told she was suffering from leukaemia.

Timothy began to spend less time away from home, turning his hand to all sorts of household tasks, doing the best he could to lighten his mother's load. Always interested in cooking, he now gradually undertook more of it. He assumed responsibility for the laundry – although he sometimes wondered if he was ironing creases into the clothes rather than ironing them out – and on Saturdays he went out to do the shopping. Maria hated seeing him shouldering these extra household burdens, but he made light of it all. When he turned thirty no one said anything about moving out.

Various treatments were tried, with Maria frequently proclaiming she was much better. But the evidence to the contrary was painfully obvious. Without complaint she struggled to do all she could, but could not hide her growing weakness. One evening the two of them were passing the time quietly together, when she decided to open her heart to her son about the two things that were weighing on her mind.

'Timothy, I've been thinking. Can I discuss a couple of things with you?'

'Of course, Mum, if you're sure you're not too tired.'

'Rubbish! No, of course I'm not. But we do have to face facts. I don't know how much longer I'll be around, and I just want to say that it would make me so happy if you could find a nice girl to settle down with.'

Timothy grinned. 'Me too – but who'd have me?'

'Stop being so ridiculously modest. You're a catch for any girl.'

'You might be slightly biased.'

'Look, I'm trying to be serious here. I know it's not my strong point. Dear me, how my poor sister despaired of me, when I was young, because all I was interested in was having fun! I didn't take anything seriously!'

'Seriously then, I'll keep in mind what you say – I promise. Not sure how to achieve it, though. As we're being honest tonight I'll admit that so far – although I've been out with some really lovely girls – I don't think I've met my soul mate.'

'I know you can't wave a magic wand. But it would make me the happiest woman in the world if I could attend your wedding before … well, you know what I'm saying.'

'I do. I do understand. And was there something else?'

'Yes. It's to do with my sister. Oh, Tim, I long to see Claudia again – especially now I'm … It's been so long, and the pain of losing her love and friendship has never really gone away. Do you think you could try and find her, and just see if you could persuade her? I'm sure if you were to speak to her … how could she refuse you?'

'I'll do my very best – at least this is a practical thing I can get on with. I'll get started straightaway. I'm pretty sure I'll be able to find her. Whether I can get her to change her mind is another matter. But I'll do my damnedest – I promise you that.'

In fact, to the surprise of both mother and son, the first concern was resolved far more quickly than either of them would have dreamed possible. It so happened that the receptionist at Timothy's office was on the point of retirement. Mary Cummings had been worth her not inconsiderable weight in gold for many years. She always knew what to do in all circumstances, helping both members of staff and the public in a hundred different ways. But now it was time for her to retire.

When her replacement turned up ripples of excitement passed all round the building. Nicola Price was young, blonde, and the possessor of a delightful figure and a glorious smile. Any oversights or mistakes she might make as a newcomer were instantly overlooked. All the men in the office found numerous reasons to go down to reception, either to offer her advice, or make her feel welcome – anything so long as they could be the recipient of that smile. The unattached ones tried to take her out – as did a few of the married ones. She would sometimes accept an invitation from the former, but it was clear that she did not view any of the men as prospective boyfriends. Rumours began to circulate that she already had someone in her life. Nicola neither agreed with this nor denied it, when she was asked. She somehow managed to sidestep the questions.

Timothy worshipped from afar. It disturbed him to see the way the other men put her under pressure. He generally kept his distance, although he always exchanged pleasantries with her whenever he could. He was unaware that she was watching him.

At Christmas time an office 'do' was arranged at a local hotel, where there would be a dinner, followed by dancing. Timothy dreaded the dancing and when that began, he went to stand by the bar. After several lively numbers the music switched to slower, more romantic melodies, and a medley of the love songs of Andrew Lloyd Webber was just beginning. There was a touch on his elbow. He turned round to find Nicola standing there.

'Would you dance with me?' Her upturned face and smile were irresistible.

'I'm not much of a dancer,' he mumbled.

'That's not important. Having a dance with you is.'

He led her to the dance area, and as he held the slim body in his arms he knew he didn't want to let go.

'Love me, that's all I ask of you,' crooned the singer, and he felt her nestle closer. Then there was a pause in the music.

'Would you like to go back to your friends?' asked Timothy, ready to guide her to the table where she had been sitting.

'I'd rather stay with you, if that's okay with you.'

'It's more than okay.'

At the end of the evening he asked if he could see her home. The underground train was packed, and he put a protective arm round her. Finally, when they arrived at her flat she asked him in for a cup of coffee. He looked quickly around, but the rumours of a boyfriend seemed unfounded as there were no signs of any other occupant.

'I need to go home soon, as my mother is ill.' He told her briefly about Maria. Her face registered concern. When he stood up to go she slid easily into his arms and the embrace was as of two people who have finally found each other.

'What a difference an evening can make,' he whispered as his cheek rested on her fair hair.

'I've been trying to attract your attention for ages.'

'Really? And I've been admiring you from a distance, but I never dared to hope ...' Thank you ... thank you so very much.'

'For what?'

'For not being put off because I can't dance like the other chaps.'

'As if that matters!' replied Nicola indignantly.

CHAPTER 42

Two months later Nicola announced, in a matter-of-fact tone, that she thought it would really be much more convenient all round if she moved in.

'It would make it so much easier for me to help with your mother,' she suggested, with irrefutable logic.

Maria and Nicola had become firm friends. Nicola proved to be a practical person who enjoyed looking after the home and did not find household duties onerous. Her background, which in many ways had been a difficult one, had cultivated the independence which characterised her.

In the past few weeks Timothy had learned a great deal about her. When she was eight her parents were both tragically killed in a car crash. She and her brother had been cared for after that by their grandmother, who had battled to bring them up despite failing health. Clive, of whom she was obviously very fond, had been protective of his little sister, and done his best to act in the guise of parent. The arrangement had worked well all the time Nicola was at school. But by the time she had completed her secretarial course and found her first job, Granny Price had become too ill to cope, and had died shortly afterwards. With the proceeds from their parents' house divided between them, Nicola and Clive had been able to go their separate ways, each buying a small flat. They always remained in close contact – Nicola described Clive as her 'best friend'.

'He's five years older than me, which seems a lot when you are still very young.'

'That's strange,' said Timothy. 'My brother was five years older, also. What a coincidence!'

'I didn't know you had a brother. Why isn't he here to help with your mother?'

Then Timothy explained in detail all that happened to the family, how Carlo had been killed in the war, and how their father, unable to live with the loss, had finally left. When Timothy spoke of the violence to Maria, Nicola was moved to tears.

'Aren't there any other relatives?' asked Nicola.

Timothy then embarked on the story of Claudia and Maria, explaining the events that had happened to cause a rift between them.

'So they haven't been in contact – for how long?'

'It must be almost forty years now. I'm thirty-four – going on thirty-five – and I was born five years after Carlo, whose birth coincided with the time that Stefano came on the scene at the girls' family home.'

'Do you think he really did pursue Claudia?'

'How do we know? But it seems their father, Hugh, was in touch with them both. He was something of a go-between. He told Maria that Claudia was extremely bitter, and heart-broken to the point that she was ill. She took herself off for a year to recover. In fact she delayed her teaching career until she had revived sufficiently to put her heart into it. But apparently, even when she returned, she looked dreadfully thin and miserable.'

'And what's your mother's take on it?'

'She's bewildered. Stefano swore to her that he had never proposed marriage to Claudia. He said she was not his type, and I'm sure she wasn't. I think my mother was pretty attractive in those days, and liked a good time. I think she would have appealed to him far more.'

Nicola was thoughtful. 'I wonder,' she said.

'Wonder what?'

'Oh, I don't know. Just my feminine curiosity, trying to work things out. What I'm wondering is, why did she go away for a whole year? It seems a long time to get over something like that. Is Maria still sad that she doesn't have any contact with her sister?'

'It's the one great burden she now carries. Up to recently she had two, but fortunately your arrival in my life cleared away one of her concerns. So now I'm working hard on trying to track Claudia down. As soon as I've achieved that, I'll go and see her, and try my hardest to persuade her to see Mum. If I told her how ill Mum is now, I'm sure … I do so wish she and Claudia could be reconciled before ….'

'Yes,' agreed Nicola. 'That would be very good indeed.'

CHAPTER 43

The ring of the doorbell took Claudia by surprise – she was not expecting a caller. Rarely did anyone ever drop in uninvited. Her visitors, such as they were, had always come by arrangement.

Claudia's home had been feeling quieter than ever since Socrates' demise – that is, until three days ago, when Fran had arrived, carrying a basket, from the depths of which a series of high pitched squeaks could be heard. Gingerly lifting the lid Fran had invited Claudia to look inside. Suddenly up popped a tiny black head with a pair of bright eyes that looked around inquisitively – then catching sight of Claudia, focused trustingly on her.

'Oh, what a lovely kitten!'

Claudia had lifted him out of his basket to examine him more closely. Then she held the tiny body against her, whereupon the kitten set about climbing up her chest until he reached her shoulder, nestling there contentedly against the nape of her neck.

'His name,' said Fran, 'is Archimedes, because he comes with a set of principles.'

'Which are?'

'He requires the best seat in the house, dainty morsels of food at regular intervals, and to have his every whim satisfied. In return he offers you his unwavering devotion for the rest of his life.'

'That's a ridiculously long name for such a tiny kitten. How can I possibly call him, with a name like that?'

'Just call him Archie. He will happily answer to the shortened version. Seriously though, you are free to decide whether you want to keep him or not. I can take him back to the pet shop if you'd rather not.'

'Don't you dare! I couldn't possibly let him go now. I wasn't going to have another cat, but now he's here – well, I just couldn't bear it if you took him back.'

The kitten clung determinedly to his position of security and began to purr contentedly.

Fran smiled. 'Glad you like him. He certainly seems to like you.'

'Oh, Fran! I think he's wonderful. Thank you so much for your thoughtfulness. Whatever would I do without you?'

Archie had quickly settled into his new home, appropriating the chair left vacant by Socrates. At the sound of the doorbell, he looked up enquiringly. Claudia was careful to shut the lounge door behind her before opening the front door.

On the doorstep stood a tall, dark-haired young man, with a pleasant smile and something vaguely familiar about him. Was it the piercing look in his blue eyes? There was no time to think.

'Miss Claudia Hansom?'

'Yes – what is it you want?'

'I'd like to have a word with you, if I may.'

'Why is that? I don't know you.'

He reached into his jacket pocket and took out a business card. She glanced at it briefly without taking it in, only noting the word 'Solicitor' and some company details before handing it back.

'My name is Timothy, and I'm a solicitor,' the young man explained. 'Do you think I might come in for a few minutes?'

'Timothy what?'

'If I could just come in for a moment.'

She led the way through to the lounge, pointing to the armchair normally reserved for visitors. At the sound of the intrusion Archie shot off his chair onto Claudia's lap, from where he climbed up to his favourite position on her shoulder, regarding the stranger with a look of distrust. Claudia removed him, putting him firmly back on his chair. Archie, who was clearly not pleased at having his wishes thwarted, managed to convey in a single look both dissatisfaction with the arrangement and disdain for the intruder.

'What a delightful kitten! How old is he?'

'Never mind that. Just tell me your business.'

'Miss Hansom, I have come on behalf of my mother – you see, I'm your nephew. My mother is your sister, Maria.'

'Then you have gained entry into my flat under false pretences. I think you had better leave, immediately.'

'Please, just hear me out. I have a particular reason for coming at this time. I know that you and my mother have been out of contact for many years. It has now become very important to her to see you, and I've come to ask if you would grant her this request.'

'I haven't seen or spoken to your mother for forty years.'

'I know that is so – she has told me.'

'Then why should I see her now?'

'She is desperately sad about the lack of communication between you, and the fact that it has gone on for so long.'

'And has she ever told you why we have been estranged?'

'She has often spoken of the times when you were a happy family, and of the events that caused everything to go wrong. But I fully appreciate that I only have my mother's side of the story, and that I may not know everything that happened.'

'You won't know everything because Maria will not have told you the story accurately – she always was one for rewriting history. In any case, she will not be able to see things from my point of view. Don't forget that I once knew her very well, and was only too aware of her weaknesses. She never could see beyond her own nose.'

Timothy winced slightly, but knew nothing was to be gained from becoming confrontational. He continued to speak in a reasonable tone.

'Then please tell me. I promise you I'll remain impartial – that's the benefit of having a solicitor's training.'

'How can you possibly be impartial when it's your mother I'm talking about? And in any case, how can you, as a young man, ever have any inkling of how a woman can suffer? You cannot know how it feels to have your hopes and dreams torn away from you. You can have no idea of the kind of life I was condemned to live. Yes, I made a good career for myself professionally. I worked my way into a position of authority – but I did not gain the respect of my colleagues. I knew they sniggered behind my back. Because I had to go through life walling in any emotions, because I dared not let anyone close enough to see the chinks, I had to remain cold and aloof. I was excluded from any social gathering that was held – after all, I would have spoilt the atmosphere. I was treated as a necessity because I held the reins, but not as a human being. They considered me some sort of freak – someone to be slightly pitied, who was best dealt with by making snide allusions. I know they poked fun at me behind my back. I couldn't have felt more different from everyone else if I had had some sort of physical deformity.'

'I see,' said Timothy quietly. There was a look of pain in his eyes.

'Of course you don't! What can you understand? I expect Maria told you I was mistaken in thinking Stefano wanted to marry me. If only she hadn't insisted on coming into the picture. It was all her fault – she flirted with him abominably, until she had attracted him and turned him away from me.'

'It may be as you say, but I am asking you to take pity on her now. I have a particular reason for coming, as I mentioned. My mother now has a terminal illness – leukaemia – and hasn't much longer to live. She wants to see you before … well, before it's too late.'

'So that's it! I might have guessed there'd be some sort of emotional blackmail behind the request. How like Maria to play out the final scene as if it were high drama. So, she's weak and helpless, and wants to make everything right before she meets her maker – is that it? What about all those years when she had a family life, and I had no one? I heard there was a child, very early on – my father wrote something about it, I remember. I didn't dwell on the letter – as soon as I saw the word "baby" I tore it up, but I think things have been pretty cosy for my younger sister.'

'Perhaps not quite as cosy as you may think. My elder brother, Carlo, was killed in the Falklands War. My father never got over that.

He frequently got drunk, and became violent and abusive. In the end he left.'

'Please don't tell me any more.' Claudia put her hands over her ears. 'I don't want to hear it. Don't say any more.'

Timothy leaned forward.

'I implore you, I beg you, for the sake of the love that once existed between you and my mother, please try to put the past behind you and grant the wishes of your dying sister. I know that once you and she were close. She has recounted much of the early days to me. I know that as children you were the best of playmates, and when your mother died at an early age you assumed much of the responsibility. She has told me she doesn't know what she would have done without you. She admits she didn't take life very seriously, but you were always there to help and advise. She looked up to you and valued you as her older sister. Now she longs to see you again. If she has hurt you in the past she regrets that bitterly.'

'If! There's no doubt about her having hurt me. And hasn't she left it a bit late to regret it now, almost forty years after the event?'

'I don't think that's altogether fair. She tried to contact you many times in the first few years. She wrote often, but her letters were never answered. She was dreadfully upset and totally bewildered by your refusal to respond.'

'I see no point in prolonging this conversation. We have no more to say to each other. I must ask you to go now, please.'

Claudia stood up. Timothy stood up also, then hesitated.

'Please,' he said, 'Aunt Claudia …'

'Don't call me that! How dare you!'

He turned and walked to the door. This time he was ahead of her, and even in her state of churning emotions, Claudia noticed that he walked with a slight limp. He had reached the door, and was stepping through it. For some reason her attention was drawn to his feet. She saw that the backs of his shoes were different – the left heel was higher than the right one.

Where had she heard something about that before? Someone

who could glide through the water, but on land walked awkwardly? Into her seething mind came a vision of a deserted beach, with a rough sea, and Fran, her beloved Fran, threatened by rolling waves, fighting for her life.

She ran out of the house and down the path.

'Timothy!' she shouted. 'Stop! Wait!'

But he had climbed into his car, her words drowned by the engine springing into life. He eased the car into gear and drove away.

Claudia turned back into her house. The roar of thundering waters pounded in her ears. Waves of emotion crashed around her, threatening to engulf her. She staggered back to her chair, cries of pain forcing their way to the surface.

Then she noticed, on the chair where Timothy had been sitting, a small white card. She picked it up. There was his name, Timothy Volpe, and his business details. She turned it over. On the back, handwritten, there was a telephone number.

CHAPTER 44

Claudia tapped gently on the lounge door. The middle-aged nurse who had answered her ring on the front door bell had shown her where to go.

'She has a bed downstairs now. It means she can be with her family when they are there, but she can sleep whenever she wants. Please don't stay too long – she gets very tired.'

A voice, barely audible, called, 'Come in.'

The voice did not sound like the Maria she remembered. Her heart beating loudly, she turned the handle. There, propped up on pillows, was a small, frail figure. Gone was the shining, golden hair – in its place a sparse layer of wispy grey strands. Gone was the youthful, clear complexion. Instead, a wrinkled skin and sunken eyes met Claudia's gaze.

Maria held out two arms – surely no thicker than twigs. Claudia ran across the room and clasped the thin body in a strong embrace.

'Oh, Maria! Please, please forgive me!'

'Oh, never mind any of that. It's enough that you are here.'

Suddenly this unfamiliar person was her sister Maria again. For some time neither could say a word. The tears flowed freely.

At last Maria spoke. 'I think we could both use some tissues.'

They helped themselves from the box and mopped their faces.

'Oh Maria, I've been a stubborn, obstinate, obdurate old woman. I'm so very sorry.'

'If you're going to start that again we shall need some more tissues. At least you're still recognisable. Grey hair, maybe, but you're still the Claudia I remember. And before you try and say it, I know I do not resemble the old Maria in the slightest. I don't look in the mirror these days, if I can help it.'

'When did you become so ill?'

'About three years ago. I was diagnosed with leukaemia. I've undergone various sorts of treatment, and I tried to believe I could fight it, but recently it became clear that I am losing the battle. But don't worry about that now. I think we've got a bit of catching up to do, don't you?'

'About forty years' worth.'

'How did it happen? How was it that we fell out? Claudia, I really want to know how it all went wrong. I've missed you so much!'

'Are you sure you're strong enough? The nurse said I mustn't tire you.'

'Never mind that dragon – she's all fire and brimstone – but she means well, and she does look after me beautifully, I have to admit. Timothy insists I have a nurse here all the time, while he and Nicky are at work – they work in the same office. Sometimes they take half a day off, at different times, so that they can be with me. Isn't that sweet?'

'Who's Nicky?'

'Timothy's wonderful fiancée. She is so lovely, and so beautiful. You must meet her soon. But come on, Dragon Drake will be driving you away before we've got going. You start.'

'Maria, do you remember my college summer ball – the one I went to just before my final exams?'

'Yes, I do. It made quite an impression on me, because you didn't normally do things like that. You were so serious about your studies – I could never understand that! I couldn't have cared less about mine. I was the one who liked all the fun things. But I do remember that when you had started teaching Stefano English, you asked him to go as your escort.'

'That's right, and I got very excited about it because he was so handsome, and I knew the other students would envy me for having such a handsome man as my partner. I found this lovely ball gown in a charity shop, and when Stefano came, looking like a film star, I was bowled over. I don't have to tell you how charming he can be. He was wonderful company, and we danced into the night.'

She fell silent. Maria prompted her. 'Go on, tell me. Don't try to spare me anything.'

'In the early hours of the morning we went for a walk in the moonlight along the river bank. There was no one around, and the path was surrounded by plenty of trees and long grass. Oh, Maria, he made love to me, and I'd never dreamed of anything like that before. Then he proposed.'

Maria gasped. 'Are you sure? When Dad told me that you claimed he had asked you to marry him I couldn't believe it. Don't get me wrong – not because of you, but because of what I was to find out later. I wonder ... can you remember exactly what he said?'

'I'm not sure. I was pretty intoxicated, partly with the wine, as I wasn't accustomed to it, and partly with the magic of all that had happened that day and evening. I think he asked me if I would like to marry him.'

'What did you say?'

'As far as I remember, I said – yes please. Then he said would I like babies, maybe five of them. And I said no, not yet, as I had a teaching career to pursue, and that was why I had been studying so hard, and I didn't want to waste all that. The babies could come later.'

'And then?'

'I'm not sure, because I was falling asleep. I think he said I would make a very good wife.'

Nurse Drake put her head round the door. 'Not getting too tired, are we?'

'No we are not!' replied Maria as vehemently as she could manage. 'We've only just started.'

Nurse Drake sighed and withdrew.

'When will she go?' asked Claudia.

'As soon as Timothy or Nicky comes back. If Timothy has to stay on at work, Nicky doesn't wait for him. She comes straight home to free me from the dragon's clutches. I'm so lucky – she's just like the daughter I never had.'

Claudia was silent for a moment. Then, in a whisper that was barely audible, she said, 'I have a daughter.'

CHAPTER 45

'Claudia!' Maria looked at her sister in amazement. 'I don't understand! How ... I mean when did you have this child? And why did Daddy never say anything to me about it?'

'Because he didn't know! No one knew. You see, I went away for a year, and I had the baby, and then, as soon as I'd given birth to her, she was ... she was taken by the adoption society. Oh Maria, no one who has not endured that particular form of torture can have any idea what it is like. I grew her inside me for nine months, and I tried to keep myself strong and healthy for the child's sake, and then, as soon as my beautiful baby girl was born, I had to give her up! Can you see now why I hated you! I heard from Dad that you also had a child ... I couldn't listen when he told me. And then later, you had another. So you had Stefano, and you had your family, and I had no one! The only time I had someone, I lost her! I was bitterly resentful, and so dreadfully jealous. The only way I could deal with it was by trying to wipe all thoughts, both of my baby, and of you, out of my mind.'

'Oh, my poor, poor Claudia! But who was the father? Oh no! Of course! That was Stefano's child!'

'You could say it was one of life's bitter ironies. Only once in my whole life have I ever had relations with a man, and it has to result in a child! You see, I was so ignorant about things of the world, I thought ... well ... now that we'd been intimate, he would certainly marry me. It never occurred to me, for a single moment, to doubt it. Though I must admit I was disturbed by the letter he wrote to thank me for taking him to the ball. It was such a stilted, formal letter. But

I tried to tell myself he wasn't comfortable writing English, and everything would be all right when I got back after my exams. But when I arrived home, I learned he'd married you, and you had gone off together to Italy. I couldn't believe it!'

Maria shook her head in disbelief. 'Claudia! I had no idea! Oh my dear, I'm so, so sorry.'

For a while neither spoke. Then Claudia said, 'I'm afraid I'm tiring you. I should go now.'

'No, please don't go – it's my turn now. I must have my turn.'

'Are you sure? It can wait until tomorrow. I'll come again tomorrow, if you'll let me.'

'Oh yes, please. But don't go yet. I've waited long enough for this. I'm blowed if I'm going to wait another day.'

She was sounding more and more like the old Maria. Claudia smiled. 'If you're sure?'

Maria nodded. 'Life hasn't actually been that easy for me. Stefano wanted a wife quickly, for a particular reason. He had a child back at home – a child he wanted to bring to England – so he wanted a wife to look after him. I assure you, Claudia, the baby you heard about wasn't mine! Honestly – I promise you, I never slept with him until we were married.'

Claudia was puzzled. 'If the child wasn't yours, whose was it?'

'It was Stefano's son, by the family's kitchen maid.'

Now it was Claudia's turn to be shocked. 'You mean …'

'Yes! I didn't know it, but I was taken to Italy to get accustomed to the baby. I was used, by Stefano and his family, disgracefully, and I was too innocent to see through it. Then, on the day we set off to return to England, Carlo was put in the car without my knowing. You should have heard the wailing, the mother, Rosa, made that day! She must have felt like you – only she had had him a bit longer, and she had to go through the slow torture of seeing me there each day, knowing I was going to replace her as his mother, and he would be taken away. I was the only person there who didn't know it.'

Now it was Claudia's turn to look shocked. 'However did you feel

– when you discovered you were being thrust into looking after a baby?'

'How do you think? I was absolutely furious, but it didn't get me anywhere. If I was cross, Stefano became unpleasant. In the end I found it best to knuckle down and get on with it.'

'Oh Maria … the whole thing's more unbelievable than one of those fanciful stories you used to make up when you were young. Only this time it's all true – and you and I seem to have been pawns in some mischievous game! I had to give up a child I wanted more than anything else in the world, and you had to take one on completely against your will! Were you able to love him, after a while? Did you come to think of him as yours?'

'Yes, I did, after a surprisingly short time, really. Carlo was a lovely little boy. And when I finally had a son of my own, Carlo was thrilled with his small brother, and that endeared him all the more to me, especially as Stefano was so disappointed with Timothy.'

'Disappointed? Why? Did he want a girl?'

'No, not at all. He was thrilled to have a second son. But physical prowess mattered terribly to him, and Timothy, as you will have seen for yourself, was born with a physical handicap.'

Claudia nodded. 'I did see there was a problem with his foot.'

'Stefano couldn't bear to think that any son of his was less than perfect physically. Masculine strength meant such a lot to him. He started taunting Tim, and humiliating him. At the same time he was always praising Carlo. Tim felt this difference in their treatment keenly, and it made me so sad. But amazingly the two boys had a good relationship. Carlo was protective and would often put paid to any school bullies who were having a go at Tim.'

'And all this time I've been envying you with your cosy family! If only I'd known … but then, I didn't give you a chance to tell me. I can't tell you how ashamed I feel.'

'We're not going to have any self reproaches. That's a rule in this house. Sometimes I get a bit weepy, at the thought of all the problems I'm heaping on my two young people – but they won't let me be apologetic. They tease me and laugh me out of it. I'm so lucky, I know.'

'Oh, Maria, you've turned into such a brave person.'

'We've both changed a lot, haven't we? I suppose that happens when life deals you some hard blows – and to think neither of us knew all the important things that have happened to the other. I'd like to tell you the rest of my story, as briefly as I can, if you can bear it.'

'Go on,' said Claudia gently, 'if you're sure you have the strength. I don't want you to get tired.'

'I am tired, but now I've started I don't want to stop. Carlo joined the army, just when the trouble in the Falklands Islands blew up. He went out there with the task force, and was killed at the battle for Mount Longden.'

Claudia, shocked, squeezed her sister's hand, her eyes moistening.

Maria paused a bit, and then went on. 'Stefano was heartbroken. He started to get very drunk, and this led to violence. When Timothy saw it he wanted to protect me. He couldn't bear seeing Stefano hit me, so one day, being quite big and strong for his age, he lashed out, and knocked his father to the floor. Stefano left the next day and I have never seen him or heard from him since.'

Now Claudia was sobbing again. 'I can't bear it! You went through all that – and I was no help to you at all! Too busy feeling sorry for myself! What a thoroughly useless older sister I have been.' She covered her face with her hands.

'Remember the rules! There's not to be any guilty feelings. Let's just be glad we're together now. I'm longing for Timothy to come home and see you. You gave him such short shrift when he visited you!'

'I know. Again, I regret it. I've been so harsh towards everyone … just horrible.'

Maria was silent for a moment, thinking. Finally, she said, 'What I need to know is this. I've been trying to find the answer amidst all we've found out about each other and I can't. Why did you change your mind about seeing me? Timothy came home from his visit to you miserably disappointed. He was certain he had failed in his quest, so we were both amazed when you telephoned to say you were coming. And you haven't answered my earlier question – did you ever find out what happened to your daughter?'

CHAPTER 46

'Did she come?'

Timothy stood in the doorway anxiously – but one look at his mother's face and he had his answer. Maria was smiling, and there was a special look of contentment in her eyes.

'She came, and it was wonderful. It was emotional, nerve-racking, chilling, surprising, almost unbelievable, and completely wonderful.'

'You're friends again?'

'We are, and so happy to be friends. There's so much I have to tell you.'

Nicola was behind him.

'I'm going to get supper ready – you tell Timothy all about it.'

'What a kind, tactful girl you have found yourself!'

'I know. I'm the luckiest chap. Look, Mum, if you're sure you're not too tired, do tell me what happened. I'm longing to hear about it.'

'I don't know where to start. Perhaps I'll try and tell it in order, although it certainly didn't come out that way. We kept getting side-tracked, or we'd have to stop to blow noses. I think you'll have to buy me another box of tissues.'

Maria recounted, as best she could, what Claudia had told her. She described the night of the ball, and it was necessary not to spare the details, because of the result of that night's liaison.

'Just think – Claudia went off to have a baby, all by herself – and none of us knew. She never told our father, or anyone. She made all the arrangements herself to have the child adopted, because she knew she couldn't pursue a teaching career with an illegitimate child – and she couldn't possibly have looked after it herself. So she had to give the child away – she said it was a lovely baby girl. She was absolutely heartbroken.'

'Did she ever see her again?'

'Hold on … I'll tell you … but I need to try and keep things in order.'

Maria went on to say how Claudia had believed Stefano wanted to marry her, and had been devastated when she came home and found he had married the younger sister instead. Then, to make things a hundred times worse, there had come the blow of discovering that she was pregnant.

'I'd no idea!' cried Maria. 'It never, for a single moment, occurred to me that Claudia would want to marry him.'

'Did the bounder actually propose to her?'

'Claudia is certain that he did. From what she says it sounds as if he was trying to find out if she would be suitable to look after Carlo. He must have decided that she wasn't, because she said something to him about being keen to get going with her teaching. As she would, naturally, after having studied so hard. But stupid Maria, with no thought of any sort of career, might well have seemed a more suitable candidate.'

She went on to tell Timothy how it had then been her turn to describe her life. As her story had unfolded she had seen Claudia's reaction at the realisation that her sister's lot had not been the cosy, family life she had imagined. And knowing nothing about Carlo, she couldn't possibly have guessed that Stefano had a particular motive for marrying Maria.

'When I told her about Rosa she immediately grasped what slow torture it must have been for that poor girl to have to watch me, day by day, being trained to take over her role as mother.'

Timothy shook his head, dumfounded by what he was hearing. 'What incredible stuff you and your sister have both been through – and yet neither of you knew about the other.'

'And all the while we both completely misunderstood each other. I was totally bewildered as to why she wouldn't see me, and why she bore me such a deep grudge. But looking at it through Claudia's eyes, it must have been blindingly obvious what the problem was, and she couldn't understand why I couldn't see it! There was I, with the twin blessings of marriage and a baby – at her expense! But of course, I didn't know that was what she was thinking, and she couldn't possibly have any idea of what actually happened to me.'

'She believed you'd deliberately hatched a plot to steal Stefano away from her! Oh dear – what a fearfully long time you two have been apart – and all because of mutual misunderstandings! How sad that it's taken your illness to clear things up.'

Maria, who was now getting very tired, was quiet for a little while. Then she went on, 'There were many things we neither of us knew about the other. She had no idea that we lost Carlo to the Falklands War, or that Stefano had become violent, and then left us. And I, of course, knew nothing about her daughter, or the pain she experienced, nor that she had vowed never to let anyone get close to her again.'

'And the baby girl? Did she ever find out what happened to her?'

'That's the marvellous part of the story. Just recently Francesca – or Fran, as she likes to be called – came walking back into Claudia's life! It seems she had long wanted to trace her birth mother, but held off doing so until her adoptive mother had died, as she knew it would upset her terribly. Then, just a few weeks ago, she appeared on the doorstep. Claudia was dreadfully shaken, and at first didn't want to have anything to do with her. But Fran persisted and gradually, it seems, they have drawn closer.'

'That's an amazing story!' Timothy smiled at his mother. 'But what I want to know is – why did Claudia change her mind about seeing you? She was pretty adamant in her refusal when I visited her. In fact she was downright rude to me. I couldn't have been more surprised when she rang to ask if she could come.'

'There's one more piece in the jigsaw which explains it all – and it's perhaps the most amazing part of the whole story. Tim, do you remember, the time when you were thirteen? Stefano had just left, and I was in a pretty poor condition. You thoughtfully suggested we had a few days away, to help things settle down. I drove the old boneshaker all the way to Cornwall, and we had a happy time together exploring those lovely coves?'

'I do remember – particularly one beach, because three noisy females invaded our space. And as if that wasn't enough, one stupid jackass of a girl went in swimming, and got swept out to sea – and I had to go in and fish her out!'

'And I tried to stop you! But it's just as well you're as pig-headed as you are, because the stupid jackass of a girl you saved on that occasion was none other than Claudia's daughter! In other words – your cousin! Can you believe that?'

'That was Fran?'

'It was indeed. Apparently she never forgot the boy who saved her life that day – the boy who wore shoes with one heel higher than the other.'

'Well I never! That is some coincidence! My goodness, that takes some believing! You mean to say you and I were on that beach at the same time as Claudia's daughter? Even so, I don't see how that comes into it.'

'It was when you were leaving Claudia's flat, and you walked out ahead of her – and Claudia noticed the way you walked. And then, it seems, she remembered the story Fran had told her, of how she had been saved from drowning, and how she watched the boy who'd saved her walk away – and she had noticed his shoes with one heel higher than the other. That all came back to her in that moment!'

Timothy shook his head in amazement.

'It completely changed her attitude to you. You see, Fran has become very dear to her now, I'm very glad to say, and since she owed Fran's life to you … well …'

Timothy took his mother's hand, still trying to take it all in.

'So you see, my dear, your courage on that day … well, it not only

219

saved someone's life, but was eventually the cause of healing the rift between me and my sister. And to think I tried to stop you going into the water after that girl!'

'I always was an obstinate so-and-so. But thanks for telling me all this. It's certainly a lot to take in. Now I think you should have a little sleep. You must be worn out.'

Maria nodded.

'Yes, I have to admit it – I am very tired – but oh, Timothy, I'm so very happy!'

CHAPTER 47

Claudia left Maria's house with a lighter step than she had had for years. Like Christian, in *Pilgrim's Progress*, a burden had rolled off her shoulders. Saddened as she was at the sight of her sister suffering from a devastating illness, her overriding emotion was a feeling of absolution. Maria had forgiven her for her stubborn refusal to allow any communication for forty years and the barrier of the intervening years had disappeared, allowing a harmony between them that was reminiscent of the old days. Laughing and crying together as they exchanged accounts of all that had happened, they could have been in their teens once more.

Claudia decided to take a longer walk home so that she could continue to delight in this feeling. She wanted to hang on to it as long as possible. Without thinking much about the route she was taking she realised she was near Kingdown Primary School – a place she had deliberately tried to avoid until today. The park opposite was a pleasant spot to sit and when the weather was reasonable mothers often gathered there to wait for their children to be let out of school. A woman was sitting on a bench, holding the handle of a pushchair, cooing over the occupant. Claudia could hear the baby chuckling, and as she drew near she thought she recognised the woman.

'It's Paula, isn't it? Paula Munro?'

The woman looked up, unsure for a moment; then recognition dawned.

'Claudia! How very nice to see you again! How are you? Were you badly hurt, after that fall? What terrible weather it was, that day!'

'Oh no, it was nothing – just a graze. You were so kind to me. I should have rung you up and thanked you properly.'

'Don't worry about it. It was the least I could do – all I did was run you home. I couldn't believe, afterwards, I'd asked you to tea! I must have embarrassed you! Jack always said it would be a good thing if I could learn to think before I spoke, but I never seem to do it.'

'So this is your new baby?' Claudia, looking at the child, saw a pretty face with a mop of curly brown hair. 'This must be Maria?'

'That's right. It's clever of you to remember the name.'

Paula tickled her daughter's tummy, making her smile.

'She's very pretty. And how's the older one – I think you said she's called Isabel? I take it she's at the school?'

'Yes, we did get her into Kingdown, and she's loving it. She always comes running out so excited and happy.'

'Your husband must have been thrilled when he finally came home and saw the new baby.'

Paula put her head down, and her shoulders began to tremble.

'What is it?' Claudia, concerned at the sudden transformation in the young woman, laid her hand on Paula's arm.

'Jack didn't come home from Iraq. He …' Paula's tears began to flow.

'Oh, Paula. I'm so very sorry. How dreadful for you.'

Tears rolled down the younger woman's face. She brushed them away quickly.

'Well, it's all right. I've mostly got over it now. I know I must keep bright for the children. I always knew there was a risk. Jack had told me before we married that the life was hard on a soldier's wife. But you never think it'll happen to you.'

The young woman made an effort and brightened up.

'Anyway, Isabel's really happy at Kingdown – I knew she would be. She adores her teacher.'

'I believe they've got a new head there?'

'That's right. How did you know that? Mrs Bentley – everyone likes her. They say she's very different to the old one. Easier to get on with. The old one was a stickler for discipline – mind you, I think that's a good thing, really. Apparently she was much admired – very good at her job, they said. But very strict.'

'I'm glad Isabel's happy there. At least that must be a comfort to you.'

'Yes, I'll go over to the school soon … it's almost time. But it was such a lovely autumn day I thought we'd have a little walk in the park first.' She hesitated. 'If you don't mind me saying, you seem different. I don't know why I'm saying this … probably putting my big foot into it again. But you seem, well, more relaxed. Perhaps it was just that it was such an awful day … and you were in a hurry. You'd been shopping at Marks … do you remember?'

'I remember it well. And I remember how patient you were with me.'

'You didn't say much. You didn't talk. Well, I suppose I didn't give you half a chance. Edith says I'm always prattling on.'

'I am different,' said Claudia, quietly. 'Oh Paula, you've had a dreadful time since we last met, and lost someone very dear to you. I've done the opposite – I've found people I lost forty years ago.'

The younger woman looked at her in surprise.

'It's a long story, and I won't embark on it now. But I was wondering, you were kind enough to ask me tea, and I didn't even have the manners to ring you up. Do you think … that is, is the invitation still open?'

'Oh yes!' Paula smiled happily. 'Will you really come?'

Claudia nodded.

'I'd love to,' she said. And this time, she meant it.

CHAPTER 48

'A party! We must have a party!'

Excited by her own idea, Nicola announced it eagerly, hoping for a positive reception. She was not disappointed.

'How wonderful!' Maria injected all the enthusiasm into her voice that her frailty could muster. 'It's ages since I've been to a party!'

'This party's coming to you,' said Nicola. 'No need to go anywhere or do anything.'

'What sort of a party?' enquired Timothy. 'Not fancy dress, I hope.'

'Don't be silly,' Nicola admonished him. 'A family party – just for our family. We'll ask Claudia, Fran and Nigel to come next Saturday evening.'

'Any chance Clive could come?'

''Fraid not – he'll be in America. He's only due back two days before our wedding.'

Timothy was still intent on making helpful suggestions.

'As Mum may be in bed, perhaps we could make it a pyjama party.'

'That wouldn't be any good,' said Nicola. 'I wear nighties.'

'No you don't,' said Timothy, and they both giggled.

'Stop it, you two! You're making me blush. Let's discuss this seriously. I think it's a great idea, Nicola, if you're sure it wouldn't be too much work for you. We don't need to feed them.'

'Of course we do! It wouldn't be a party otherwise. But don't worry – I'll enlist the help of my two good friends Mr Marks and Mr Spencer, and they'll do all the preparation for me.'

Timothy still had another proposal.

'What about a bring-a-bottle party?'

'No!' Maria was adamant. 'I don't want them feeling they have to make a contribution – that is, if you're sure you can manage, Nicky. But I've got a good idea. What about a "Bring-your-own-memory" party?'

'That,' said Nicola, 'is absolutely perfect.'

* * *

Fran and Nigel picked Claudia up, and Claudia made the acquaintance of the disembodied voice she had spoken to several times on the phone. He looked quite a lot older than Fran, although Claudia knew there was only six years' age difference. She supposed it was the beard, which, together with the moustache, hid most of his face.

'It's good to meet at last,' he said. 'Fran hasn't stopped talking about you since she found you.'

'I don't know what to say to that,' said Claudia. 'When you meet people in the flesh it can be disappointing.'

'Quite so,' he agreed. 'I apologise for any disappointment.'

'Oh dear,' said Claudia, feeling she had got off on the wrong foot, 'I didn't mean ... that is, I wasn't referring ...'

'Don't worry, Claudia,' intervened Fran. 'You'll soon discover Nigel is an awful tease.'

'I hope I can manage that,' responded Claudia. 'You see, I think I lost my sense of humour a long time ago.'

'Then it shall be my life's mission to find it,' replied Nigel. 'I don't suppose you remember where you had it last?'

'You see what I mean?' said Fran. 'He never stops! But wasn't it nice of Maria and her family to ask us along? I am so looking forward to meeting them.'

'I think I should warn you, so you're not too shocked when you get there.' Claudia felt anxious about this meeting. 'Poor Maria, well, she does look very ill. She might well be in her bed.'

'Don't worry.' Fran was reassuring as ever. 'We'll take it just as it comes. And I promise you we'll be ready for whatever we see when we get there.'

Maria was not in bed. She was sitting in an armchair, propped up by many cushions, wearing a lovely pink dress. Her hair had been brushed and curled, and her lips were bright red. Make-up was bringing colour to her cheeks – but still nothing could disguise how pale and thin she was. She was smiling, and her eyes shone with happiness. Claudia held her hand as she introduced her daughter. Fran knelt beside her chair.

'It's just wonderful to meet you, Aunt Maria.'

'Oh, don't bother with the Aunt bit – just call me Maria. I can't tell you how pleased I am that you've come, you and your husband.'

Nigel bowed slightly as he took her hand.

'And you can call me Nigel.'

'With all that fuzz on your face you'll be lucky if I don't call you Bluebeard.'

'As it happens I have my eye patch in my pocket. Fran, what did you do with the parrot?'

Soon all the introductions were completed. Fran had been looking round the room and had spotted a vase standing by itself on a small table.

'That's a very beautiful vase! I adore that ruby red colour, and the petal effect round the rim. It's so elegant – I'm wondering if it's Murano glass?'

'How clever of you,' replied Maria. 'It's a treasured possession – I brought it back from my honeymoon in Venice. I bought it as a gift … that is, it was intended to be a gift, but I liked it so much I kept it for myself.'

Claudia spoke quietly. 'My guess it that it was bought for your sister, but as she stubbornly refused to have any contact with you, it couldn't be passed on.'

'Now Claudia, we are not going over any of that,' said Maria as firmly as she could. 'The past is all over, and now you are here, and that's all that matters to me. And today I am completely happy. Not only do I have my beloved son and my dear soon-to-be-daughter-in-law living with me, but my beloved sister, and her daughter and son-in-law are here, in my home, too, and my cup of happiness is full.'

Fran stepped in to fill any awkward gap that might have arisen.

'It's strange, really – I've always loved Italy, and all things Italian – and now I've discovered that I had an Italian father.'

'You love Italian food, too, don't you, darling,' interjected Nigel. 'I'm happy to say my wife has a healthy appetite, especially recently.'

'Talking of food,' said Timothy, 'we have some plain English fare set out in the kitchen. We'd like you to come and help yourselves, and then bring it in here, and I'll see you have something to drink.'

There were all sorts of savouries and salads, and everyone had their fill. Many appreciative comments were expressed, but Nicola modestly disclaimed any credit. They all noted that Maria's plate held only a minute portion, and very little of that was consumed, but no one commented.

When the plates and glasses had been cleared away, Timothy announced that it was now 'share a memory' time. Claudia opted to begin.

'I always wanted to be a teacher, for as long as I can remember. I started practising at a very early age – possibly as young as five, if my memory serves me correctly. My class consisted of my sister, Maria, and all the dolls and stuffed toys we possessed.'

'And I was the most woolly-headed of them all,' said Maria.

'Certainly, at the age of two, concentration was not your strongest point.'

'Nothing changed throughout my school life. I never could see any point in bothering with my studies. I just wanted to have a giggle with my friends. But I did admire you, Claudia, because you were so single-minded, and seemed to have a goal, and you directed all your energies to that. I was rather in awe of you.'

'And I envied you your beautiful curly hair, and attractive appearance, and the way the boys all came flocking round you. You seemed to know what to say to them, whereas I felt shy and awkward.'

'But look what a success you made of your professional life!'

'Be that as it may, this is my memory, and I want to thank you for being part of the first class I ever taught.'

'Mum, do you still remember anything you learned from those lessons?' enquired Timothy.

'No, I'm afraid I don't, but can I do my memory next? I remember how, when I was twelve and Claudia fifteen, our mother died. It was very young to be left motherless, and our father, Hugh, was a rather distant figure. What I remember is the way my big sister slipped into the role of mother. She looked after me in a way that I now realise was far above her years. She would make sure I had all I needed for school every day, and although we had a housekeeper, it was Claudia that I always turned to, and I felt secure because I knew she would sort everything out for me.'

'Oh,' said Claudia, 'I didn't know … you felt like that … I'm glad.'

'Now it's time for the younger generation.' Timothy was anxious that Maria did not become overtired. 'You start, Fran, if you will.'

'I remember a beautiful summer's day, and an attractive cove where the rollers pounded in on a deserted shore. The sea looked so inviting, with the sun dancing on the water. I couldn't resist it, and although my two friends chickened out, I struck out for an invigorating swim through the waves. It was only when I turned round and saw the shoreline rapidly receding, and felt the strength of the current dragging me further out, that I realised what a fool I'd been. Then I saw a figure streaking through the waves towards me, and as I held on, literally for dear life, a pair of incredibly strong arms and legs forged a pathway back, until I was finally on the beach once more. He was only a young lad, in his early teens, but he was my hero, and I shall never forget.'

'I think I should go next,' said Timothy. 'I also remember a lovely Cornish cove, which my mother and I were enjoying in peace, when suddenly it ceased to be deserted because three giggling females, shouting and laughing together, came down and ruined the atmosphere of seclusion completely. What's more, one of them, who I must admit was devastatingly attractive – which was perhaps why I was watching her – forgive me Nicky, darling, I was but a lad and I hadn't met you then – behaved in a foolhardy manner by taking a dip, and was in serious danger of disappearing beneath those rolling waves. So I thought I'd better hoick her out, which I did. After all, she was rather pretty, and it seemed a shame to let the fish have all the fun.'

Everyone laughed, relieved that the atmosphere had been lightened. Nicola then recounted the night she and Timothy had found each other.

'It all happened when we started dancing together to some Andrew Lloyd Webber tunes. I shall never forget, because the music, and being in Timothy's arms, felt so romantic.'

'I well remember, and how striking you looked in your green dress.'

'Actually, I think it was blue.'

'Oh, no it wasn't.'

'Oh, yes it was.'

'I think I'd better have my turn,' intervened Nigel. 'I well remember the day I first met my new mother-in-law.'

'But you only met her today,' objected Fran.

'Exactly so,' agreed Nigel. 'And I haven't forgotten it yet. And talking about not forgetting, I'd like to suggest a team photo, so we have a lasting memory of a very special day.' He took his digital camera out of his pocket.

'Oh no!' groaned Maria. 'I don't want to go down to posterity looking like this!'

'You,' said Nigel, 'are the star, and we all want to remember being together today.'

'But if you take it …' demurred Timothy.

'No problem. I have a self timer, so I can be in it too.'

Nigel grouped them round Maria's armchair. He put a dining-chair on either side, and sat Claudia on one side, while the other three stood behind the chairs, with Timothy in the middle, flanked by the two girls.

'I shall sit on the other side of Maria once I've pressed the appropriate button. First I need a table to put the camera on.'

The precious glass vase was carefully moved, and the table placed the right distance in front of the group. Nigel squinted at the back of the camera until he was sure he had it placed correctly. Then he pressed something and began to head for the chair, but made the mistake of hesitating and looking back, so that the camera flashed as he was just turning to sit down. There were various comments about treasuring pictures of Nigel's behind.

'Try again!' he said cheerfully. This time he had ample time to sit down with the others as the camera failed to flash.

'Must have done something wrong. Third time lucky.' But the third time wasn't lucky because it transpired that Claudia had blinked.

'Once more with feeling,' urged Nigel, and at last the picture was a success. By this time the guests were aware that Maria was looking very tired.

'Before we go,' said Claudia, 'I'd like to say something.'

She paused, moved by the occasion, momentarily unable to continue. Claudia, who had made many speeches throughout her life and who had never feared standing up in front of people, confident that she always performed competently, was today searching for words. Finally she spoke, in a way that was new to her – as it clearly came from the heart.

'I'd like to thank Timothy and Nicola for welcoming us all here, and, of course, my dear sister. I have spent the last forty years believing that I didn't need anyone, and I was perfectly happy on my own. I know now that I was quite wrong. Today, here with my new family and a part of a bigger family, I have felt I belonged. This has been the happiest day of my life.'

Maria squeezed her hand. Then Timothy spoke.

'As you know, Nicola and I are looking forward to our wedding day in two weeks' time. We would like to invite you all, Claudia, Fran and Nigel, to come and share our special occasion with us. You will be our guests of honour.'

'That would be just amazing,' whispered Maria.

CHAPTER 49

How could the sun fail to shine on such a special day as this? How could the sky be anything but brilliant blue? True, there were one or two dark clouds on the horizon – but they would not be allowed to encroach on the brightness of the day. Today was too important to everyone involved. Today Timothy and Nicola were going to be married, and the ceremony would be witnessed by all the people who mattered most to them.

Timothy was there, standing at the front of the church, dressed in his hired morning suit, as devastatingly handsome as a groom could look. His best man, Ben – a friend from his school days – hovered ready to lend his support. Nervously, Ben kept fingering the ring in his pocket, to make sure it was still there. He would be glad when they reached the part where he had to hand it over.

The pew behind Timothy was reserved. Several cushions had been placed in the aisle corner of the pew. Ten minutes before the appointed hour there was a flurry of activity. A nurse appeared with a wheelchair, in which sat a tiny, bent figure with the biggest smile of anyone present. As the wheelchair progressed up the aisle, it was followed by Claudia and Fran. Nigel stayed at the back with his camera poised.

Timothy and Ben gently lifted Maria and placed her among the cushions. Maria had insisted that she wasn't going to spend the whole time in the wheelchair. Claudia sat next to her and held her hand. Fran was next, and a space was reserved for Nigel who wanted to wait at the back and capture the moment of the bride's arrival.

The organ struck the notes of the *Wedding March*. All heads turned to look. There stood Nicola, a vision of loveliness, her

'It's a lovely story – elegant writing. There's an intricate web of relationships with some twists in the plot I certainly wasn't expecting.'

The Bookbag

'Attractive characters and a feel-good ending.'

Jackie Wilkin, Book Reviewer and Denman College Lecturer.

'A dramatic take on a universal theme.'

Shan Lancaster, Freelance Journalist

he Gol*d*en Th*r*ead is available *fro*m all g*o*od b*o*okshops, from *Ama*z*o*n a*n*d als*o* as an e-book.

*97*8 17*80* 8088*0* 167   £7.99

For *infor*m*ation* *o*n on on how to

c*o*m*e* a car*ee*r*y* rly.c*o* com

A New Novel by Monica Carly

The Golden Thread

MONICA CARLY

Two sisters, Claudia and Maria, grow up as happy playmates and the best of friends. Claudia, the elder by three years, is protective of her sibling, whose fun-loving ways often lead her into trouble. When their mother dies, Maria feels secure in the knowledge that Claudia is there to help and guide her. Then handsome Italian businessman Stefano Volpe enters their lives and everything changes. bond between the sisters is stretc to breaking point – Claudia refus contact with her sister for the years. But a chance encounte eventually to a miracle – an sisters find happiness just i exquisite white dress ending in a small train that trailed behind her as she walked steadily up the aisle on the arm of her brother, her bridesmaids behind her. Timothy was clearly bursting with pride and happiness as he watched her approach. Nicola paused just before she reached him, and bending down, kissed Maria. Then she smiled at Claudia and Fran, before joining the man who would very soon be her husband. Timothy gazed at her, unable to take his eyes off her, and took her hand in a firm grip, as if he would never let her go.

'Doesn't she look amazing!' whispered Maria to her sister.

'And Timothy looks so handsome!' responded Claudia.

'What a wonderful couple they make! They look so happy!' breathed Fran.

'Anyone like a large hankie?' enquired Nigel.

The vows were exchanged and the ring was produced without mishap. There was some dabbing of eyes in the family pew, but they were tears of joy. The wedding had taken place, and Maria had been there. The bridal party moved off to the vestry for the signing of the register.

They had agreed, previously, that there would be no attempt to bring Maria forward at that point – it would have been too much for her. Timothy had worried that she would not last until the day – her illness was clearly marching inexorably onwards – and although she never complained, he knew that the pain was becoming hard to bear. He had discussed this with Nicola, and they had even tried to bring the ceremony forward a week, but changing the arrangements had proved impossible. Nicola had said she thought the will to live until the appointed day would carry Maria through, and she was proved right.

Claudia was glowing for more than one reason. It wasn't just that the ceremony had been so moving. On the way to the church Fran and Nigel had imparted some news, and she longed for the chance to share it with Maria. But this was not the moment – nothing must detract from concentrating on Maria's thrill of seeing her son marrying Nicola.

Someone gave a signal and the organ struck up once more, the triumphant notes of Widor's *Toccata* resounding through the building. There stood the bride and groom, arm in arm, broad smiles on their faces, beginning their walk back down the aisle. All those present rose to their feet – except one. The bride and groom broke with tradition, stopping as soon as they reached the second pew. A great deal of hugging and embracing, and expressions of good wishes took place, mingled with not a few tears. At last the procession continued on its way.

In all the bustle and commotion, with the organ tones ringing in the rafters, only those close by saw Maria keel forward. Claudia grasped hold of her, and managed to prevent her from collapsing completely.

'I'll ring for an ambulance,' said Fran.

Maria seemed to be unconscious, but then she opened her eyes. With great difficulty she said, 'Tell them they must carry on – that is my wish. They must continue to be happy – that was what they promised me.'

Fran went to tell the best man, and the ambulance drew up round the side of the church. Strong arms lifted Maria on to a stretcher.

'I'll go with her,' said Claudia. 'Please, Fran, you stay – then you can tell me all about it.'

The ambulance men were just shutting the doors when Timothy and Nicola appeared. Once again Maria found the strength to speak. Claudia stood apart, knowing they were saying their goodbyes.

Timothy spoke to Claudia.

'We shall do what she has asked, and what we know she wants. She wants this to be a joyous day for us, and we shall make it so. Thank God she was there – that makes it possible for us to carry on.'

They both wiped their eyes, before going back to smile for the cameras.

Claudia climbed into the ambulance and took Maria's hand in hers. There was no strength in Maria's grip. At the hospital they put her in a small, private room. A doctor came and gave her a morphine injection.

'I'm afraid it is only a matter of time,' he said.

Claudia spoke softly. 'Maria, my dear, the wedding was just wonderful! And what do you think? I'm going to be a grandmother!'

But Maria did not speak again. Claudia went on sitting there, holding her sister's hand. She sat there long after the hand had become quite cold.

At last she stood up, bending to kiss her sister's brow. Then she went to find her daughter, and the new life that was just beginning.